PLANET NO-X

The Red Door

David Alley

PLANET NO-X: The Red Door
© Copyright 2025 by David Alley

Published by:
Peace Publishing,
Rockhampton, Queensland, Australia.

Distributed in Australia by:
Peace Publishing
Po Box 10187
Frenchville, Qld 4701
Phone: 07 4926 9911
Email: mail@peace.org.au
Web: www.peace.org.au

Author's Website
www.davidalley.com.au

ISBN Numbers:
978-1-920780-15-9 - eBook
978-1-920780-16-6 - Paperback

CHAPTERS

CHAPTER ONE:
THE RED DOOR

It was the year 3234. Colin Philips looked at the group of nine people before him and knew with certainty it would be the last time he would ever see them. They knew what he was thinking, and he knew what they were thinking. His wife Sophia and son Gregory were there, as well as family friends, Nathan and Bridie, some neighbours, and work colleagues. Leaving them was the hardest part of this decision. But he was determined to go through with it. Over time, he had come to the realisation that this decision was unavoidable, although there was nothing easy about it.

He looked right into his wife's eyes, his expression an amplified plea. His face begged her to join him. They had already talked about this many times, but she disagreed with him. They were stalled by an ideological standoff. Maybe she would change her mind after he had gone. He hoped so.

He said just one word, the name of someone he didn't believe in.

'Jesus.'

He hadn't said or thought the name Jesus in any outward way for the last twelve years, and even before that it was not something he would think about often, much less speak. Even in his church-attending days back on Earth, he never said the name Jesus if he didn't have to. And saying that name now had nothing to do with a prayer, or any type of appeal to God. He hadn't changed his opinion about that. Even so, never before in his life, had this name had such a dramatic and instant effect.

That word, and a few other similar words, were an offense punishable by deportation. They got you 'voted off the island.' Colin had wanted to leave the planet for some time, but his dear wife wanted the family to stay. Within himself he hoped that her love for him might be greater than her love for this wonderful planet, Utopia. He wanted all three of them to leave together.

But she had a son to think of now, not just herself. She wanted him to grow up on the best planet in the galaxy. He didn't have to pay the 2.5 billion Valens price tag to immigrate here like they both did. He was born here. But more than that, she also didn't want to go back to the rest of the galaxy with all of its constant 'god talk.' That was why they left in the first place, plus of course the luxurious lifestyle that awaited them here was appealing. This place was heaven, a real heaven, not like all that Christian talk of some future paradise out in space somewhere.

But for Colin, it was too late now, he had done the deed. He had said the word that would deport anyone from Utopia, no matter how old, or young. Even if they were unaware of what they were speaking, it would have the same effect. He had passed the point of no return.

And when he said it, he was heard. It was the nature of the technology of not just Utopia, but most of the galaxy. Things both said or thought in public, were public in every way. There were ears, and not all of them were human ears. Most people were careful about what they said and thought. If you had something to hide, you had to be discerning. What Colin had kept private for so long, was now public.

So, like when the wind changes direction, or when curtains reveal a new scene at a live stage production, everything was in a moment, different. Nobody else present said anything. Some reacted with shock, not sure if they could accept what they just heard, but some like Sophia dreaded this moment, knowing it would come. But regardless of their feelings, all of them turned their backs on Colin, and looked away. It was as if he didn't exist. Some started to leave, but most stayed in the room not sure whether to go or stay..

Within a few minutes, three law enforcement officials arrived, each wearing matching light purple full body suits with one-way face masks. They could see out, but you could not see who they were. Scanning the room and judging from the posture of everyone there, they summed up the situation, and knew who to take into custody. They would have known anyway because each voice has a digital signature, but it was obvious without any verification.

Sophia had also her back turned on her husband, a tear had formed in the corner of her eye, she dared not say a word. She put her hand over her young son's mouth; it was not safe for him to speak either. She didn't want to lose him too.

The law enforcement officials took immediate action. Firstly they disabled Colin's thought control processor unit which enabled him to interact with elements all around him. He was now disconnected from the infrastructure on Utopia, which meant that he could not control anything, and now all of his thoughts were private. Next they opened his mouth and inserted a jawlock. It was a device which once inside the mouth held the teeth closed, and was locked shut by the thoughts of the law enforcement officials. In accordance with Utopian law enforcement principles, he was not to speak or to communicate by thought. He was now incapable of speaking or publicly thinking, unless the chief official granted thought permission.

Next Colin was cuffed, which clicked onto his hands like old-fashioned cuffs, but unlike them had no key. The cuffs could also be unlocked once the officials approved it with their thoughts.

The majority of infrastructure from fridges, transportation, communication and more were controlled by thought on the planet of Utopia. This wasn't a unique innovation for Utopia, but it was more prevalent here than elsewhere.

Finally, they slid a purple fabric bag over his head so his face could no longer be seen. He did not fight them, he didn't know what to expect, and it was more cut-and-dried than he imagined, but given he had broken the cardinal rule of Utopia, he wasn't surprised at the treatment. He was now isolated from all human connection, except for the touch of the two officials who held both of his arms as they now marched him out of the room. There were no goodbyes, not even the possibility of a glance. It was as if he had never existed. Nobody who had been present in that room would ever see him again.

Once he had been taken away, everyone knew they were permitted to speak again, but nobody did. There was just one noise that could now be heard, the sound of soft crying. It came from Sophia. It had happened. He had done it. She wished she could have stopped him.

She knew why he had done this. They had argued about it many times, but her appeals had no effect. If anything, the harder she pushed, the more resolute he had become. It was nothing like the early days when they had first known each other. He always listened to her ideas back then. As the years had rolled by on this planet, something had gotten into him. Crazy ideas about government conspiracy and lack of personal freedom. She knew it just wasn't true. They had lived elsewhere in the galaxy and there was no place like Utopia. But she just couldn't change his mind.

She didn't want to go back to the cold winters in Estonia. Once her family had died, she had no ties left on Earth. She had friends on Utopia, and Gregory had friends as well, especially since starting his education. Plus, going back to Earth would mean she would be surrounded by all the god stuff everywhere. She liked it here on Utopia and loved the freedom from having to believe in anything.

There were too many thoughts in her mind at that moment. But she was also overwhelmed with feelings. She felt grief at her loss, and her son's loss. She was angry at Colin for leaving. How could he do this to her and to Gregory? Yes, what about him? Now he would have to grow up without a Dad The emotions were too much, and she couldn't process any of them right at this moment.

Then a little voice spoke.

'What happened to Daddy?'

Sophia gave no response. Just tears.

'Where's Daddy gone?'

It was a question that would linger, not just in the boy's heart, but in the private thoughts of many people.

-- -- -- -- --

Far from everyone else, Colin was taken to a secluded room by the three purple-clad officials. They stopped before a red door with a white frame. The room was circular, not spacious, was painted white, and in addition to the red door, there were two other doors, three in total. Apart from that, the room was empty.

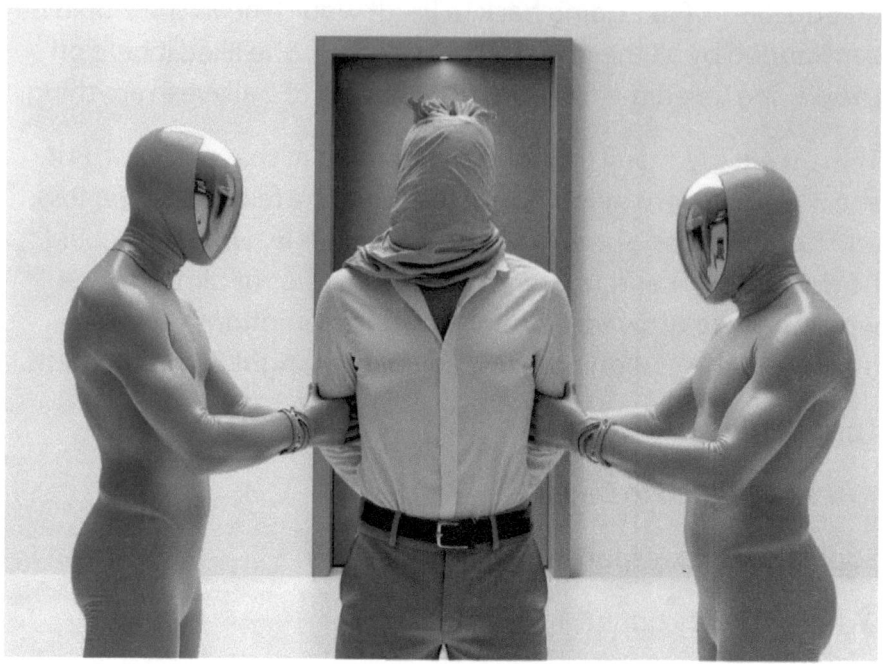

His purple hood was removed by the law enforcement officials. The first thing he noticed was the red door, and he knew where he was. He had been here before, as had every single person who had immigrated to Utopia. It was the first room you arrived in when you left Earth. Coming through the white door, travellers were greeted by immigration officials, who required a verbal confirmation of immigration approval, which was intended to be permanent. This was the last moment someone could change their minds, and go back. After that there was no possibility of return, and no refund of the huge fees. Nobody did of course because Utopia awaited them. Once they had confirmed their decision, immigrants were then taken through the purple door and to the planet of their dreams.

But it was the red door that Colin was before this time. Within a few minutes he would walk through that door and forever be gone from Utopia, the planet that had been his home for twelve years.

If Colin was honest with himself, he didn't know where the door would take him, and in fact nobody knew that, or at least nobody was able to say where it would go, but everyone assumed it was a doorway back to Earth, somewhere. On Earth there was a Grand Hall of Doors which connected all the fourteen inhabited planets, a kind of grand central station for interplanetary travel. On Earth, the door to Utopia was considered a one-way door. Hundreds of thousands of people had walked through that door when they emigrated to Utopia, but unlike the other planetary doors, nobody came back through it. Or at least nobody on Earth could ever recall seeing anyone come back from Utopia, but then nobody on Utopia had tried to return, as far as anyone knew anyway.

Now that he had arrived in the room of three doors, a troubling thought entered his mind. If incoming travellers came to Utopia through the white door, why did they leave by a different door? Why didn't they just go back the way they came? And why was the door red? He realised that he had no assurance whatsoever about where he might end up if he went through that red door. If he had a chance to speak or think in public, he might have asked about the white door.

It was too late anyway to entertain such ideas. He tried to push the thoughts away, and concentrated on the good things he was certain were ahead of him. Somehow, he figured he would be the first to walk through the red door, and arrive back on Earth. He looked forward to talking to his parents again and his other family and friends he hadn't seen, and his brother. He might have left them behind on semi-disagreeable terms twelve years earlier, but those issues seemed smaller now. And it would also be good to eat ordinary food again; he couldn't wait for that.

While all of this was going on in Colin's mind he remained gagged and cuffed.

Two of the officials remained next to Colin, one on each side. The third official stood in front of him and read a statement. The statement came from his thought processor, line by line, but he could not think it, in this case he was required to read it out to Colin.

'This is an official and recorded pronouncement on behalf of the government of the planetary commission for Utopia. Colin Lawson Philips. On the 2nd day of July, 3234 you were guilty of breaking the second of the foundation rules. According to your consent on the day of your immigration to this planet, you agreed that the actions that will now occur, are just and appropriate. There is no recourse for the outcome now to happen, which is final and irreversible. You will never be able to return to Utopia, and you forfeit all claim to all currency and personal assets that remain here.'

'In a minute we will remove your cuffs. And you will walk through that door. Your jawlock device will remain in your mouth but will deactivate once you exit the room. At that point you can remove it yourself, and can talk again. Do you understand?'

Colin nodded.

And just like that, he was unshackled, and the cuffs were gone. The two officials guided him to the door, expecting resistance, but there wasn't any. He walked through and was forever gone from Utopia.

CHAPTER TWO:

THE GREAT NICK JONES

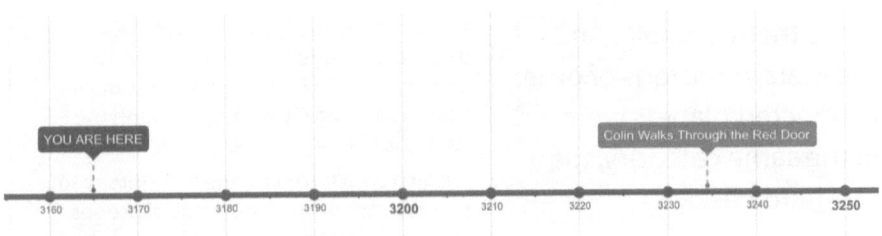

Sixty nine years before Colin Philips had walked through the red door, Utopia did not exist. It was nothing more than an idea in the mind of a handful of hopeful atheists. Wouldn't it be wonderful if there was a place you could go to get away from all the spiritual nonsense that was everywhere? Wouldn't it be 'heavenly' if there was a planet where all religion was outlawed? It was no more than a lot of 'what ifs'.

Nicholas Jones was no atheist, but if it weren't for him, the atheist planet would never have come into existence.

As a child, he had grown up hearing about the terraformation of Kepler and Kepler Second, and the other four planets that had already been inhabited, Barnard, Wolf, Lalande and Luyton. Many more planets had been discovered, connected, visited, and even explored, but the inhabited stellar-system remained at just seven planets. He dreamed of working to terraform planets, and studied subjects that would take him that direction, but that wasn't unique. A lot of people wanted to work in planet tech.

Planets like Mars were close to Earth, but too complex with current technology to civilize. Both Mars and the Moon could be visited, and plenty of people did, especially children on school excursions, but it was too big an effort to transform those places and make them liveable. And like Mars, hundreds of other connected planets were in the same category, the too-hard basket.

Nick dreamed of being involved in terraforming, but it was a dream that many children his age shared. Everyone loved the idea of terraforming your own planet, like people in the twenty-first century loved the idea of having their own tropical island. In this case, it was something not even the rich could do, it was limited to governments.

Beam Me Up Scotty? Not Quite.

Unlike in Star Trek movies you cannot just beam around anywhere in the Universe you want to. There has to be a connection established between both points. So to travel to the moon, you can get there instantly, if the technology required is already in place on the moon. This means that expanding civilization through the galaxy is a slow process.

The first step is to send the technology to places in advance. Thousands of probes are released every year which travel at good speed, about 20% of the speed of light. To reach Kepler, the first planet ever connected, took less than twelve months by this method. Once both endpoints of a translator were in place, travellers could jump between the two (like Star Trek) but only between those two points. Moving between these two points is called translation, and the technology behind it is called 'pairs' because there are two halves of the equipment required to make it work.

In the year 3234 when Colin walked through the red door, there were over 500 planets connected in this manner, but only 14 that had been civilized and to which regular travel took place.

The first six inhabited planets other than Earth were the work of significant time and effort. Since the discovery of super-entanglement in 2545, which made this possible, generations of people had spent centuries on these planets making them what they were. But the so-called 'wave of terraforming' came in the thirty-first century because of one man, Nicholas Jones.

In his lengthened career of ninety years, Nick was responsible for the transformation of another six planets, Enaiposha, Cathedral, Utopia, Verde, Gileasie, Silica and a seventh planet, Carbon One which was making progress. He had a lot of help from millions of willing volunteers, but in one sense, he was single-handedly responsible for doubling the number of habitable planets in the stellar system. And it was because of him that the atheists eventually got their planet.

As a tertiary student, Nick had studied system planning, which was something like the ancient art of town planning, except that it was nothing like it in reality. While completing his studies, he had an insight that would change not only his life, but the lives of billions of humans both alive and yet to be born.

His inspiration came one morning in Port Sudan, when he lay in a cantaloupe field enjoying an unusual patch of cool weather as the breeze blew across his face. When the chance occurred, Nick loved to go outdoors to think private thoughts, and then write them down in a notebook. It was old-fashioned.

It was true that everyone loved to think, and in fact they wasted huge amounts of time thinking, but this was not the type of thinking that Nick loved to do. While they loved to be entertained, connecting their minds to the thoughts of others, and watching video in the mind's eye, and communicating with others in public thought, Nick loved private thinking. He loved to contemplate, and to record his contemplations.

His friends said that private thinking was an overrated pastime. What was there to think about anyway? But he found it relaxing, and there were actually endless things to ponder. For example, where have all the birds gone today? Does the wind have something to do with that?

He not only thought about what he observed, he was also philosophical. He thought about God. Why did God make everything? It seemed such an unusual thing for Him to do. Surely He had better things to do than worry about people. And why didn't God leave more obvious clues about Himself? And why did he allow atheists to say such nasty things about Him?

There weren't many atheists in the stellarverse any longer, maybe no more than five percent, but some of them were vocal with their atheism. There were also some prominent and wealthy atheists, such as Richard Heibermann, and Kurt Luise. Nick sometimes thought about the things they said, and wondered why God was such a problem for them.

Sometimes he thought about his family and the behaviour of people. His father was obsessed with his research into longevity. Civilization had a kind of unofficial collective goal of extending life to 300 years of age. Many people now lived into the high 100's and a handful had lived to the elusive two. But despite his father's genius, he ended up not even living to ninety. It was a case of stress and burnout. How ironic that his father's focus on longevity shortened his life.

This particular day he was thinking about the cantaloupes all around him. They were a delicious melon that grew on vines, and were exported from Port Sudan all over Africa, and many other places too. On rare occasions, such as Christmas each year, they would load up the spacerail to Silica with carriages of melons. It would shoot through the railgate and arrive on that other planet and stock the underground supermarkets there, to the joy of the Silicians..

Today he had cantaloupes around him, and from his melony repose, he could observe the Red Sea, with its sparkling azure water, and brilliant white coral sand. A smallish pleasure craft bobbed near the edge as undersea divers, with the latest gilltech suits, dived in shallow reefs for lobster.

But as Nick lay in the melons he was not thinking about lobsters, or diving, or the beautiful scenery, but he was thinking about water. In particular he pondered, where does all the water come from to water these melons?

When he looked to his right, he could see billions of gallons of water, and when he looked left he could see dry land, although covered by millions of mellons? There was a system in place to get water from there to here, and probably to desalinate too, but what was it?

All of this thought led him to a parallel question. He thought of the water-rich ocean planet of Enaiposha, which evaded terraforming because there was no usable land, and the dry, gorge-filled spectacular planet of Cathedral. Nobody could live there either because the atmosphere was thin, and there was no water on the planet at all. He wondered, just like with the melons, was there a way of getting some of that surplus water out of Enaiposha and getting it to Cathedral? It seemed there should be a simple way of doing that too.

If he could take just some of the water from the ocean planet and send it to Cathedral, it would create

> **Gilltech Suits:**
>
> Although a gilltech suit was mostly easy to put on, it required the insertion of a cannula into the bloodstream. As the wearer swam with the suit, it extracted oxygen out of the water, placing it into the blood. The lungs were bypassed, and breathing in was not required. But the diver must still exhale the accumulating carbon dioxide. The diver needed training on breathing out, but not breathing in. It took practice, and one could breathe in a lungful of water if one wasn't careful. Early experiments had produced catastrophic outcomes. Training took place standing in a pool with the head out of the water. It took most beginners an hour or two to become proficient.
>
> The benefit of the gilltech suit, meant that as long as the diver stayed in water shallower than about six metres, they could dive all day long without having to surface. Below six metres of depth, the oxygen under water pressure became toxic and the divers risked oxygen toxicity poisoning. Thankfully, lobsters were plentiful in Port Sudan in the shallower water.

oceans, improve the atmosphere and give them a water source. Then they could add insects, birds, fish and animals, plant crops and trees, and voila …he would have used one planet's resources to terraform the other.

But how would that happen?

Then it hit him like a lightning bolt. He knew exactly how it could be done. In fact it wasn't even technical or challenging, although it would be expensive and time-consuming. Why had nobody thought of it before? They needed to build a super-entangled door, and have it placed on Enaiposha, not in the air, or atmosphere like it had been done other times, but under the oceans. Like emptying a bath, they could pull the plug, and drain the water to Planet Cathedral where it could drop in and create oceans.

They needed to build an aquadoor.

Not only that, but once the ocean levels on Enaiposha dropped, land would start to appear, and they could terraform that planet too. One idea could lead to the transformation of two planets.

And so it was that just months later a large number of gears in the terraformation engine for both planets began to turn. An underwater depth survey of the entire planet of Enaiposha was commenced, which determined the amount of water to remove, and the future shape of continents and islands that would emerge. Detailed mapping of Planet Cathedral took place to determine where the oceans would end up being located. After this, engineers calculated the best location on both planets for the aquadoor to be situated, and the size of the door was calculated, a tradeoff between cost and speed.

The preliminary work took a few years, and in that process it was calculated that 53.7 metres of water would be removed from Enaiposha which would produce 2 continents and numerous islands. It was estimated that after the removal of that water, the highest 'mountain' on the planet would be just 52.9 metres in height, and there would still be more than 90% of the planet's water reserves remaining, sufficient to remove more later if needed on other planets.

An aquadoor 44 metres by 22 metres was to be built, approximately the size of two tennis courts, and was placed in a location where the sea depth was about 60 metres deep. It was positioned on twenty-seven submerged concrete posts, at precisely 53.7 metres under the water. Tides were not well understood on an all-water planet, so the figures were calculated based on what would be considered the probable low-tide mark. No more than about 58 metres of water would be moved in total.

Mapping was also done on Planet Cathedral, which was a smaller planet. The equivalent amount of water would produce on that planet more than 74 metres of depth on average, where oceans were to exist. A door was bonded above the deepest gorge on the planet, known as Central Gorge. When the aquadoor was opened, like a giant waterfall it would pour down the gorge creating one of the most interesting sights in the galaxy.

In September 3168, the plug was pulled on Enaiposha and the water began to drain away. A giant whirlpool formed rotating clockwise which sucked water into itself at ferocious speed. It was not safe to approach the whirlpool above water. Like the supermassive blackhole at the centre of the Milky Way, nothing near on the surface was safe. But venturing near it was not only dangerous, legislation was passed to also make it illegal. On the ocean floor underneath the aquadoor, all was calm, but just a few feet above, water roared into the portal with the ferocity of a freight train at full speed. Engineers relied on submersibles to maintain the aquadoor, approaching from a distance below the depth of the gate.

34 Light years away on Planet Cathedral a door had been opened in the sky, and water majestically appeared as if from nowhere. There on the edges of the Central Gorge spectators came from all over the seven inhabited planets to admire water plummeting kilometres below into the depths forming a river. It was either the first river on the planet, or the first for a long time.

After a full day of draining the ocean, the water level on Enaiposha had dropped by nine millimetres. There was no visual difference to speak of, but there was something to see on Cathedral where water was now visible. But it was 89 days later that the first land appeared on Enaiposha, and the first rocks came to light. The water had by this time dropped just 80 centimetres. The process was going to be a long one.

Three years later the water level on Enaiposha had gone down 3.2 metres and genuine islands existed. But a more amazing thing had happened on Cathedral where it rained for the first time, even though it was just a sprinkle. Clouds were becoming more common, and each time a cloud was sighted, cheers went up.

> **Stages in Creating a Civilized Planet**
> 1. **Identification:** Planets that are potentially habitable are identified.
> 2. **Connection:** A probe is sent to create a physical bridge in space. This can take many years travelling at just 20 percent the speed of light. Thousands of probes are launched annually.
> 3. **Certification:** Once a physical bridge exists, robots visit to take readings and test if humans can visit.
> 4. **Visitation:** Humans visit and determine if a planet is worth exploring, or researching, or inhabiting.
> 5. **Exploration:** If a planet has terraformation potential, it is explored to create an inventory of its geography and resources.
> 6. **Terraformation:** Work to transform the planet as required to make it habitable.
> 7. **Construction:** The development of initial infrastructure to establish civilization, including a gateway to connect to the Grand Hall of gates in Delhi, India.
> 8. **Habitation:** The establishment of a political process, including a founding parliament, rules for migration, and an economic basis to manage the planet.

5966 days had been allowed to drain Enaiposha, but it ended up taking less than that, because as the water lowered the process sped up as more and more land appeared. Instead of it taking 16 years it took just 14 before both planets had completed the water adjustment process. Enaniposha still remained 90% a water planet, but Cathedral now had oceans, evaporation, rain and life.

But long before that had completed, fish had been introduced to both planets from Earth, as had insects, birds, and plants. Within 20 years both planets were ready for construction and handing over to the Stellar Habitation Authority which handles the last stages of planetary transformation.

After Enaiposha and Cathedral were handed over for construction, Nick Jones was something of a hero. He was published, and became a household name. Everyone thought about him in their public thoughts, and many in their private thoughts. Opportunities opened to him that he would never have expected.

It was then that a message arrived from Richard Heibermann, that avowed atheist. He had just one question.

'Mr Jones, would you be willing to help us? We have an idea for a new planet?'

CHAPTER THREE:

SNOW SUNSET

Colin Philips had been born into an involved church-going family. They were more than devoted. It wasn't unusual to be 'churchy' because most people were, but something had never settled with Colin about it. His father Gary was sincere in his Christian faith, Colin could see that from the way he cared for other people in needy times, and how he shared and gave money to the less fortunate on developing planets. Colin's mother was Colleen, and he was named after her. She was kind, softly-spoken and never forgot the little things that mattered to him, like tomato soup on a cold morning, or cutting his sandwiches into triangles. She always thought of others, and it was hard to not have affectionate feelings for her. Once he had woken up in the middle of the night and found her kissing him on the forehead. He knew that both parents loved him, but even though they were both good people, Colin just could not understand how they could believe in a God they couldn't see. He thought they were nice people, but like most of the people around him, he felt they were a bit deluded.

Of course, growing up in a church environment, he had heard all the usual explanations for why God was real even though you couldn't see Him. 'He is a spirit,' they said, 'But if you want to see God then you need to think about Jesus.' He was a real person, and that was how God revealed Himself. Colin just couldn't understand how a man called Jesus who lived over three thousand years ago, could be the same as the invisible God they also talked about. The reality was that he didn't care to try to figure it out. It was irrelevant to him. And that of course was the real issue; he didn't want to understand.

It was late in the work day. Colin was a mathematician, who worked at ICE, the Intergalactic Communication Exchange. His job sounded exciting, with his title of Chief Relativity Mathematician, but was the most mundane of all the jobs that existed at ICE. He had a team of mathematicians that worked alongside him, but life was predictable and routine, nothing different happened day by day.

Relativity and the Keeping of Time

It was popular in the twentieth and twenty-first centuries to believe that time itself was relative. Albert Einstein had theorized this, and certain experiments seem to prove he was correct.

A clock taken nearer to stronger gravity would run slower for example. This seemed to demonstrate that time ran slower nearer stronger gravity.

However it is now understood that it was not time itself, but the clock that was affected by the gravity. If a clock is taken too close to a black hole for example, the clock itself will be destroyed by the black hole, but time will not have stopped. It is the measuring device that is affected by the physical conditions that surround it, being heat, magnetism, atmospheric pressure, wind, and most certainly the strength of gravity.

In the thirty-first century at places like ICE, Colin and other mathematicians work mathematics, not to adjust time, but to adjust the measurements of time, so that a universal time is able to be kept consistently everywhere in the galaxy.

Their task was to analyse new locations in the galaxy, to calculate the physical conditions of those locations and how the measurement of time would be affected, and then to feed that information into the galactic gravitational database. It was a part of maintaining the metric time system that allowed not just communication, but calendars and programming and so many of the features of modern life. They also had to review every inconsistency in the timing of communication or synchronicity and update the maths behind the code so that there was constant improvement taking place right across the known part of the galaxy.

Early in the 20th century Albert Einstein had a brainwave that time was relative, and everyone believed it for a hundred years or so after his death. Later it was discovered that time actually wasn't relative, but that physical conditions like gravity, temperature, atmospheric pressure and more, all affected the physical systems that measure time. (See Inset on Relativity - Previous Page) So their job at ICE was to update the growing database of gravitational measurements, pressure measurements and more so that time could be consistent for everyone. The maths kept all the clocks in synchronicity. It allowed communication, scheduling, event recording and more to happen with precision.

It sounded exotic, but was as boring as laying bricks.

Colin had graduated with a Masters in Relativistic Mathematics, and then landed his special high-paying job at ICE. His friends slapped him on the back and congratulated him, and his parents celebrated by buying him a translator set he could use to jump to work and back. He later concluded it was all a terrible curse.

Day in and day out, the same boring routine happened at the office. They would translate into work sometime before 9am. The first hour would be in review of the situations that had come in overnight. Colin would decide who would tackle what problems, and take some of them himself. They would then make coffee and start their calculations. One joy had been the new coffee that had been circulating the last few years. The new 'green coffee' was grown on Verde, a planet with a gravity fifteen percent stronger than on Earth, making the plants shorter but stronger. It affected the coffee somehow and made it nicer.

After a cup of that special 'green' coffee was acquired, it was time for maths. Having worked so long at ICE, Colin and the team would often have the problems solved and the database updated soon after midday; and then they had hours to kill before being able to go home. It didn't matter whether they were working, or passing time, all of it was boring. Plain Boring!! Most of the team spent the rest of the day in the public thinking space, but Colin found that had grown dull for him.

At the end of the day, Colin would just activate his translator and arrive at home in a blink like everyone else. He would have dinner with his parents, talk about the day, always with similar conversations, then read something in a good old-fashioned book, and go to bed. But occasionally, like today, he just had to do something different. So he decided to walk home instead.

Colin lived and worked in Tallinn, which was formerly in the nation of Estonia, but now a part of Greater Europe. At the right time of the year, usually in late February, he liked to walk along the edge of the water, and admire the sunset and its reflection as he went home. It was about five miles, and sometimes the sun had gone down, and was

Metric Universal Time.

Time had been historically imperial, using different arbitrary units like 24 hours a day each with 60 minutes an hour with 60 seconds a minute. But with the future came metric time, and the abolishment of timezones. Now there was just one time everywhere in the galaxy, and it was metric.

Each day contained 100,000 metric seconds, based on a day on Earth, and that was it. If your planet spun twice a day, and you had two daytimes and two nightimes in the span of 100,000 seconds, it was still just one day.

With just one timezone, an event could be set at a certain time anywhere, and everyone there or anywhere else also knew what time it was. If a transit vessel departed the moon at 20,000 seconds, it was also 20,000 everywhere on Earth, and if it arrived at 39,000 on Earth, it was the same time on the moon. Having one time zone simplified life for everyone, especially the mathematicians at **ICE..**

replaced with cool crisp night long before he made it home. Other times he would find a quiet place and eat dinner as it went down. As the year dragged on, the sunset was later in the day, so that in June it didn't set until 11pm at night. Seasonal changes in the northern latitudes could be dramatic.

But it was February and the sun was due to set just before 6pm. He wasn't hungry, but just needed to stretch his legs this night. He was soon walking along the edge of the water. After a few moments, he came across a magical spot with a bench overlooking his favourite view. He sat down, and watched as the sun dropped lower towards the horizon. The shadows started to grow as they lengthened across the ground near him. Winter was nearing its end, and the snow was just starting to thin, and the sun setting over the white world was remarkable. The sky cast a pink hue into the many variegated clouds that dotted the sky.

Then a soft female voice spoke.

'Pretty isn't it?'

He turned to see a young red-haired woman with a light blue winter suit and a light brown patchwork scarf with matching brown gloves. She smiled at him.

'Yes it is.'

'What brings you here?' she asked again.

'Do I know you?' he queried.

'Yes you do, I've seen you at ICE. I work upstairs in the boardroom.'

'Wow, Upstairs!. You're important,' said Colin, his mind racing. In his mind, he started to sift through all the names and faces he knew at ICE, just as a secretary rummaging through an old-fashioned filing cabinet might do. But he came up empty.

'I do apologise, but I'm struggling to remember when I met you before.'

'It's ok,' she said. 'Everyone forgets me. My name is Sophia.'

'Ahh, Sophia,' he remarked. 'Of course, how could I have forgotten such a pretty face.'

She blushed, at his attempt at a compliment. But Colin felt embarrassed that he had to ask for her name despite knowing her already. The truth was she did have a pretty face. He knew he had to say something else.

'Tell me about yourself,' he said. 'What do you do? How did you get a job at ICE?'

Sophia sat down next to Colin. 'I never had the idea of coming to work here. It was my grandfather, Sören.'

'Sören?' He interrupted. 'You mean Sören Saar, the founder of ICE?'

'Yes.' She didn't like saying that she was the granddaughter of the founder.

'Wow. How did I not know who you are? You're work royalty.' It was now Colin's turn to be embarrassed. He had to admit, he had found his work so dull that his mind was disengaged from his work environment. He hadn't paid enough attention to those around him.

She said nothing. She didn't know how to reply.

He lifted his head and looked right at her. 'Please tell me more. Not about your grandfather. Tell me about you. How long have you been at ICE? Do you like it there?'

'Well I've been at ICE ever since I graduated, so about 6 years now. I don't mind it, and I am paid well.' She paused, not sure if she should say the next part. 'Although, if I had the chance, I wouldn't mind doing something different.'

'What would you do instead?'

'Oh, I don't know. Just go somewhere different, and get away from all the cold weather.'

'But it's not that cold, we do have good weather control systems now.'

'I know, I just want a change.'

Colin looked at her and knew how she felt. He was wanting a change in work himself. He understood her. All of a sudden he wanted to ask her a personal question, but he wasn't sure if he could. Would she be open to hearing it? What would her response be?

He decided he would ask. It was a gamble. Normally such a question would never be asked except in romantic relationships. But he had a hunch that he could. He sensed something in her that he had not felt in any other person before, certainly not in any woman.

'Would you be open to giving me permission to access your feelings?'

Sophia looked back and surprised Colin. She was willing. She didn't have to say anything, she consented in her public mind, and the technology did what was needed. In just a few seconds, he felt what she felt. He knew her feelings. Her inner world was his. She was lonely, tired, and ready for a change in life. He felt her ache and her desires. He also realised something that she had not said. The truth was that in her feelings, she liked him. He was encouraged by that.

For a moment he just sat there and took in all of those feelings. It wasn't awkward, but was the way to respond when feelings were being shared. She allowed him the minutes to feel. He not only felt them, but he thought about what the feelings meant, and he tried to understand them. She watched him as he felt her feelings, and knew he was receiving them.

Understanding someone else's feelings wasn't a science, it was more of a developed skill. The more practice you had the better you became at it. But Colin thought he understood them. By looking at him, she thought he did too.

Sharing Emotion

In the old days, people shared feelings by talking, such as 'I feel sad.' But technology in the future, aided with mindchips in the body, and thought processing servers outside the body, meant that emotions can be replicated in another person. This is called 'sharing feelings,' and can be done with each person giving permission.

When they are young, humans are given a brain to software interface, a mindchip. When permission is given to share emotions, which is done by a public thought of approval, the brain interface then can read the varying physical levels of chemicals in the brain, and share that information with another person. The other person can then utilise their own software to replicate those hormones, or chemical levels, and recreate the same feelings.

Sharing feelings is not permitted outside of a family until a child becomes an adult.

Initially humans tried to control their feelings, and feel good all the time. Studies determined it was bad for the body to stimulate the brain either positively or negatively too much.

'Would you like to feel my emotions too?' he asked. This was the way of replying, not with words, but with feelings in return.

She nodded.

And in that moment he shared with her his sympathy. He was sorry for her, and she could feel how genuine he was. He also felt lonely, and detached from his work too, and he also needed to find something beyond it. She knew that feeling well. In that moment their hearts were knit together somehow in an unexpected way. They both felt the same things, and they knew each other felt the same, and they knew that they understood each other. They experienced the feeling of belonging together.

Before them the sun went down over the water, its rays reflecting on the snow around them. Colin moved across closer to her, and put his arm around her, and pulled her close to him. It was sudden, but felt natural, like they had known each other a long time. It was a magical moment, one they would never forget.

CHAPTER FOUR:

THE TERRAFORMATION OF UTOPIA

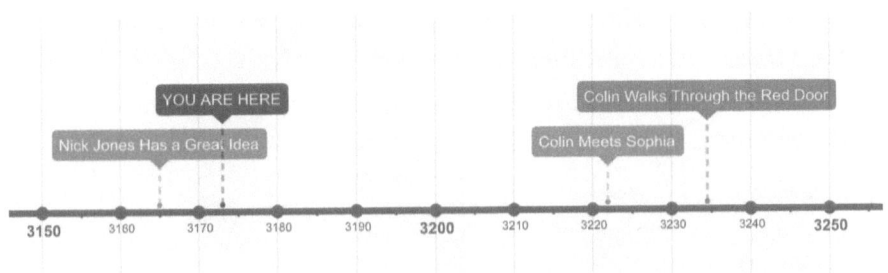

Nick Jones sat in the lounge with his parents, and with his girlfriend, Jay. They had known each other since secondary school, and spent many weekends together ever since. They often spent afternoons in conversation together, but not today. His head was in his hands, and he wasn't talking.

His parents' home was in North Africa where generations of his family had lived, and Africa in general was a popular place. It was sunny, fertile, and well-connected to the rest of the world. The economy was doing well, most people were happy, literacy was up, education was up, wars had been non-existent for centuries, poverty didn't exist either, society was well-to-do and people helped each other, mostly. But despite that, Nick Jones was struggling with something which for him felt almost existential.

How could he, a believer in Jesus Christ, consider helping people like Richard Heibermann and his atheist friends start their own planet? He was attracted to the idea they had proposed from a planetary point of view. They wanted to build the best society from the ground up, with all the latest technology. Nothing about Utopia would be second-rate. It was going to be a galaxy-class destination when finished. Who wouldn't want to help with that?

But on the other hand, they wanted to build a society that excluded most people. They wanted this place to be for atheists only. It wasn't just that Christians were disallowed, but anyone who didn't reject all forms of religion. It felt so wrong to want to help them. It felt like he would be working for the devil, tearing down the foundations of civilization itself. His conscience bothered him.

'What's wrong Nick?'

Jay asked the question. Having known him since he was ten, she was well-acquainted with his personality, his faith, his work and hobbies which were mostly the same thing. In reality, she didn't have to ask the question. She already knew what was wrong. Her question wasn't about obtaining information, it was about getting him to speak, to say something, to say anything at all.

> **Atheism**
>
> Unlike atheism in the twenty-first century, atheism in the future is about living a life that leaves God out of it. It is not a denial that God exists, or that God created, but a denial of God's importance for living now.
>
> Atheism is a worldview that says God is no longer relevant to us. There is no evidence he cares about us, or shows any attempt to be involved in our lives. The resulting conclusion of these beliefs by atheists, is that they can live their lives however they wish, without the need for moral commands.

He didn't answer.

This had been going on for a week. If anyone could get Nick to talk, it would be Jay. But her charm, good looks, and long-standing friendship didn't make one bit of difference. This trouble was soul deep for Nick.

When Richard Heibernmann, the noted atheist, and Nick had first met, the matter of the societal exclusion of people with faith hadn't come up. It was more a discussion of the technology that would be used to build what was going to be the galaxy's premier planet. Nick got excited by the things that were being proposed. That day in the coffee shop in Khartoum would always stick in his memory.

'I want a planet where it's daytime all the time, so that people can play and have fun as much as they want,' said Richard.

It sounded ridiculous, but Nick pondered that wish. And, it didn't take him long to figure out how it could be done.

'We either need to find a planet that is tidally locked in the right part of the habitable zone, or we need to change a planet to make it tidally locked.' Nick said.

'Tidally what?'

'A planet that doesn't spin,' said Nick. The planet will certainly rotate around its sun, but as it does, the same side of the planet will always be facing towards the sun. One side of the planet will have permanent daytime, and the other side will have permanent night. And there will be a twilight zone, where it's always sunset or sunrise depending on what you call it.'

'Do you know of any planet we could use like that?'

'Not really,' said Nick. He paused, and looked out the window where he could see water flowing by. It wasn't just any water. A few miles upstream, two rivers joined together, the Blue Nile and the White Nile, their waters merging together to become the Great Nile which flowed near the cafe where their conversation took place.

When Nick terraformed Enaiposha, and Cathedral at the same time, he had learned a life lesson. It often took two planets to help terraform each other, and the key was using doors to connect the planets in interesting ways. Likewise, outside his window was a big river, created from the mixing of two lesser rivers. There was something powerful about that idea of using two things together to create something greater..

'I have an idea,' he said, 'of using a second planet to slow the spinning of the first planet so that it will come to be still. We can create a tidally locked planet with the help and power of another planet's spin.'

'Go on.'

'If we build four, or six, or maybe eight big doors along the horizontal axis of the direction of spin on the first planet, and match doors on the other planet with spin, we can cancel out one planet's rotation and slow it.'

It made little sense to Richard. It was gobbledygook. But he was interested, as long as it worked.

'Then as the doors line up on the two planets, both of which are spinning, we release a pound of negative magnetism to slow the spin of the planet slightly. Not a literal pound mind you, just as much as we can generate with electromagnetics.' His thoughts were faster than his mouth. 'As it progresses, the planet will slow its spin over the course of many months. It may take half a year. Eventually we can get it to stop and it should then hold right where we want, until we are ready to close off the doors.'

Richard knew enough to get the basic idea of what was being said.

'Won't it slow down the spin on the other planet too?'

'If we wanted it to we could,' said Nick. 'But we won't have all the doors lined up in the same direction on the donor planet, we'll put some of them in the one direction, and some in the opposite so that the forces balance out. The recipient planet will slow, but the donor planet won't.'

Richard didn't understand that part either, but he didn't have to. This was Nick Jones, the terraformation expert.

But now it was Nick's turn to ask a question.

'Won't it be annoying to have permanent daylight on half the planet?'

Richard's face smiled; he had thought about this.

'That's what we want,' he said. 'we want permanent night too.'

That still hadn't answered the question.

'For every house on the planet, we plan to build two separate buildings, one on the light side, and one on the dark side. We then plan to connect them by a hallway portal door, so that inside the house it's like one house. The bedrooms will always be night, and the living room and kitchen will always be day. So if you want to sleep for three days straight you can, and it will be night the entire time. But then you can wake up and go out fishing for three days straight and the sun will never go down.'

Nick understood immediately. He nodded.

'It's brilliant,' he commented. 'But, there are some downsides to having a tidally locked planet too.'

'Go on.'

'The part of the planet closest to the sun will get hot and nothing will grow there. It will also generate high atmospheric pressure, and wind currents that affect the whole planet will be generated.'

'Go on.'

'If you don't want that, we need to create other doors in the atmosphere to regulate atmospheric pressure and minimise the wind.'

'I think we will need that.'

'And the other side of the planet farthest from the sun, will be cold. It will be hard for anything to live there too.'

'Don't worry about that,' said Richard. 'Apart from the night rooms, we don't have any plans for the dark side. Maybe we'll build an observatory at some point, but our goal is to make the light side like heaven, and the dark side isn't needed apart from somewhere to sleep.'

'Do you realise it's going to be expensive?

'We've been planning and saving for this for a long time. We want to do this once and do it well.'

And so that initial meeting had gone well, and so had subsequent meetings. But it was later that Richard's ideas for societal change were mentioned, and it was this that bothered Nick. Richard was honest about their intentions.

'Nick, we respect you as a terraformer, but there is something about you that we struggle with. It's your faith in God.'

Nick, who had never once brought up the subject of faith, was surprised.

'Why is this even a question?'

'It's not a question for you, but for us,' said Richard. 'You see we don't believe that God is a part of this world, and we want to build a place that we can go, and create our own society, without having any Christian or Bible influence on our lives.'

'As you know, throughout history people have tried to get rid of God, but it hasn't worked. The communists in the twentieth century tried hard to do that, but they were in a world surrounded by theism. But for the first time in history, we have an opportunity to create a planet free of God.'

Richard seemed pleased with himself as he said that.

'How will that work?' Nick asked cautiously.

'There will be no tourism on this new planet. People can only immigrate, and only people who have agreed to reject theism can do so. And so it will be a place where everyone agrees they don't want God. That's what will make it work.'

For the first time, Nick felt that sick feeling in his stomach. He didn't want to be that person that helped remove God from society. He didn't want to be known as the person who helped start the atheist planet.

'What's wrong Nick?' Jay's voice asked again.

This time he lifted his head up from his hands, and looked at her.

'If it was you,' he said, 'would you help them build a planet to remove God?'

'Yes I would,' came the reply.

He didn't expect that answer. 'Why?' he asked. 'What possible good reason can there be to say that?'

'Because you are not building the society, you are just building the planet. You can't be responsible for how people use what they have. But you can certainly do the best job you can with the task you have, and you can even do it in your heart as if you were doing it for God.'

He hadn't thought about it like that before. He looked at his parents who were sitting there, as if asking them for an opinion too.

'We don't mind what you do, and I don't think God minds either. In fact, if you think about it, God made you and me, knowing we wouldn't do everything perfectly. God even made people like Richard your atheist acquaintance. He knew what Richard would want to do, but God still gave him the ability to do it. If God can help atheists, then you can help them too.'

For the first time in days, Nick felt the possibility of moving on from this. It was true that God knew everything, and he helped atheists. He knew those people who would reject him, like the atheists did, but he still made them, and let them have their choices. Maybe it was OK to help after all.

That little moment was like when a child takes a pin and pricks a balloon. Next thing, no more balloon. The weight of that worry was just not there anymore.

Nick resolved, he WAS going to do the best job he could of building an atheist planet. He would work as if he was working for the glory of God. And so it was not long after, that work began on two planets using one to terraform the other, to build a heavenly place for atheists to go, to get away from God.

What Nick didn't know was that this planet would suck him and his family, even though they were not atheists themselves, into its story for generations to come. History would be written by the decision he was making today.

CHAPTER FIVE:
EMOTIONAL VIRGINITY

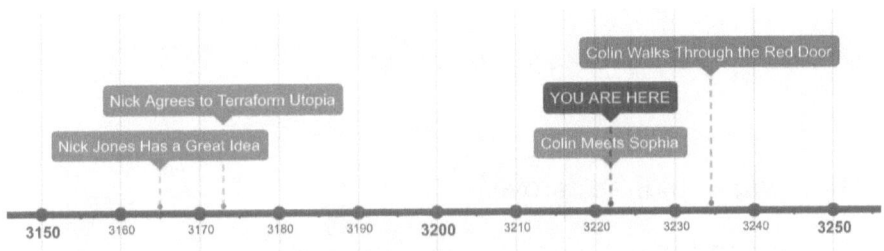

Sophia called her friend Bridie. She had to talk. Bridie and Sophia were close, like sisters; their friendship was deep and trusting, and longstanding. She had to tell her about Colin.

Calling didn't require any device or gadget. Everything she needed to make that call was already with her. She willed to talk with Bridie, and if Bridie willed back, they could start 'speaking' with their public thoughts. It didn't require any actual vocalisation, although it could if they preferred that. Women usually did prefer, so the conversation would have sounded one-sided to someone in the room trying to listen in.

Sophia spoke out loud, 'Bridie you won't believe what happened tonight.'

Bridie was in Sweden, not far on the global map from Estonia. In the good old-fashioned times it would have taken a long day of driving to get together, which included a ferry ride, but being best friends, they had not only shared their thoughts with each other, and their emotions, but also bought each other a translator for their birthdays a few years back. They often spent the weekends at each other's house.

'What happened?

Bridie replied out loud, but Sophia didn't hear it with her ears, but in her public thought space. And so the conversation went, both of them speaking out loud, but hearing in their thoughts.

'I shared my feelings with a man tonight.'

'WHAT!!'

'I knew you wouldn't approve.'

'How can I approve? You don't know any men.'

'Well, this guy has been at my work for years, so I do know him.'

'Who is he? Why have you not told me about him before?'

'His name is Colin. He is the chief mathematician. He works downstairs. Tonight I actually got to talk with him.'

'See. You don't know him, you only know who he is.'

Sophia looked embarrassed, and Bridie knew it. Even though they weren't sharing feelings at that moment, Bridie just knew. What Sophia really wanted to share wasn't her embarrassment, but her excitement. But she just paused for a moment as that embarrassment hit her.

Bridie broke the silence. 'Come on, what did you talk about?'

Sophia was glad to respond. 'Well, the sun was setting over the snow, and he sat there looking lonely, and I knew I could talk to him.'

'Go on.' Bridie softened a bit.

'I came up behind him and said, 'Pretty isn't it?'

'That's all?'

'Well, it was a magical moment and we connected. And, after just a few minutes, he asked if he could feel what I was feeling. As we looked at the sun setting together, it seemed like the natural thing to do.'

'Sophia, you can't give in to a man that easily. It's like losing your virginity. You have to protect yourself. He wanted to take advantage of you.'

'He didn't. He shared his feelings with me too. And, we had the exact same feelings as each other. We both felt what each other felt, and we both felt the same. He cares about me.'

Bridie knew how dangerous that could be. What should she say back? But before she could say anything Sophia spoke again.

'I've kind of liked him for a while, you know seeing him at the cafeteria at work. But when I shared my feelings, he found out. After that, I think we joined our hearts,' said Sophia.

Now Bridie was worried. 'My Darling Sophia, do you remember when we were teenagers, we were given strong warnings about sharing feelings with someone too soon. You know it can bond you in the wrong way. There is a reason why parents tell us these things. There's no way your Dad would have approved of it.'

'Bridie!!'

Sophia had intended to think her name, but it just came out loud, and with emphasis. 'My Dad isn't alive anymore, so it doesn't matter. Anyway, I know I need someone in my life, and don't ask me how I can be so certain, but I really can trust him. Sharing our feelings with each other proved it. And guess what?'

Sophia continued her talking with a sort of question, sort of statement. 'Tomorrow, I'm going to ask him to share his thoughts with me too.'

Bridie was silent for a moment as she privately considered what her friend had just said. As she contemplated it all, she had a horrible creeping sense come all over her. It came with goose bumps.

'You didn't lose your actual virginity to Colin did you?'

Now it was Sophia's turn to be horrified.

'Why would you even think such a thing? Of course not. There is no way I would even consider doing that until we are married. Do you think I'm mad?' She flung that last question right back at her friend.

'No,' came the reply. 'I don't think you are mad.' The accusation stung.

> **Public and Private Thought**
>
> In the same way that feelings are shared using technology via the mindchip, communication can also happen by just thinking.
>
> Thinking is either public or private. Public thinking is still inaudible, but available to thought processing servers for use in communication. With private thought, nobody knows what you are thinking.
>
> Because thinking is so automatic, to learn to think in public takes practice, and this skill is often developed in the first six years of schooling.
>
> Sharing thoughts with another person is a permission-based form of communication reserved usually for people who are close relationally, or in some rare cases in work circumstances.
>
> A child laying down in bed at night can tell her parents what she needs. Her parents can also tell her to get back in bed without leaving their own bed or without anything audible being heard. With the exception of parents or siblings, children do not communicate in thought with anyone until they are eighteen.

Bridie then reconsidered her answer. 'Well, maybe you are mad. I never heard of any woman sharing their feelings with a man the first time they met. It would be easy to have his feelings overwhelm you, and make a mistake that you would later regret for the rest of your life.'

Sophia didn't answer, Bridie kept talking.

'How do you know that he understands his own emotions and thoughts? What if he is immature? How do you know if you can trust him? What if his feelings are fooling him, and fooling you at the same time?'

Sophia still didn't answer. There was a long pause.

'I'm going to ask him to open his thoughts to me anyway,' she replied.

'Goodbye.' Bridie was finished, and left. It was an abrupt end to their conversation. It had not gone the way either of them would have liked. Bridie felt like she hadn't been heard, and Sophia felt attacked.

Sophia figured she wasn't going to wait until she went to work the next day to talk to Colin; she would talk to him straight away. Strike while the iron is hot, her father would have told her. She twisted her memories of him in her mind and he became a supporter of her actions rather than an opponent. Act now, she decided.

She had never communicated with Colin before, except for that conversation while the sun set the previous evening. So she needed to message him the 'old-fashioned way' by sending a direct message to his thought system, kind of like an email from the twenty-first century. She didn't know when he would 'read' it or reply. As well as that, she didn't know how to get a message to him either. What was his address? Maybe she could use his work address, but it would mean going through the work servers. It was going to seem like work was contacting him. It was her only option.

Meanwhile elsewhere in Tallinn, Colin realised an internal message had come through from his work messaging system. His thoughts told him it was from work, so he ignored it. He would check it the next day.

CHAPTER SIX:

THE GRAND HALL OF DOORS

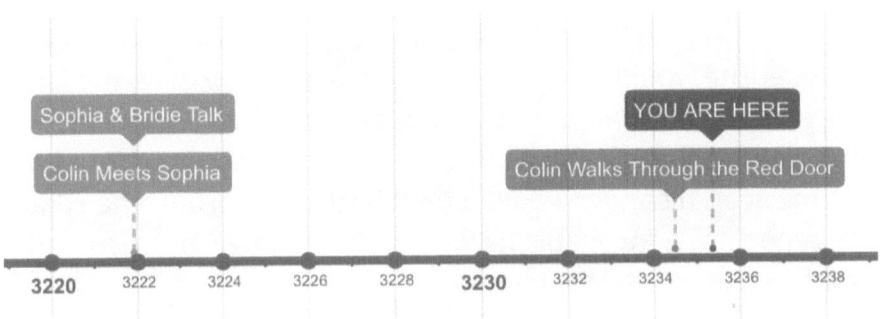

Judson and Silas were identical twins, but were nothing like each other. Yes, it was true they were born on the same Tuesday morning, April the 14th 3219, nine minutes apart. It was also true they looked similar, but once you had met them, it soon became apparent that they were different. It was hard to believe that despite being raised in the same set of circumstances, they had turned out so unalike.

Silas, the younger of the two, was cheerful, an extroverted and mischievous young man, who teased his brother all the time. In a word, jovial. He loved nothing more than playing jokes on his fellow classmates. He could be serious, and like most other people living in the thirty-first century, he had real faith in God, but like many younger people, he also wanted to enjoy life. Within himself, he knew he should take God seriously, but it was a little thought, hard to hear above other more prominent voices.

Judson was likeable, friendly and pleasant to be around, but enjoyed spending time alone. He was a manly young man, showing interest in all the things men did, such as the history of war, guns and fighting. But despite having an interest in conflict, he avoided personal conflict, and was happiest when other people seemed to be cheerful. If others were happy, he was happy. If others were upset, he was upset. His feelings depended to some extent on the feelings of others. Occasionally, when provoked, he would lose control of his feelings, and the less peaceful side of his nature would appear for a short while, cause havoc, and in that state he would say things he regretted. Then, in no time at all, his anger would retreat back to calm, but when that happened it was inevitable he would feel ashamed and want to avoid people.

And so the twins who looked superficially similar, had the potential to get on each other's nerves. One provoking and antagonising, the other ignoring, the first provoking more, the second losing control. There were joys to be experienced in learning and growing together.

On this particular day, their Aunt Angela was coming from Lalande to spend a few days with them. Mr and Mrs Jones needed a few days away to rest and recover, and were going somewhere they didn't want to reveal. That was the point, having a genuine get-away without anybody being able to track them down. But they wanted someone trustworthy around the house to keep an eye on the boys. Yes they were sixteen, and capable enough, but they could also be mischievous. And that was why Angela was coming in from the Planet Lalande via the Grand Hall of Doors.

The Grand Hall of Doors was a unique room. Each planet had its own hall of doors, but Earth's was the biggest, and the grandest, and was also the first. Silas and Judson had never been to the Grand Hall before, and most people, as part of their ordinary regular day-to-day lives, would never have a reason to visit the Hall of Doors. Each planet needed a place like this that did the necessary job of allowing travel between the worlds. Because of rapid growth and advancement in the galaxy, it was often the case that newer planets didn't yet have a connection to all the other planets, and so a return to Earth was often required before leaving to go elsewhere. The Grand Hall operated as a type of hub to a wheel, and on Earth it was physically in North India. So, it was off to India.

To get there, the twins first visited their local 'hall of doors' in Port Sudan. Each town had these local halls, a kind of room with sets of doors. Usually they contained doors to the major cities of importance for them. The local hall in Port Sudan had a doorway to Khartoum, the capital city of Sudan, and a doorway to Alexandria in Egypt, and a third door to Pretoria, in South Africa. In this way they could transport to the major hubs in Africa, and then from there enter other doors to get to other continents, or to other countries or cities in Africa. It was efficient, and fast, at least in Africa. Most local doors charged a basic toll of 500 Valens each way, and nobody checked too closely who you were. Passengers had to place their left hand on the handprint scanner, which tracked location, checked permission to travel, and charged their Valens balance at the same time.

Stellar ID

Stellar ID is a combination of money, roles, permissions and identity. Rather than having multiple sets of 'papers' needed, one set works for everything. There is one identity per person in the galaxy, and everything one does, or applies to do, owns, sells, gives or goes, is connected to this.

Firstly, the ID number is assigned a day after birth. The ID is connected to DNA upon registration. As a person ages, the left hand handprint is added at 12 months, and updated at 5 years, and 18 years. Eye Prints are added at 5 years and updated at 12. Biological ID markers are used in multiple locations.

This was all possible through the use of Stellar ID.

After leaving Port Sudan, and arriving in the African Hall of Alexandria, they ported to the International Hub in Delhi, which cost another 7250 Valens each. A short walk from the International Hub took them to the Grand Hall, where they paid 1000 Valens for entry. It had taken them only twenty minutes, and less than 9000 Valens to get there.

Had they continued past this point and endeavored to leave the planet, that is when it would have become complicated. It wasn't the travel itself that was complicated, no more than using any of the other doors, but when leaving Earth, requirements for travel had to be in place, and sometimes there were delays. The travel tolls were also significant, depending on which planet was the destination.

Planets with a high population tended to lower their fees to encourage tourism, but new planets charged higher fees, to help offset the costs of building and development. Cathedral was an exception. It had a low population but contained the Cathedral Cathedral, the biggest church structure in existence, and visits were encouraged for spiritual purposes, but donations were welcomed. The huge numbers of visitors to Cathedral, especially at Christmas and Easter, meant that the incoming donations exceeded the travel income of all the other planets combined. It allowed genuine development of the Cathedral Cathedral, a building big enough to seat twenty million people at once.

As the twins walked into the room, they stopped to look all around them; it was obvious that it really was a grand place. They had heard many things about this place. It was as though they had just walked outside, when in fact they were indoors. It felt as if they were standing in a giant field on top of the Swiss Alps in the spring. Alpine flowers grew everywhere, asters, orchids and bright blue gentians. The mountains all around were covered in snow and ice, but the field they stood in was verdant and alive. The air was filled with birds and butterflies. It felt real.

The Grand Hall was a large square room with high sides about twenty metres high. The ceiling sloped upwards on all four sides towards a point in the middle. It gave the impression of being inside a pyramid, but with the entire thing hollowed out. The entirety of the floor, the walls, and the sloping ceiling, with the exception of the tip of the ceiling, were a digital display which adjusted visually every 1000 seconds, or about every 15 minutes in analogue time. It gave visitors the feeling of being somewhere else, and it was easy to lose the sense that one was inside a building.

Cost of Travel

Depending on which planet one was planning to travel to, the permission and costs vary widely.

Planet	Price in Valens
Earth	None
Kepler First	120,000
Kepler Second	125,000
Barnard	99,999
Wolff	100,000
Lalande	495,000
Luyton	410,000
Enaiposha	115,000
Cathedral	Donation
Verde	None
Utopia	2,500,000,000
Gileasie	150,000
Carbon One	None
Silica	5,000

No sooner had the twins entered the room than they were lost in the grandeur of the view. But within 80 or 90 seconds of having arrived the display adjusted and they were now on the surface of the sea somewhere in the middle of the ocean with waves all around them. It was a strange feeling of being unsafe, and yet they were safe.

Sometimes visitors came to the Grand Hall simply to be there for the experience. They might go to the Sahara, or the Weddell Ice

Sea, or to deep space, all without leaving the room. It was worth the entrance fee.

The digital display did not extend to the tip of the pyramid. The highest part of the ceiling, instead of being a display, appeared to be a glass structure of some sort. While it was small on the inside, it contained a prism positioned in a precise way to allow a thin beam of sunlight through, which moved across the floor of the big room like a sundial. Instead of the shadow marking time, the beam of light marked time. At whichever point the light beam touched, the digital display would mark the time next to it in seconds, in accordance with the metric system of keeping time.

At different seasons of the year, as the Earth rotated around the sun, the 23 degree tilt of its axis caused the sun to strike the prism on the pyramid in slightly differing ways. The result was that in January, the light timekeeper would move across the floor on one side of the room, but in July, it would transit on the other. All of this was adjusted for by the digital display and gave people an otherworldly feeling. It was like being outside while inside.

Around the lower walls of the Grand Hall were thirteen doors, one for each of the thirteen other planets that had been civilized beyond the Earth . There were also blank spaces where future doors would at the right time be opened, when future planets were ready.

While more than five hundred planets and many moons had been connected, building a door was something special and unique, and reserved for a planet that reached a certain point of readiness. The majority of planets didn't have the population to warrant the building of a door.

Each door in the Grand Hall was large in size, more than five metres in width, and each was trimmed with elaborate white marble mouldings. This made each door stand out clearly against the dramatic visual decor of the wall displays. Each door also had a label etched in silver with onyx outlining into the white marble, written in block style similar to Roman numerals. In this way each of the doors identified where it would take the traveller.

The left wall of the room had five doors, for the first five civilized planets in order being Kepler, Kepler Second, Barnard, Wolff and Lalande. The back wall of the room had another five doors, for the next five being Luyton, Enaiposha, Cathedral, Verde and Utopia. The right side of the wall had just three doors for Gillease, Carbon One and Silica. There were two other blank spaces for two future doors on the right wall. There was no door for Earth, because each of the thirteen doors was an Earth doorway in that other place.

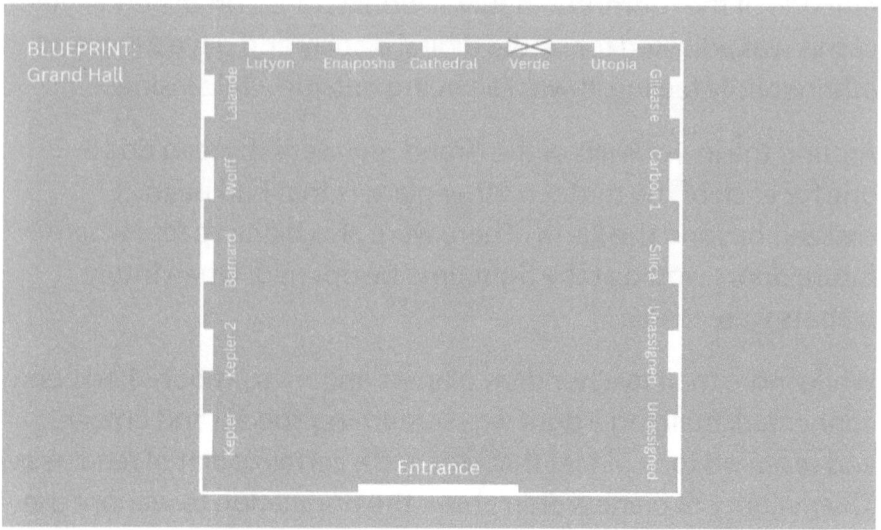

The Grand Hall was open to the public, a place for migration, tourism, and travel management. Aside from being a visual spectacle, it was also a place of hellos and goodbyes. And that was the reason that had brought the twins to the Grand Hall this particular day. Their Aunt Angela was arriving from Lalande.

The boys made their way to the back left corner of the Hall, and stood not far from the door for Lalande. Other people came and went according to their permissions, each scanning their left hand on arrival or exit.

Then, there she was. Angela was before them, right on schedule.

'Nephews!' she called out. 'You've both changed, but still look the same.' She laughed at her own joke.

'You haven't changed, and look the same too,' said Silas with a grin.

Judson smiled, and there were hugs all around.

'It's so good to see you both, and so good to be on
Earth again too.'

'How was your flight?' Silas asked, once again with a cheeky grin.

'Fine, you goose,' came the reply. The flight question was an
antiquated expression from more than 500 years earlier.

'Can we help carry your bag?' asked Judson.

'Yes you can, young man.' She handed the bag over. As he took the
bag from her, she straightened and looked around the room.

'I remember this place,' she said. 'It's been many years since I was
here. What an amazing site.'

'How many planets have you been to Aunt Angela?' Judson asked
a second question.

'Just three of the planets in this room,' she said. 'Earth of course
was my first, and Lalande is where I live, but I also did some
volunteer work on Carbon One for Nicholas Jones. Have you boys
heard of him?'

'Of course we have,' replied Silas. 'Everyone knows about Nick
Jones and his work terraforming planets. We learned about
him in school.'

'He's quite a man, and I really enjoyed working with him on
Carbon One. Do you know that we planted more than one billion
trees? Of course I only planted about five hundred of them.' She
gave a sheepish smile.

'Boys, changing subjects, do you remember who your
Uncle Terry is?'

'Uncle Terry?' Silas quizzed.

'Yes, Uncle Terry. My brother and your Dad's brother.'

'Yes,' they replied in unison. Judson continued, 'But we have never met him. We only know what Dad told us about him.'

'Ok then,' said Angela. 'Do you see that door over there? The door marked Verde. That's the door to the planet where your Uncle Terry lives.'

She pointed at a door on the back wall, four doors away from where they were. It was closed, and clearly not in use.

'It's closed,' Silas noted, stating the obvious. .

'Yes it is, and it won't be opening any time soon.'

Angela signalled to the boys to follow her, and then walked across to the back wall of the room where the door to Verde stood, tall and elegant, with its white marble trimming and elaborate silver writing. There was a note, also framed in silver, with elegant black writing that was fixed in the middle of the door.

TRAVEL TO VERDE

*In accordance with a planetary agreement
between Utopia and Verde, development of
Verde has ceased. Travel to the planet Verde
is no longer possible through this door.*

The twins read the sign, and read it again.

'Is Uncle Terry stuck on Verde?' asked Judson.

'Sort of,' said Angela. 'Terry was living there when the agreement between the planets was signed. He had the choice to leave, but didn't. He can still leave if he wants, but if he leaves, he won't be allowed to move back again. People can leave, but not return, and the planet isn't developing any more.'

'Does he like it there?' asked Silas.

'He does. The planet has minimal infrastructure. There is no communication system, no thought control servers, minimal health care, and most people grow their own food. It is primitive compared to Earth. But it does have good coffee.'

'So why does he want to live there?' asked Silas.

'He likes the quiet life and working in the garden. He also loves to pray, and the little church they go to on Verde is a happy place. But if you ever get to visit, he'll put you to work in his garden.'

'Sounds interesting,' said Judson.

'Sounds terrible,' said Silas.

'Anyway, now you know where Uncle Terry is. I wanted to show you before we left.'

Judson picked up Angela's bag and they turned to walk towards the main entrance, when he noticed the door adjacent to Verde, the door to Utopia. The door was open, but unlike the other open doors, nobody was using this door. A simple white sign was posted on a small round silver stand.

UTOPIA
Visit by Immigration Only,
Cost V2,500,000,000
Proof of Atheism Required.

'Aunt Angela, what is atheism?' Silas asked.

'It's a belief system that people have, that God is not a part of our world.'

'But God is a part of our world.' Silas stated back. Judson kept staring at the door.

'Yes we know, but they would prefer to avoid things to do with God and church and Jesus.'

'Why do they have their own planet?' Judson queried.

'I don't know exactly,' she replied, saying less than she knew.

As they walked away, and left the Grand Hall behind, both Judson and Silas, separate from each other, had a curious feeling. A strange desire to visit that forbidden place came over them both.

CHAPTER SEVEN:
THE ROMANTIC TIERS

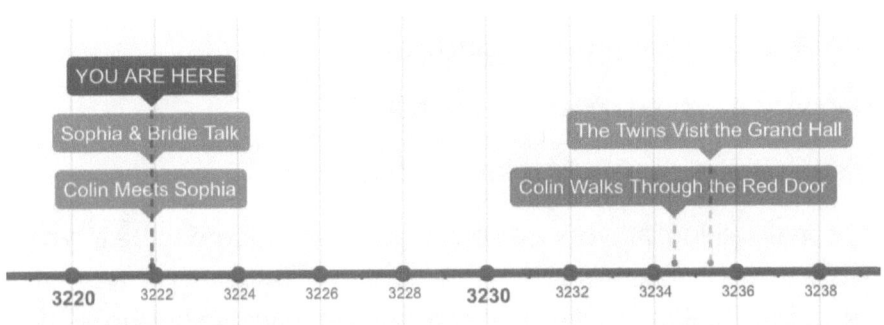

Next morning, Colin got to work a few minutes early, which wasn't standard for him, but he couldn't sleep the night before. He had Sophia on his mind all night. He had never met anyone before who he felt so connected to. He hoped if he was a little early to work, he might spot her in the break room.

She wasn't there. Oh well. He decided to check his messages and was surprised to see a message from her.

Sorry to communicate through work channels, but I didn't know how to talk to you. Would you be willing to share your thoughts with me? We can talk all the time then.

It was a little forward, but he liked it. He didn't know of the conversation with her friend Bridie the night before, which rather than putting the brakes on the situation, had poured gasoline on Sophia's emotional fire. Colin knew that he felt good about her, so of course he was willing to share his thoughts. Noting her Stellar ID tagged in the note he gave permission, and within a minute she had reciprocated. He didn't know where she was physically in the building, but they were now able to talk, inaudibly, by thinking to each other. This would happen, even while they were working, and nobody else would know except for them.

Colin walked to the coffee station to get his morning green coffee, but his mind was running.

'How are you this morning Sophia?'

'Happy and excited now that I can talk to you.'

'I couldn't sleep last night thinking about you.'

Personal 'talking' at work was prohibited, considered to be a type of cheating on an employer. It was hard to know the extent of the public thinking that employees were involved in during work hours, but most employers tended to not worry overly as long as the work was completed. As long as it didn't interfere with their productivity, it wouldn't cause a problem.

'Want to have lunch together?' she asked.

He did, and they decided to have souvlaki, Greek food, at a place not far from their offices. Within a minute, via public thought, they had booked a table, ordered the food, and it would be waiting for them at midday.

At midday, Sophia walked out of the front door of the office block. A large row of glass panels ran across the entire front of the building, above an elevated courtyard with wide marble stairs leading down. A fountain with a statue of Sören Saar stood fifty metres away from the bottom end of the stairs, with a stone walkway around and dotted with bare deciduous trees, whose leaves had long gone. Snow and ice covered the landscape. In that frigid scene, Colin stood already at the base of the stairs waiting for her. She knew where to find him because he sent her a mental picture of the location. They started walking towards the fountain and Colin reached down and grabbed her hand. He didn't ask her either out loud or by thinking, so it was a surprise, but she was delighted to feel his hand again.

They walked along in the middle of the day, when shadows lay sideways on the ground. The more northerly position of the sun did that to their shadows. Colin felt at peace and she felt that feeling within him too. She felt excited and he loved that he was the reason for such excitement in her. She felt that love, and so their feelings were reciprocated in such a way that both of them were swimming in oxytocin. In a strange way, even though they had only known each other for less than a day, their future together was already determined. They had started down the slippery slope from where it was inevitable they would end up together for better or worse.

Over lunch they talked and started learning about each other. Couples liked talking out loud. Most people did. It felt more authentic, real, and personal. You could hear the tone in the other person's voice, and got a sense of what people were feeling. But over lunch Colin and Sophia talked verbally, and also shared emotion inwardly. Using both at once, it was the most intimate method a couple could use in communication.

'Where were you born?' Colin asked.

'Right here in Tallinn.'

'So, have you ever been or lived anywhere else?' he asked.

'Not really. Since my grandfather Sören started ICE, the family was tied here, and they were such workaholics we never really had any holidays. Nope, just Tallinn.'

But then she remembered Bridie.

'Oh, I have been to Sweden many times to visit my friend Bridie.'

'Bridie?' Colin quizzed.

'Well we met during secondary studies, and then she ended up doing different things at tertiary level, but by then we were best friends. We talk almost every day.'

'Did you tell her about me?'

'Yes I did,' she answered. 'She thinks I'm losing my mind to share my feelings with you this fast.'

'Well she might be right,' said Colin, and he winked at her. 'Because I sure am losing my mind for you.'

Sophia laughed, and felt at ease. She could tell him anything, and so she updated Colin about everything that Bridie had said.

'You are lucky to have such a good friend who cares about you,' he surmised.

Colin went on to tell her about his family. He had grown up in Germany, but he was actually English. He had an older brother that was still in Germany and was married. When he was offered the job at ICE, his parents moved with him. They were concerned because he was single, and wanted to be near him and make sure he was OK.

'I really am OK,' he said. 'There's no reason why my parents need to be here in Tallinn. They have grandchildren back in Germany, so they should be with them.'

'You sound bothered.'

'I guess I am. I really do like them. They are good people. But I want to be myself and not have people checking on me all the time.'

'Well I don't have anyone checking on me. Except for Bridie. My parents died last year and it's just me now,' added Sophia.

It was the first time that Colin felt in his body, her feelings of sadness. It wasn't a strong feeling, just a tinge, like when a faint smell of something like bacon or popcorn is discerned in an unexpected location. But he sensed it was a sorrow that hadn't gone away.

'I feel sad for you.'

As Colin said that, she felt that sadness come back. When this type of thing happened, sometimes the sharing of feelings could become strange. Was she feeling her own feelings echoed? Or was he actually sad for her? It wasn't always possible to tell. Often when someone did feel the feelings of another, they felt so authentic it was like it was your own feeling.

'Hey, would you like to meet my parents?' Colin suggested. He knew that once he was married, they would give him space, and once she was married, she would no longer be lonely. Maybe they could do this? They could even do it now.

In his excitement, his thoughts betrayed him. He had intended to think those things to himself, but he failed to differentiate between his private and public thoughts, an easy mistake when excited.

Everything he had just been thinking, she had heard.

She looked at him with wide eyes.

'Did you just propose marriage to me?'

'Well I was definitely thinking about being married to you,' he smiled with a guilty expression. 'That part of my thought was supposed to be private. But I guess I'm an open book. You know everything I'm thinking. I sure would love to be married to you, not just because it would solve our personal issues, but because you seem like the nicest, sweetest person I have ever known. I can't imagine being with anyone else.'

'Well I accept,' she said.

What would Bridie say?

He beamed at her, and she hugged him, and both of them were filled with happiness, their own and each other's.

'Now I definitely have to meet your parents,' she said again.

And so over lunch they made plans to meet Colin's parents that evening for dinner.

And that was that. Within just 20 hours of meeting each other, they had gone from not knowing each other to being engaged. Right at that moment Bridie was in Sweden and had no idea what was happening. If she had known, she would have been horrified. They had done a thorough job of messing up the romantic tiers.

Romantic Tiers

There are widespread expectations in culture about how young men and women would behave toward each other in an appropriate way. The first major study into sexuality by James Unwin in the 1900's had demonstrated the societal dangers of playing loosely with sex. At first society ignored that study, and the aftermath of the sexual revolution that followed proved Unwin to be correct. Later it was realised there was in fact more personal liberty when one controlled oneself. The result of this was the informal development of Romantic Tiers, an unofficial, but commonly held set of levels through which a couple could pass on their way to marriage. Not every circumstance was the same, but for a younger man or woman, still living at home, the typical tiers were these:

1. Meeting each Other
2. Parental Approval to Proceed
3. Dating - Talking in person
4. Sharing Public Thoughts with Each Other - ie silent communication.
5. Holding Hands - Limited Physical Affection
6. Engagement
7. Sharing Emotions with Each Other
8. Marriage
9. Consummation of Marriage.

The last few tiers were held by almost all of society to be correct and in the correct order. For a young man or woman to lose their virginity prior to marriage was considered a disaster. It wasn't because they were not accepted by society as people, but because they might not be able to find a partner to marry other than the person they had lost their virginity to, or someone else like them.

The ideal of marrying someone with intact virginity was so highly prized, that the chances of marriage if you had lost it slipped dramatically. It was foolishness to risk giving up such a prized possession.

Not only that, but the attempt to convince someone to give up their virginity, was a signal that this human was not trustworthy. If they tried to convince you to give up what you had to offer only to one person after they committed to marriage, then how could you trust them to remain faithful later in marriage, if they couldn't be faithful before. In this manner people dared not give up their virginity, nor dare to even ask for it until it was safe to do so, which was within a marriage.

CHAPTER EIGHT:

IT'S FUN TO BE TWINS

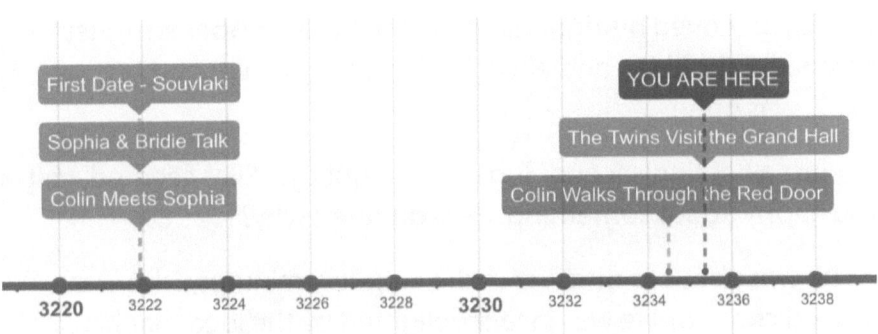

Mr and Mrs Jones had gotten away on their holiday the day before, and the twins were under the care of their Aunt Angela for the next few days. They could take care of themselves, but it made their parents feel better knowing someone was there. It also gave them a chance to see their Aunt, who they hadn't seen for many years. It was a school day, and the boys were off to school.

Being a Friday, it was the only day in the week that both boys went to the same school, their base school in Port Sudan. Because of the way that secondary level education operated, they attended different schools and classes most days, but not on Fridays. And on this particular day Judson had woken up later than usual. He wasn't worried about how long it would take to get to school, because all the students at his school had been issued with personal translators. Once he was dressed, he only had to activate the switch on the strap around his upper left arm and he would in an instant, translate into his classroom.

Silas was already dressed, and about to go.

'Silas, would you say sorry to Mrs Adams that I will be fifteen minutes late today?' Judson asked.

'Sure,' came an enthusiastic reply. 'It would absolutely be my most wonderful pleasure to tell her that for you.'

Silas then moved his right hand over to his left upper arm, just below the shoulder, and engaged his transfer chip. And in a blink, was gone.

For just a fleeting second, Judson thought that Silas seemed a bit too happy about something. He wondered why?

As he was about to discover in the next few minutes, Silas was indeed cheerful. He was in fact delighted by the idea that his brother would be late. He had been waiting for such a magical opportunity as this to present itself. Not only was Judson late for school, but it was a day they were both together, and Silas would be at the school before Judson. And not only that, it was one of the rare assembly mornings. A guest speaker was coming to speak to the entire cohort of students. So Judson would not only be late for class, but be late to assembly. The circumstances were perfect. The planets had aligned. Nobody could stop him now.

Silas arrived on his grid at school, a section of the room with no furniture and a white grid marked on the floor with each person's name on it. When people arrived they landed on their square and it was not permissible to stand or walk on any other person's square in case they also arrived at that moment causing a physical displacement. It wasn't safe, and if anyone was caught crossing the grid, either deliberately or accidentally, there were school consequences, most often extra work..

Silas looked around for Mrs Adams. She was busy with her head down. He then looked at his classmates, then looked around the room. Nobody was watching. He put his hand into his pocket and pulled out a small knife. He then bent down as if tying his shoelaces, but reached across to the square on the grid next to his own, to Judson's square. He cut a small incision into the carpet right in the middle where the translator pair ending was embedded, and extracted it.

He had to be quick. He had to move the other half of Judson's pair. If Judson arrived at school while it was in his pocket, not only would they both be hurt, but his pants would be ripped.

'Excuse me Mrs Adams…. Uhh, toilet.' He bolted out the door, not intending to go to the toilet at all, but headed straight for the assembly room where in a few minutes the entire school would be gathered. It wasn't far away. Making his way onto the stage area itself, some other students were already there setting up seating and equipment. He tiptoed behind the rigging and curtains and inched forward to a place where the curtains had been pulled across to the side. If the assembly was happening right now, he would be out of sight on stage right, but he wasn't going to give that same privilege to Judson.

He put the half of Judson's school translator he held in his hand on the floor, and pushed it out into the main stage area. It slid across the polished timber flooring, and came to a resting place in the middle of the stage, right in front of the speaker's podium. If a guest was speaking, Judson's pair half was on the floor about five feet in front of where they would stand. It couldn't be more perfect. When he did appear, the entire school would see him arrive.

Hundreds of fellow students were now gathering ready for the special morning. Silas slipped away back to his room in time to join his class, and advised his teacher that Judson was late today.

The class then made its way to the assembly hall together and the morning got underway.

* * * * *

A few miles away, Judson finished putting his shoes on and walked to the mirror to check himself. He looked acceptable. He reached up to his left shoulder and pushed the little blue button.

Blink.

Judson arrived with his back to the assembly, and at first didn't realise where he was. He was puzzled to notice a large unfamiliar woman standing in front of him, dressed in formal attire, and wearing an academic gown, as if she was giving a lecture. The thought never occurred to him that he was anywhere other than his base classroom, or that she was giving a speech. But looking down he noticed he was not on the grid, there was no carpet, the floor was wooden. Something was different.

Then he heard the noise of laughter behind him. Surprised, he spun around to see who was there. His mouth dropped open, as he took a few slow seconds to work out what was going on. He struggled to process the context of the situation. He was standing on an elevated stage, along with a large well-dressed woman, and before him were 1200 students, and every single one of them was looking at him, with the widest variety of facial expressions. Some of them reacted with hysterical laughter.

'Get off the stage,' came an exasperated voice from the side of the room. He looked across and noticed it was Mrs Adams, his teacher. Then Judson noticed Silas in the crowd fist punching the sky with a look of pure delight on his face.

'Haha. Got you brother,' came the public thought from Silas to Judson across the room. He heard it too. Nobody else heard it, but Judson knew who it was.

He was embarrassed. He didn't like being in front of crowds. He was scared of public speaking; it was too much. There was only one thing he could think of doing. He reached up to his right shoulder and pressed the little blue button and in just the same way it had brought him here, to this side of the pair, it now took him away to the other side. He was now back home as fast as he had come. He didn't have the courage to return to school that day.

He plonked on his bed and trembled. After a few minutes he sat up. Then, sitting at home in his room he now started to have other feelings come from within. In a stew of emotion, he found he actually did have some courage after all. He was going to plan a little prank of his own. Silas would arrive back home after lunch, and he was going to get his brother back, and he knew how.

Walking into Silas' bedroom where he kept his half of his school travel translator, Judson stood for a moment looking to work out where he kept his school travel translator half. He then noticed the small bump on the floor in the carpet which housed the home side of the pair. He bent down to pull it out.

'Back already?'

It was Aunt Angela. She didn't expect to see either of them until after lunch.

'Yes, I'm not feeling well.'

He straightened up and stood looking at her, as he lied. He hated lying. It wasn't OK to lie, but he felt so angry he just had to get his brother back. He had to make up something.

'Why are you in Silas' room?'

'I'm looking for the painstick.' It was another lie. The painstick was a pain relief controller in the form of an electronic stick, like a television remote.

The reality was that Judson was not sick, and did not need the painstick.

'You don't look unwell.'

'It's the muscles in my back. That's why I was bent over.'

'Hmmm.' said Aunt Angela. She had children of her own too. She looked at him. She suspected something. 'When you find the painstick, take the reading, and then show me before you reduce the pain.'

'Yes Aunt Angela.'

Angela left the room, and Judson's mind started whirring. What was he going to do? How was he going to fake his pain and also pull off

---

The Pain Scale/The Painstick

A mindchip can sense nerve activity to determine or measure the level of pain in the human body. This is useful in medical situations, both for diagnosis, and triage.

Pain is measured on the Dolor Scale, from zero to one hundred Dolor. Zero Dolor represents no pain whatsoever, but that is not always the case for everyone. Most people live in the 5-15 Dolor range. Pain starts to become noticeable in the 20-25 Dolor range, but many people are still able to function at that level. Pain around 50 Dolors is significant and people take remedial action, and pain above 80 Dolors interferes with one's ability to think.

Pain can be turned off or turned down by controlling software. Children need the approval of parents up to 25 Dolors. Parents often buy their children a painstick, which they can use anytime it is needed. Adults can make their own decision to minimise pain up to 30 Dolors. Medical approval is required to dull pain above these limits.

---

his prank of revenge? He could only think of one thing that would trick Aunt Angela. It would take real pain to pull this off.

He grabbed the half of the translator from the floor in Silas' room. He needed that to finish his prank. Then he pretended to be in pain, and walked out the door, and down the stairs to the hallway cupboard. He knew for sure that he would find the painstick there. Angela sat in the lounge nearby and could see him in the hallway.

Grabbing the painstick from its resting place with the other first aid equipment, he then did something which took a fair bit of courage. He slammed the door shut, but left his fingers in the gap. The door crushed two of his fingers between the two doors. He bit his lip so he wouldn't make a noise. The door didn't make a noise either because his fingers had perfectly stopped the bang.

He wanted to scream at the top of his lungs, but he managed to control himself. With his other good hand, he pointed the painstick at his head, and pressed the measure button.

Beep. 47 Dolors.

That amount of pain was too high for his purpose. He waited five seconds and pressed again.

Beep. 42 Dolors.

He waited another few seconds.

Beep. 39 Dolors.

He hobbled out to Angela and showed her the screen.

'39 Dolors!! Are you OK?'

'Yes I'm OK.'

Judson continued talking, 'Can I minimise my pain by 25?'

'Yes you can. Why don't you go and lie down for a few hours?'

'Thank you Aunt Angela.'

Judson hobbled up the stairs towards his bedroom. Once in his room, if Angela had still been watching, she would have noticed that he seemed to have recovered. How amazing! He walked to the window and opened both it and the insect screen. He then reached far out and threw Silas' school translator half high into the sky, in an arc above him, onto the roof of the house. He heard a satisfying thunk as somewhere up there it landed on the metallic roofing.

What Judson didn't see, or didn't realise, was that the translator half he had thrown didn't stay where it landed, but slid down the metal roof, and into the gutter on the edge of the house. From there it would have fallen two stories to the ground, except for the guttering that held it in that precarious position.

He closed the window and laid down on the bed. He wasn't alone, or bored, or tired, and not in pain either. He lay there thinking and watching mental videos, something that any boy his age would love to do on a school day. But the day was far from over for him.

About three hours later, Judson was laying there, when suddenly he heard an intrusive, loud and unexpected noise above him. It sounded as if someone had dropped a large rock on the edge of the roof, which was in effect what had happened. Then he heard a boyish scream, more like a terrified yell, as Silas arrived home, realised where he was and fell off the edge of the roof. About two metric seconds after came a thump, and a groan sounding from below as Silas landed on a concrete path which ran outside his window. He had fallen five metres to his landing place on concrete. Judson jumped to his feet and raced over to the window and as fast as he could, pulled it open. There on the ground below was Silas, in pain, holding his right leg with both hands. He noticed that his leg seemed to bend about halfway between his knee and ankle as though something had snapped it. Silas had broken his leg.

At that moment Judson had a sinking feeling in the pit of his stomach. He wished today had never happened at all. He wished all of this would go away. How he wished he had never retaliated against his brother. He even wished Angela had caught him lying and stopped the entire thing. He didn't want his brother to be hurt, and he knew, he just knew there were going to be terrible consequences as a result.

Angela raced out the back of the house. Hearing the noise, she had come to investigate. Finding Silas lying on the ground. At once she summoned paramedics, who were there within sixty seconds.

The medical professionals ran through their triage with the use of a triage stick, and assessed that Silas was not in a life-threatening situation, but was in pain. They administered pain relief through his brain chip, and he started to feel better. They told him not to move and then inserted a chip into his translator manager, alerted the hospital that he was coming and to prepare a bed, and then activated his light blue button.

Within two minutes of having fallen from the roof, Silas was free of pain, and in an emergency department being seen by doctors.

'Silas, I'm Dr Livingstone.'

Silas smiled at that.

'Is that your real name?'

'Yes it is, but my first name isn't David.' He smiled too. He had said that line many times.

'You have a broken leg, both tibia and fibula, snapped right through. How did it happen?'

'I fell off the roof.'

Paramedics

Paramedics in the thirty-second century had an enviable record for speed and quality delivery of proper medical first aid. More lives were saved by paramedics than by doctors.

Many people have a paramedic subscription. This means they keep a translator half in their home in case of an emergency, and the paramedics have the other half. In many cases this allows instant arrival of paramedics to a situation within just minutes after an emergency had occurred.

In the year 2940 at speed olympics, paramedic teams competed from all over the known galaxy. A record was set of seventeen seconds for paramedics responding to a home with a paid pair subscription service. Across the entire galaxy, the average response time was less than two minutes from request to the arrival of help.

'Didn't your parents tell you not to go up there?'

Silas could have been angry, but he wasn't. He thought he heard a sorry coming through from Judson in his thoughts. Sometimes it was hard to tell someone's thoughts when a lot was happening inside the mind. He forgave his brother. He loved jokes, and never kept a grudge.

'I think it was a joke that went wrong,' He told the doctor.

'Intentional or not, your leg needs an exoskeleton.'

'An exo-what?' asked Silas.

'It's like a bone on the outside, a shell that wraps around your leg. It does several things. It holds everything inside together so it doesn't move. It also acts as bones for you, so you can walk around like normal. You won't feel any different.'

The doctor kept explaining.

'The exo-skeleton contains an electronic component that speaks with your mindchip. It will automatically manage pain for you, but only in your leg. It will also provide periodic micro-massage to stop muscle deterioration from lack of use. It also has a numerical counter that signifies how long it must remain on. It will keep a track of your healing and can only be removed when the counter reaches zero.'

Over the next hour, Silas was given a micro-sleep. They had aligned his bones. They had given medicine straight into the bones for quicker healing, and had fitted an exoskeleton and locked it with a thought key, connected to the hospital administrative systems. Silas was brought out of his sleep and was able to see he had a shiny white leg, maybe a little thicker than his real leg, but with an electronic display, which stated. '45 Days'

'Forty fiv e days and it will unlock on its own,' said Dr Livingstone. 'But if you have any issues come back here and any of the staff are able to unlock it for you.'

'Why do you lock it?' asked Silas.

Dr Livingstone grinned as if the answer was obvious.

'To keep the exoskeleton safe from teenage meddling.'

And that was that. Silas now had what seemed like a whole new body part.

An hour later, other family members started arriving. Jonathan and Connie cut short their holiday and went straight to St Luke's hospital in Khartoum. They were relieved to see he was fine. Angela had arrived, and apologised multiple times for what had happened on her watch.

'It's not your fault Angela,' said Jonathan.

'I feel so terrible,' she said.

'Not as terrible as the boys are going to feel when we send them to Verde for the summer,' chipped in Connie with a big grin. 'Uncle Terry will put them to work.'

Verde! That was a shock.

But they were not kidding. When summer break arrived in a few weeks time, both Judson and Silas were being shipped off to Uncle Terry on Verde, to learn some of life's important lessons: The value of hard work, the joy of boredom, and how to be nice to your brother.

CHAPTER NINE:

THE JESUS QUESTION

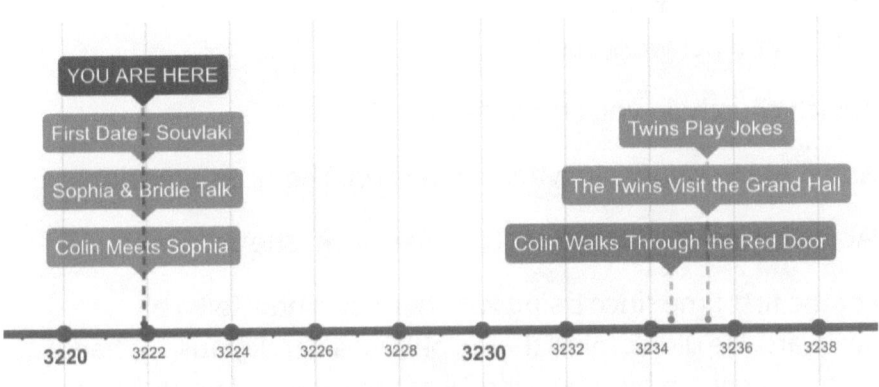

Sophia was expecting the question, and she knew the question was going to be asked at some point; it was inevitable. Colin's family were churchgoers. Even non-church families asked these questions, and so she knew at some point sooner or later, they would want to know where she stood with Jesus. And like everything with Colin, it was sooner.

They sat around the table in the Philips' living room. It was a small rectangular table in a small white living room. The house itself was small, that wasn't unusual because most people had small homes, especially in Europe where the population was higher. The walls inside were plain but decorated with a few nice pieces of artwork from the late twenty-second century and some modern art pieces as well. It wasn't common to have actual art; most people had screen art.

Dinner was modest but tasty, prepared at the last minute. Potatoes, corn, greens and lamb, all home-cooked by Mrs Philips. She cooked most evenings, but sometimes the men themselves would make something.

'So tell us about yourself Sophia?'

Sophia told them about her significant family, her upbringing in Tallinn, and her work at ICE.

'Which church do you attend?'

And there it was, the inevitable question. The Jesus question.

'Actually I don't attend church, I never have,' she answered.

For the first time since being with her, Colin now felt a bit awkward. He didn't mind that Sophia wasn't religious. He had attended church his whole life, but faith itself had never been important to him, it was a social thing, a weekly family event. If Sophia didn't want to go to church, that was OK. 'In fact,' he thought privately to himself, 'She might be my reason for skipping out on Sundays too.' He liked the idea of having some more time to himself.

'Better not admit to that just now,' he also thought to himself.

'Isn't that a bit unusual for you not to attend church?' asked Colleen.

'Not for my family. I don't think we have ever attended church. Maybe if you went back in our family tree. I know my grandparents and parents certainly didn't.'

'What about Christmas and Easter?' asked Gary. 'Everyone goes to church, at least some of the time.'

They were a little pushy.

'The truth is,' she paused, 'My grandfather Sören was against churches. I don't know why, but he never attended one, and never let my father go either. He made sure my dad found a wife who thought the same. When I got older, he sat me down and told me that churches would waste my life. He said if I wanted to achieve anything substantial, my time would be better spent doing other things.'

She was more or less being honest about the reality of how she felt.

While Gary was thinking about what to say in reply, Colin wanted to jump in and defend her, but he didn't know what to say either. His upbringing hadn't prepared him to be an apologist for not attending church.

Sophia continued. 'Sören, my grandfather, said that spending one entire day each week on prayers and scriptures could be spent better in other ways. Imagine that, an entire fifteen percent of your week used up on religion. He spent his life, including Sundays, working on building a mathematics database so we could have consistent interstellar communication. I mean I do see his point. You can see how it benefitted him, and all of us.'

It was Colleen who came to the rescue of what was turning into a difficult moment.

'I know,' she said, 'Why don't' you join us this Sunday at our church? We'd love to have you come along. Would you do that for us?'

It was a bold move by Colleen. Sophia wasn't expecting that at all. She looked at Colin, to see what he was thinking.

'You don't have to,' he thought. 'Only if you want to.'

She was still silent, although contemplating in her private mind what to say. At that moment, Colin sent her a quick thought. Neither of Colin's parents sensed it or knew they had connected in that way.

'If you say yes, it will make them happy,' he thought to her. 'Later when we are married, we can both stop going to church. I agree, it's a waste of our time.'

Sophia then answered Colleen's question, 'Sure. I'd be happy to come and see what your church is like, and share your religious experiences.'

So, it was the morning after next, and church was scheduled to start at 48,000 metric seconds, (Equivalent time 9:52 on the old imperial time in Tallinn). Gary and Colleen arrived at church about a thousand seconds early. They didn't need to find a seat for themselves because they sat in the same place each week as did most people. But they would need to find a seat for Sophia, which meant they would all sit somewhere different this time. There were few spare chairs in churches, because the majority of people in society already attended a church, and not many visitors were expected.

The history of Christianity was something that was both strange and marvellous. Christian historians said it had a duality to it, both human and divine. From its beginnings with Jesus and the twelve disciples it seemed popular and politically threatening. Jesus did miraculous things that seemed so divine. But then Jesus died, which happened to humans. The movement appeared to be over, but then the disciples saw Jesus once again and he was very much alive, which could not be more divine. Not everyone accepted there had been a resurrection, but the disciples certainly believed they saw him, and lived convinced and convincingly. The early Christians had many problems; they were persecuted and misunderstood and often poor and mistreated, all human predicaments. But within three hundred years the Roman Empire had fallen to Christendom, a true miracle, and an unexpected divine outcome. And so the story continued with the strange mixture of humanity and divinity, of human failure and miracles combined. And now Christianity had more or less conquered the planet, and it seemed the planets. Churches were everywhere and 90% of people attended church often.

The jewel in the crown of Christ was the former nation of India, at one point a polytheistic mega nation with more than a billion humans, and a million 'gods.' India was now thoroughly devoted to the worship of Jesus. Not only that, but Delhi had become the capital of Christianity and the de-facto capital city on Earth. It was an unexpected change, and something that felt divine.

But what Sophia had not shared was that her grandfather Sören was one of those few avowed atheists. In his reading of history, he did not observe the divine hand at all, but a combination of human interest and fortune that favoured the greedy and the brave. For him, it was people who took advantage of the divine idea to push their own selfish interests. God had not played any part according to Sören.

One summer's day many years earlier, when Sophia was just a young lady, Sören had a conversation with her in a grove of pear trees. During those moments he gave her guiding principles for life.

'Sophia, listen to me,' he said. 'There is no dispute that a God of some type created everything. Everyone knows that. But what does it mean for us now? Christians will tell you that it means we belong to God, and must worship Him. They will use this to control you, and in fact they already control everything.'

He continued.

'The fact is there is no evidence that God is a part of our lives at all. We don't see him anywhere, he doesn't do anything. He is an absent father, who brought us into the world, and then left home. He is a God who wound up the clock of the universe and then went somewhere else to leave it to tick away. Perhaps he will come back sometime, but isn't it reasonable to conclude that we don't have any obligation to him?'

Sophia had to agree; it made sense to her.

As she grew, Sören continued to fill her mind with the atheist worldview, which revolved around a universe with no God in it. He taught her that morals were important for civilization, but not divinely commanded. You could do whatever you wanted and God would not be offended, but if it caused harm to others, it might well harm you back. Atheists were good people as far as their public behaviour was concerned, but they had no love for God. He didn't matter to them at all. Why make an effort for something that wasn't there? If it was true, then it was logical and reasonable.

And so one way or another, attending church was going to be something new and different for Sophia.

She stood next to Colin in the snow out the front of the building. It was a modern building, built with glass and stone, but with a traditional church appearance. It had a high roofline and a steeple. A sign outside on the right of the path read 'Church of St James.'

Colin reached out and with his left hand took a hold of Sophia. He held her right hand and pulled her nearer to him. Then together they walked in through the double-glazed glass doors at the front of the worship facility. Inside was another pair of glass doors leading from the foyer into the sanctuary. The right door had an image of a fisherman emblazoned on the glass. It was St James. On the left door, an image of Christ on the cross covered the glass. Jesus looked remarkably well for someone who was being executed. Sophia knew who Christ was and knew the story of the crucifixion. She didn't know anything about St James or why he was emblazoned as a fisherman.

As Colin entered the building, with a new female face by his side, the regular attenders, all who knew him, were curious about this woman. A few parishioners greeted them with friendly faces, and soon they were seated with Colin's parents. The service was due to commence in 300 seconds.

Sophia looked around the room. She had been inside a church building a few times in her life, for funerals and weddings, but still, the scene was unfamiliar. On the walls were signage with what seemed to her spiritual slogans. A big sign read 'Jesus Saves.' She thought to herself that it made no sense at all. 'He saves what?' she thought.

'Sophia,' it was Colin. He spoke out loud.

'Yes.' She answered out loud too.

'This church, St James parish, is a traditional church. We follow the ancient liturgies, although we follow them in English, a modern language. Soon we will start to read scriptures, sing songs, and repeat sayings that have been used for thousands of years.'

He continued.

'Other churches are modern churches, they sing modern music, and have modern prayers. It makes no difference to faith, it's simply preference. All the different churches have the same God and generally agree about most things.'

'Why do you come here?' Sophia queried.

'It's my parents, they like the old-fashioned style.'

And at that point, the minister motioned for everyone to stand, he said a short prayer, and one of those old songs started.

Praise to the Lord, the Almighty, the King of creation!

O my soul praise Him, for He is your health and salvation.

As they started singing, Sophia noted a few things. There was that word 'salvation' in the song. Curious! Next, she noted that somehow right before the words were sung, everyone knew what to sing. It was a clever use of public thought sharing. She had never encountered that before. But the thing that most got her attention was how happy everyone was singing. The song continued.

Come all who hear, now to his temple draw near,

Join me in glad adoration.

'Glad adoration,' she thought. 'That's what it is.'

She looked across at Colin who was singing along. He always did sing along. 'They are happy,' she thought to him. 'Even if they are completely deluded, at least they are enjoying themselves.'

'May as well enjoy yourself,' he thought back with an accompanying grin. And so she decided she was going to enjoy herself too.

After the song finished, the minister stood up, and looked at them. It was then that Sophia had a brilliant idea.

'Colin.' She didn't call out. She thought it out, and nobody heard a word except him.

'Yes.'

'Why don't we ask the minister right after the service to marry us?'

'Today?'

'Yes today.'

'He won't be able to marry us today,' Colin clarified.

'No, I mean ask him today.'

'When do you want to be married?' He wanted to know what her answer was, and was also curious what it would be.

'As soon as possible,' came her reply.

Colin tried to remember what the rules were for marriage. He felt like in Greater Europe a month's notice for marriage was required, or it would be something like that.

'How about in a month?'

'Yesss.' If she could have squealed her thoughts, she would have done it. It was the silent equivalent of mental delight.

'Where would you like to be married?'

Sophia had no hesitation in her answer. She had planned her wedding ever since she was a little girl. In fact Bridie had helped her plan it.

'Malta,' came the reply.

'I like the sound of that. Where do you want to honeymoon?' As Colin asked that last question he was hoping she would want to travel. It wasn't that he wanted her to choose everything, but he did really want her to have what she dreamed of. He wasn't fussed about what type of wedding they would have, or even where the wedding would be located, but he wanted to travel somewhere off the planet for the honeymoon, somewhere unique.

'I like the idea of a honeymoon on a boat, sailing the oceans,' she replied.

Colin had to admit, it did sound nice. He wasn't sure how he would be able to give her that, and also travel, but right there, in church, he realised there was a way to do both.

'I know where to take you,' he thought to her. 'Would you be willing to trust me, and I'll surprise you with the location.'

'I do trust you Colin. Surprise me.'

And so it happened that while the minister was praying, and teaching everyone about Christ, they were ignoring it all. A thousand years earlier it would have been considered rude, but nobody knew that they were thinking to each other in church, and Colin's parents had no idea they would soon be attending their son's wedding.

And so, wedding bells would peal, one month hence.

CHAPTER TEN:

UNCLE TERRY

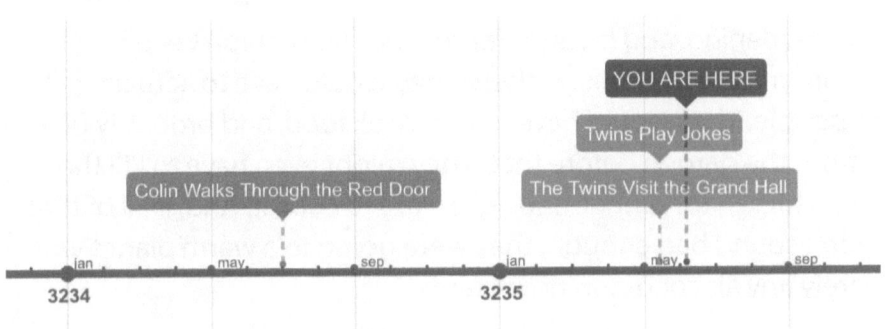

The day had arrived. Silas and Judson were going to Planet Verde to spend the summer with their Uncle Terry and Aunt Joy. Both of them were in rip-proof jeans, and light summer shirts. Judson wore blue, and Silas wore red, which were typical colours for them. Growing up, they had often differentiated between their things with colour, and it continued as they got older. Judson had a black letter J badge which he pinned on his pocket, and Silas had the same but with a black letter S. This had become a convention for them when they were both going somewhere together. It helped others. They didn't want Terry and Joy to be confused, except of course if they did, and then they could take them off, or even switch badges.

> **Verde... Pronounced Verday!!**
> Verde is the Spanish word for Green, and the planet Verde is GREEN. In the galaxy there were millions of planets. Names became commonplace, and sometimes a planet would have a very ordinary name, such as the name of a colour, like Verde does.

They were excited because it was something different to anything they had done before, but they were nervous too, for the same reason. Neither of them had left home before, so there was that excitement about travelling, but the other was because of where they were going. This wasn't your typical planet with all the conveniences of Earth. They were going to the most basic of all the planets, to a non-automated life, to a place with cleaning, and gardening, and buckets for toilets. They couldn't even communicate by thinking there, they would have to actually talk to people. They would have to also cook food, and probably pick it from the garden before that. They might even have to kill their own chicken for dinner, and light a fire to cook it. And, if all of that didn't sound bad enough, they were going to a warm planet with barely any air conditioning systems.

'Verde will be good for you both,' said their Dad.

'You'll both come back as better people,' said their Mum.

'We know,' said Silas standing there, still with his exoskeleton under his trousers and his lack of enthusiasm evident to anyone with ears.

Judson sat there thinking privately. He loved the idea of coming back to school after the summer, and being able to tell his friends he had been to one of the hard-to-get-to planets. Who ever gets the chance to go to Verde? But on the other hand, his friends were just as likely to laugh at his bad luck too. It wasn't exactly a fun way to spend the summer. Plus that heat. Even they, who lived at Port Sudan and were accustomed to the warm temperatures, knew that Verde was next level when it came to heat . Not only was it hot, there was no transportation system on the planet, so it required walking, in the heat.

'Walking? Nobody walks these days,' he thought privately. He imagined himself talking back to his parents.

'Can't we be disciplined here? We could start a garden here, and cook old-fashioned food here. We don't have to go to Verde to do those things, right?'

He also imagined them talking back to him, getting angry, and it becoming a big deal. Better to avoid all of that. Coming out of his mental daze, he realised his Dad really was talking, explaining details about the travel to come.

'Strap the connector around your arm. Make it firm. Translating to Verde will be the same as going to school, but if you lose your band when you get there, you can't just walk home. Make sure it is nice and tight. Then place the strap lock so it cannot be removed.'

He had been given similar instructions when he first went to school, but he had no memory of those. And it wasn't as if anything different was happening technology-wise. Perhaps it was just the distance they were going that made it seem more important.

'Now slide your chip in to connect yourself to the pair,' said Dad.

Normally, the boys didn't worry about this level of technicality. The translators they used for school were provided ready to use. Things didn't go wrong very often, and when they did, the school was nearby for troubleshooting. And, if it broke, you were still on the same planet. In fact, if a translator broke a student often had to get picked up in some kind of vehicle, and that was exciting. Everyone loved the idea of having rides in vehicles because of how uncommon they were.

But if something went wrong in this case, there would be no car to take them home. The consequences were potentially life-threatening, or if not, seriously inconvenient. This was of course why most travel between planets was through public doors and not with translators. But this was Verde, and there wasn't a door that could be used. If they wanted to go, it had to be with a translator pair.

The process of acquiring translators and permission to travel wasn't hard. Uncle Terry had provided permission for the boys to use the translators. Not only was he Jonathan Jones' brother, he was also the Mayor of Verde. Being Mayor wasn't an official position. There weren't enough people living on Verde to have a functional political system, but as a longstanding resident, he had somehow collectively become a voice on behalf of them all, all two thousand people who lived there. His approval opened the door, and they were able to collect two sets of translator pairs from the proper government department in Greater Europe, and here they were putting them on.

Their Dad was still talking.

'Uncle Terry knows you are coming. He has placed the other half of the pairs in his lounge room on the floor, so the first thing you will see is the inside of his place. Are you happy with that?'

'Yes Dad.'

'Do you have everything you need?'

Judson nodded.

'Ready to go?'

Another nod.

'We love you both,' their Mum chimed in.

'Now both of you press that blue button on your arms, and we will see you in a few weeks.'

Both boys reached to their left upper arms. Judson pressed the light blue button first and was gone. From his parents' perspective he disappeared. But to him, it seemed as if he hadn't gone anywhere. Rather, in a microsecond, the walls and floor around him changed. It felt like he hadn't travelled at all. He didn't feel sick, tired, jetlagged, nauseous, or anything, just normal. He was used to that, because he had done it every single day when going to school. Interstellar travel felt far less incredible than he had imagined it to be. He could not believe he was now on Verde, dozens of light years from Earth.

He was standing in a smallish room, with regular white walls, clear shiny windows, and a tan coloured, but thick and luscious carpet. The windows were filled with green plants of every description. In fact outside it looked 'jungly' like nobody had mown the lawn in a thousand years, or maybe it had never been mowed even once.

All of those were fleeting impressions, but the thing that got his attention the most was the heavy feeling. It was like the ground had grabbed his legs and was holding him down. It reminded him of when one of his younger cousins would stand on his shoes and want him to walk around with them on top, except it wasn't just his feet feeling heavy, but all of him. It was an effort just standing there.

And then he saw Terry and Joy with huge smiles looking right at him.

'One of my favourite nephews.' said Terry with a sparkle in his eyes. 'Which one are you?' He laughed. He knew of course that it was Judson because of the letter J on the collar of his shirt, but they had never met before this. He stuck out his right hand to offer Judson a big strong Verde hand shake.

'I'm Judson.'

'I guessed from the J.'

Joy didn't offer any handshakes, it was hugs for her. 'It's good to see you Judson, and I'm so glad you are able to come here. We don't get visitors, and I'm so glad it can be you.'

Then Terry said, 'Well I guess I better give you a hug too.' He then proceeded to squeeze the air out of Judson's lungs with a ferocious bear hug, but the feeling was of squeezing even more love in. Even though Judson had never been here, or seen his Uncle Terry and Aunty Joy before, it felt like they were family, because of course they were. He felt loved, even though he knew Terry was one tough guy.

'It's good to see you in real life,' said Joy, 'You know we have seen all your baby pictures. Sometimes we get things in the mail. Now, where is your brother Silas, what is holding him up?'

'I'm not sure,' said Judson. 'We've been playing a lot of jokes on each other. He might be up to something.'

Uncle Terry gave a knowing look.

'I'm aware,' he said. 'I've spoken to your Dad about that. We are going to put you boys to work around here, and teach you to be men.'

They guided him into the adjoining room. Judson walked slowly, each step was a challenge, like walking underwater. Terry looked at him and laughed.

'Ahha, you've just discovered the famous gravity of Verde. You know it's stronger than on Earth. Everyone walks like that when they first get here, but you soon get used to it. In no time at all you become stronger yourself and it feels normal. Of course that won't help you if you only visit occasionally; you will have to come and live here a little to adjust properly. But don't worry, after a week or so you will start to notice it less.'

In the dining room, a table had been set for their arrival. It had a small but fabulous array of food, some that Judson knew well, but a few that were strangely different. Judson noticed a pile of five or six white ball-like items on a plate

'What are those round white things?'

'Would you believe they are actually white oranges?' Joy grinned.

'Why do you still call them oranges? You should call them whites.' Judson laughed at his own joke. It wasn't funny to Terry and Joy because everyone who had ever seen them had said the exact same thing.

'Here we call them tangerines. We also have orange oranges too,' answered Joy, 'It's an easy way of differentiating.'

Joy then set about showing what else was different.

'At the end of the table is maamoul. You may have seen that in Port Sudan at some point. Next to that is freeze-dried ice cream, which is popular in Verde, and lasts all year long if we don't get a delivery from Earth. Then there is fruit cake, tangerines of course, bananas, and mangoes. Fruit grows really well on Verde.'

'I want to try it all,' said Judson, starting to get excited, 'But before I do, show me your place. What is it like living here? And what do you do every day?'

'Hold your horses young man,' chuckled Terry, 'Let's wait for your brother to get here shall we?'

They sat at the table and waited. After about five minutes he had not appeared.

'Want a cup of tea?' asked Joy

'Why don't you offer him some of our famous Verde coffee?' suggested Terry.

Joy got up from the table to heat water in the kitchen, and while they were waiting for her, Judson walked over to the window.

'It's really green out there' he observed.

'Yes it is,' replied Terry. 'Did you know that the word Verde is the Spanish word for the colour green?'

'Oh.'

'This planet was named Green because it was atmospherically and geologically ready for vegetation, and once we started planting grasses and trees, they exploded. The planet was covered in green in just a few years.'

Terry continued.

'I think that is what makes the coffee so good. It's some kind of combination of gravity and minerals, and atmospheric pressure,' He was sounding like an expert.

'You know a lot, Uncle Terry,' said Judson.

'I used to help as a terraformation worker years ago.'

Joy came walking back into the room with a pot of coffee.

'Silas still isn't here?' She queried.

'Judson, would you shift back for a minute, and see how he is going?' suggested Terry pointing at Judson's little blue button.

Judson stood up, so that his posture was a standing posture. It was always important to adopt the posture you needed on arrival at the other end. He then reached his right hand up to his left upper arm, pressed the light blue button to switch to the other side of the pair and was gone.

Terry and Joy took their seats in the lounge once again, where the incoming half of the transfer pairs were located, and where Judson and Silas would soon appear. They waited. But Judson was taking his time too. What was he doing?

Five minutes…

Ten minutes…

Fifteen minutes…

Suddenly Judson reappeared.

'Silas has gone. He is nowhere to be found.'

CHAPTER ELEVEN:

BOTTOM OF THE LAKE

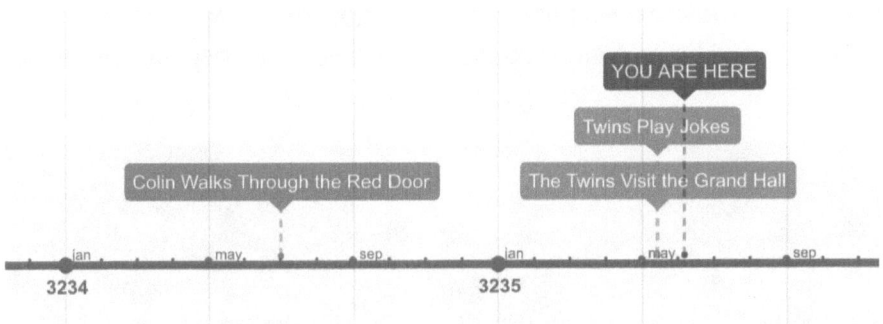

Silas reached up and pressed the little blue button on his upper left shoulder, and was gone.

Nothing could have prepared him for the surprise he encountered on the other side. When a fish bites bait, assuming it to be food, and then a moment later is pulled out of the water on a line and hook, it could not be more shocked. That type of twist was what Silas now experienced, but in the opposite experience of the fish that was caught. Silas now found himself somewhere underwater, and unable to breathe.

One minute he was on Earth in his living room, with his brother and parents, preparing to visit his Uncle Terry, and the next minute he was in a watery world. And not only was he surprised, but the fish that swam in that water were surprised to find a human had just appeared next to them.

Silas had to find the surface, but which direction was it? And how far was it? Gaining a sense of which way was up was not easy. He remembered something he learned in scuba classes. Bubbles always go up. He exhaled, just slightly, and saw his breath going away from him.

He had to follow those bubbles. He could feel his lungs tightening. How far was it to the surface? How far underwater was he? Too many thoughts rushed through his mind for him to think about them all. After what seemed longer than it was, his head broke through and he took a deep breath of the crisp air. It was pure relief.

He could see that he was in the middle of a little lake. The water was clear, but bitey and cold, and he knew he could not stay in the lake for long. It was maybe just a few hundred yards to the shore, which looked warm, and green, and inviting. Further away were mountains that looked misty and mysterious, but on the other side of the lake in the far distance were other mountains with snow on them. How curious. He was in a unique location.

While one part of him was enthralled by the new scenery and the dopamine hit his new visual surroundings were giving him, he was also confused about what had just happened. Where was his brother? And where was Uncle Terry? Why was he in this lake? And how did his translator device place him here, in a lake? Didn't Uncle Terry know that placing a pair underwater was illegal? Maybe this was another of those Judson jokes.

That last thought made him angry. He wasn't angry the first time Judson played a dangerous joke on him, when he fell off the roof and broke his leg. But now he wanted to punch his brother. How could he play such a mean joke a second time?

His leg? He remembered the exoskeleton. He knew it could handle a certain amount of water, because he wore it in the shower each night. But being submerged that far underwater. Was that OK? He wasn't even sure how deep the lake was.

Trying to peer down into the water, his leg seemed fine, even though it was still submerged. It wasn't possible to get a thorough look as he tread water. The seals around the top and bottom seemed to have worked, and the display was still working. He was able to see, even through the water, that it could be removed in 29 more days.

Looking up, he noticed a little boat in the middle of the lake behind him, not far from where he was, perhaps just fifty yards away. He started paddling toward it. In no time a friendly middle-aged man with a full orange beard, and a bit of a belly, was helping him climb into the punt. He looked every part the fisherman, comfortably seated in his small though fully-decked-out fishing vessel, replete with equipment of every type. It was a little brown skiff with oars for transport, several fishing rods lying unused, but one in use, line in the water. He could see a bucket of bait, containing little creatures that were worm-like, but different to any he had seen before. It was barely big enough for the fisherman and his equipment, let alone to give it the responsibility of staying afloat with a second human added to the cargo.

'Make sure you sit right in the middle of the seat. She's a wobbly girl with the two of us in here.' The fisherman looked at him and kept talking. 'I didn't know anyone was going swimming. I'm a bit surprised to see you here in the lake. You're not dressed for a swim.'

Silas smiled, but felt a bit awkward.

The boat wobbled and he put his hands on each side to steady himself, trying to avoid taking another dip.

'Well I didn't expect to be swimming either,' he said. 'I translated here. Someone put the receiving end of my pair in the lake.'

The fisherman raised an eyebrow.

'You mean to tell me that you travelled here just now?' he queried. 'By a translator, you say?'

'Yes' said Silas pointing at the strap on his upper left arm for proof. 'I think I'm lucky to be alive because some goose arranged for me to arrive underwater. I have a feeling it was my brother.' He said this matter-of-factly because he wasn't at all surprised by the idea that he was once again smack bang in the middle of a joke. He was about to proceed to tell the fisherman about their saga of pranks, when he noticed the shocked expression on the fisherman's face.

'What's wrong?' asked Silas.

The fisherman held his finger up to his lips, as if to indicate that he should stop talking. He then reached into his bag and pulled out a pen-like object. He wrote on the back of his hand and then held it out for Silas to see.

It read, 'people could hear us.'

The fisherman then with the use of hand gestures indicated that Silas should lie down on the floor of the boat. As he tried to lay low, the boat got another case of the wobbles. The boat was too small for effective hiding. The fisherman then proceeded to cast his gaze along the banks of the land to find a place they could land. He headed for a small pebbly beach, near a patch of bushes.

After rowing for what seemed like half an hour, but which was just a few minutes, Silas felt the shore underneath the boat as the keel scraped on lake rocks. The water was getting shallower. The fisherman jumped out and pulled the boat up higher out of the water and then proceeded to use a chain to anchor the boat to the base of a nearby tree.

He turned around, and then with a grin smiled at Silas.

'I'm Nathan,' he said. 'We can talk now. We are away from microphones. What a genuine pleasure to meet you. Where do you come from?'

'I'm from Earth,' replied Silas. 'Or at least that is where I was about twenty minutes ago. Right now I wish I was back there again.'

'You'll probably get your wish,' said Nathan. 'You definitely can't stay here, but I would dearly love to ask you about Earth.'

For the first time, the thought entered Silas's mind that he might in fact not be on Verde. He looked around at what he could see. It was green and pretty. He knew that Verde was also green and lush. But he did see elaborate looking buildings in the distance. He knew that Verde was plain, and its inhabitants lived in simplicity.

'Is this Verde?'

'Verde? Don't be silly. This is Utopia.'

'Utopia!' Silas reacted with surprise. 'I'm not allowed to be here.'

'I know.' said Nathan 'That's why I told you to be quiet.'

Silas was dumbfounded, but soon regained his composure.

'How did I even get here?' he asked.

Nathan looked at him with a blank expression.

'Err, perhaps there is some glitch with your translator thing. Maybe it is paired to the wrong end?' suggested Nathan.

'My translator!' Suddenly Silas realised he could leave. How could he have forgotten that? All he had to do was press his little blue button and he could go back safely and with no fuss.

'Uh, sorry. I'm not supposed to be here. I better go now.' Silas reached up and pressed the little blue button on his shoulder.

Nothing happened.

Press, press, press. Still nothing.

'What are you doing?' asked Nathan.

'Trying to leave,' he replied.

'You might not be allowed to leave,' suggested Nathan in a nonchalant tone. He wasn't bothered at all. 'I think they block people from leaving.'

'Why didn't they block me from coming then?' Silas retorted. Fear started to rise within him. Soon, he was overcome with emotion. As terrible, and hot, and difficult as Verde might have been in his mind before, it now didn't seem so bad after all. How he wished he was there right now. How wonderful it would be to be with his brother, and to spend time with his Uncle Terry. He knew it was all his fault. He was an idiot. If only he had stopped playing pranks when his parents had told him to. If only he had controlled himself when Judson was late to school that day. Why did he always ignore that little voice on the inside?

He pushed the button again.

Nothing.

Push.

Nothing.

Push push push push.

Nothing.

Silas just stood there dumbfounded. Was he trapped here on Utopia?

Nathan spoke again, 'What is your name?'

'I'm Silas Jones.' His head hung down. 'I want to leave.'

'Come with me,' said Nathan. 'I know a place you might be able to stay until we figure something out.' Nathan started walking down a path between the bushes, heading towards the mountains.

Silas started following Nathan. He didn't want to at first, but it was obvious he didn't really have any other option.

'Are we going to your house?' he finally asked.

'No,' came the reply. 'I would, but my wife is a stickler for the rules, so I think we'll go to the shed. Don't worry, it's a nice shed.'

That reply by Nathan raised so many questions in Silas' mind. What were the rules that Nathan was speaking of? Why couldn't he tell his wife? What type of woman was she? And hiding in a shed, really?

They walked a few hundred more metres in silence. There was a lot on both of their minds. Then Silas broke the quiet.

'What are the rules you talked about?'

And so began another whole conversation about the rules of reporting. Silas learned about the ban on speaking of God. Nathan was very clever in the way he talked about the thing he wasn't to talk about. He spelled God's name out as G-O-D. He then described his wife Bridie. She had moved from Earth to Utopia about twelve years ago with her friends. They had met one afternoon gardening, and spent more and more time together. Eventually they married. But, Nathan was careful to point out, Bridie was conservative. She had come from Earth, and did not want to be deported. She followed the rules super carefully. So he couldn't risk telling her a thing.

Nathan went on to describe his friend Colin who had been deported just a year ago for saying the name of G-O-D's son, and they had not seen him since.

Silas interrupted Nathan's explanation. 'So if someone says something they are not supposed to say, do they go to jail?'

'I don't think it's jail,' replied Nathan. 'No one knows for sure, but we think they are deported and can never come back.'

'That might not be bad,' thought Silas. He might get to go home. He looked ahead at the path, and noticed it was heading into a forest and the light was starting to thin.

'How far is it?' Silas asked.

'Not far, my shed is in the forest. You'll be comfortable there.'

They kept walking another half kilometre and came to the shed. It was a square timber structure in the middle of a pine forest, almost like a small log cabin home. In fact, people in Alaska lived in houses that were not as nice as this shed. Junk was piled up on the verandah, and looking through the glass he could see there was junk inside too.

'I'm going to be safe here right?' asked Silas.

'Well yes,' replied Nathan. 'As long as my wife doesn't find you here. But she probably won't, don't worry.'

'The shed is a long way from the house,' said Silas. 'How could she find me?'

'The shed and the house are connected by a door,' Nathan answered. 'Do you have doors in your world? I don't mean normal doors you walk through, I mean special doors that take you from one place to another.'

Silas nodded. 'We have those.'

'So the shed and the house are a long way apart on the planet, but they are just a few metres apart on the inside. So you can walk right into the shed from our lounge room.'

'O dear,' said Silas. 'She is going to see me for certain.'

'She never goes into the shed,' countered Nathan. 'It's a big mess and she hates it. If she needs me, she just thinks to me, and I come out.'

'But what if she does see me?'

'Oh, if that happened, she will certainly report you. She would assume you're one of the rats.'

'The rats?'

The more they talked, the stranger a place Utopia was sounding. The rats were people that once lived as normal Utopians, but had fallen afoul of things. Some of them had been selected for deportation and run away, others had been disenfranchised. All these people had gone to the darkside of the planet and now lived there in caves. Sometimes they came to the dayside of the planet to steal food.

Even though Utopia sounded weird, as Silas looked around, everything he saw seemed fabulous. Everything was clean. Everything in its place. He had never seen a place that felt more organised. Even the temperature was perfect as though there was a planetary climate system at work, which of course thanks to Nick Jones, there was. But even with the obvious beauty of what he could see, and his recognition of it, he felt anxious.

They opened the door to the shed. Nathan was starting to relax. Silas wasn't such a threat, it seemed to him. He started to get into a chatty mood. Now inside the shed Nathan started showing off his cabin. He pointed out the features of his shed, its beds, its lounge, its storage and it even had a kitchen. It was like a second house, but kind of for men.

'This fridge is the most amazing thing,' said Nathan. 'I grew up here on this planet and I still think this fridge is unbelievable. It's got a door.'

'Of course it has a door,' stated Silas.

'No, not a door you open to get food, a shopping door.'

Silas looked puzzled.

'So if you need a drink, you open the fridge and take one, but that drink doesn't come from this fridge, it comes from the supplier. The back of this fridge is connected to a giant retail fridge. They restock every night. We tell them what things we like and they are always in the fridge. What do you think about that?'

Silas imagined his favourite drinks always there whenever he wanted.

'I like that,' Silas agreed.

'I like it too,' said Nathan. 'Now while you stay here in the cabin, you can eat and drink whatever you need and I'll pay for it.' He pointed across the room. 'Back there is a bed; make yourself comfortable. I had better get back to my dear Bridie or she will be wondering what happened to me. I will come back and check on you later.'

Nathan exited the shed by a back door, different to the one they had both come in. He must have gone home straight into the house, rather than walking back through the forest.

Silas turned and looked around the room. It was comfortable here, even for a shed, and he was glad for somewhere to stay, but he hoped they could figure out some way of getting him back to Earth. That is what he preferred.

He walked over to the fridge and opened it. There were drinks he had never seen before. There were snacks in wrappers in the fridge. He noticed something that looked like a muesli bar. He could eat that. There was also a red cola drink. It wasn't Coca-Cola, which he knew he enjoyed, it was Utopia Cola. He wondered what that would taste like, and took that. He cracked the can and took a sip.

Not bad.

Walking back to the bed, he stumbled over a piece of lumber laying across the floor, but caught himself, spilling cola all over his shirt. Annoyed with himself he looked around for a towel. Finding one hanging behind the main door he dried off his stained shirt. Then he noticed that some cola had also splashed onto this translator manager on his left upper arm.

'I hope the liquid didn't damage it,' he thought to himself.

And that is when it hit him like a bolt of lightning. Of course he couldn't leave the planet when he tried earlier. His translator controller had been dunked under water just the same as he had. It wouldn't work when it was wet. They had been told over and over as children not to get the translator system wet. If you wanted to swim, you took it off. If it got wet, it could take hours to dry out.

He had a hunch it was going to work. He reached up his right hand to press the little blue button, and just as he was about to, a little thought flashed into his mind.

'What about Nathan?'

He badly wanted to leave right then and there. But what to do? He couldn't leave without at least saying goodbye, or trying to at least keep some communication going between them. He would leave a note.

Looking around the room, he noted a poster on the wall, or at least it was a type of postery thing. It was harder or firmer than paper, but still thin and hung on the wall. He took it down and turned it over. It was a surface he could write on. There were no writing implements in sight. Looking around he then searched for something he could scratch with. In a cupboard he found tools. He took a sharp pointy tool like an awl. and began to scratch words into the back of the poster.

Nathan, my translator is working now. I must go. I might come back and see you again in a few days if my parents let me. Silas.

Then with that, he reached his right hand up to his upper left arm where the little blue button was located and pressed it.

This time it worked, and he was gone.

CHAPTER TWELVE:

WHIRLWIND WEDDING

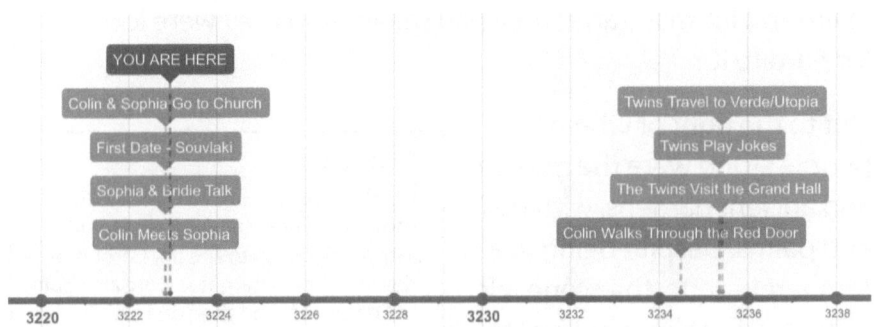

One month ago, the idea of Colin and Sophia being married was not on anyone's radar. They didn't know who each other was, and yet here they were. Bridie took some convincing, but once she saw the wedding dress, and the plans started coming together, she was won over by the mood of it. She was all in support.

It was a glorious day as a crowd of about one hundred and twenty people gathered early in the morning at the Lower Barrakka Gardens in historic Valletta, Malta. Out to the left was the sparkling Mediterranean Sea with its shining blue water, and the entrance to the Grand Harbour of Malta. From that place many ships had come and gone over the millennia, and St Paul in his missionary travels had been shipwrecked. Malta located in the middle of the Mediterranean had always been a hub for sailors and travellers. But just thirty years ago the first of Earth's watergates had been opened right here, connecting Earth to Enaiposha by connecting the two oceans. From where the crowd stood, they could see the big circular gate through which ships and boats would traverse on their way to that water world.

In just a few hours, Colin and Sophia would be married, and would board a small yacht, and sail through that watergate on the honeymoon of a lifetime, although Sophia didn't know just yet where they were going. They would have their first experiences of life and intimacy after they had sailed. And they were looking forward to it.

Out to the right of where the people stood were the majestic and ancient gardens, with figs and palms. Despite being in a temperate zone, the scene felt so tropical. In the middle of the greenery stood an elaborate monument to Vice Admiral Alexander Ball, who more than a thousand years earlier, had helped bring Malta under the control of the British. But right now, St Paul, and Alexander Ball, and the fig trees, were the last things on anyone's mind, because before them the stage was set for a marvellous ceremony to take place. Colin

Watergates

After Nick Jones conceived of a gate under the water on Enaiposha to drain part of the ocean to the dry Cathedral Planet, other watergates were also built on Enaiposha, and then on Earth to other planets.

Most watergates were for the purpose of freight, but in the case of Enaiposha, also for tourism. Watergates often feature a quick dry lock, or a series of locks that work in a similar manner to the Panama Canal. A few had no locks at all.

The Malta to Enaiposha watergate was a gate with no dock or lock, and allowed magnificent mid-size cruise liners to sail straight through from one ocean to the other. As a ship sails through, it appears to spectators to disappear into nothing.

was standing there, with his brother and best man Nathanael, and they awaited the arrival of his bride-to-be Sophia, and along with her, Bridie, her close friend, and Matron of honour.

Weddings were an in-person thing. You didn't watch a wedding, you attended. The benefit of doors and translators was you could hold your wedding ceremony anywhere in the visitable galaxy.

And, you invited even distant family and friends because it wasn't that hard for them to come. Colin's minister from Tallinn was there, and he was pleased to be the celebrant on this fine sunny day.

Colin stood there looking anxious. Nathanael had a grin on his face, enjoying his brother's nervous mannerisms. The ceremony was scheduled for 50,000 seconds, which was late morning in Valletta. Colin and Sophia had not seen each other today. They had agreed not to share their thoughts or feelings for the entire day right up until the moment they were standing together in front of their invited guests. So as a result, both of their minds, and hearts, were running wild. They had no idea what each other was thinking, except by imagining what it might be. The last month had been a whirlwind, and they had been inseparable. Even when they were apart, such as at work, they had been together in thoughts and feelings, except for today.

It was normal for couples to share their feelings and thoughts on a one-by-one basis, in an ad-hoc manner, if and when they were required. But Colin and Sophia had come to trust each other with everything. One morning Sophia had poured boiling water on her hand in the staff kitchen. She was upset, and even though Colin was downstairs, he knew something was wrong; he felt it. They were in tune with each other. Another time he had solved a challenging mathematical puzzle at work, to do with fluctuating gravitational fields around the rings of Saturn. He was pleased with himself, when he heard Sophia's thoughts coming from upstairs.

'Feeling happy about something?'

They were both in touch even though they were apart most of the day.

So it was a morning of anticipation, but also of mild anxiety for Colin. He looked up at the sun. It was bright, getting warm, and there were no clouds today. The sun had just about reached the middle of the sky. He knew the ceremony should have started by now. He mentally checked the time, and the thought servers returned a reading of 50790. She was almost a thousand seconds late. Where was she?

She was in fact ready, but was having one brief last minute conversation with Bridie.

'Sophia, I'm going to miss you a lot.'

'Come with us Bridie.'

'It's a lot of money.'

'Don't worry about money Bridie. You know how much money my grandfather left me in his will. Bring your parents too if you want.'

'Thanks Sophia, you are so kind. I will think about it.' She stopped talking, and looked Sophia up and down all over. 'You look amazing darling, let's go and get you your man.'

And with that Bridie turned and began the walk out of the building they had hired. Sophia followed and both of them walked down the pathways through the garden towards the place where everyone was. She desperately wanted to send Colin a thought, but she held it in, for just one more minute.

Reaching the designated starting place, Sophia stayed out of sight. The music commenced, the gathered people stood up, and Bridie began to walk. Around from behind the foliage she appeared, now walking in time, matching her pace with the music. She headed off down the central aisle between the gathered onlookers. About twenty steps behind her, Sophia commenced her slow walk too. As she came around from behind the figs, she saw him. He saw her too.

In that moment, both of them let their feelings go, and both were hit with waves of emotions. Both their own emotions at seeing the other, and the feelings of the other hitting them too. It was pure reciprocated happiness.

Bridie reached the front, but Colin barely noticed her for his eyes never left Sophia. She looked magnificent, and he told her right then, but not verbally. Nobody knew for certain they were having a conversation in that moment, but everyone suspected it, because all those previously married had done it at their weddings, and all those too young to be married thought it would be the most romantic thing to do.

'You look wonderful Sophia.'

'Thank you darling, you do too. You make me so happy seeing you.'

'I wish you were allowed to walk faster.'

She blushed, and looked away. She didn't want to look away, but she felt as though it was all too good to be true.

'It is true, and it is real. You're about to be mine, and I'm so glad to be yours.'

She looked back at him. It really was happening.

She reached the front. He took her right hand with his left hand and they faced the celebrant. The music quieted and came to an end.

The celebrant spoke.

'Dearly beloved. We are gathered here today, in the sight of God, and in the presence of these witnesses, to join together this man and this woman in holy matrimony. Marriage is to be honoured, an institution from God from time immemorial, significant because it speaks to us of Christ and his Church.'

And so the ceremony began.

Weddings, even those not held in church buildings, were Christian, even for people like Sophia with no Christian background. For her, these were just words. Colin was used to the words, and didn't think about their meaning. Both of them had been to weddings before and heard similar words. The important thing for them was, they were to be married.

'Colin Lawson Philips, do you take this woman Sophia Saar, to be your legal wedded wife?'

'Yes, I do.'

'Sophia Saar, do you take this man, Colin Lawson Philps, to be your legal wedded husband?'

'Yes I do.'

Near the vegetation to the right was a small portable table. Now it was lifted and brought forward. A cloth was removed to reveal a hand scanner. A time traveller from the past would have found this moment to be so strange and a break with tradition, but for the Philips' and Saar families, and for all people who married at that time, scanning the hand was the same as signing the marriage register with a pen.

'Colin, would you place your hand on the scanner, to confirm that you are today married to Sophia in accordance with your will?'

He had done this many times before when entering doors, paying for items at a store, or voting at an election. Today something different was happening. Not only was his ID verified to make sure the right person was present for the marriage, but his Stellar ID would be bound with Sophia's. Now while both of them retained separate ID as people, their ID's now were tagged as married to each other.

That data would be entered into the quantum blockchain and became a part of the permanent unalterable record of what happened, and part of the history of humanity.

Colin placed his left hand on the scanner. The blue light coming from the scanner verified his data and did its work.

'Sophia, would you place your hand on the scanner?'

Sophia did the same and her ID and records were now updated too.

The celebrant also scanned his hand, to authorise what had taken place. He then stood and made his final declaration.

'I pronounce you man and wife. You may now kiss the bride.'

And they did.

At that moment bells began to ring, and joyful music erupted. The ceremony was over, and the couple embraced and began to greet family and friends.

That afternoon they had photos in various beautiful places in Valletta, and then everyone gathered together late afternoon for an early dinner, featuring a true delicacy, the Dodo, acquired from one of the officially uninhabited planets, a real treat.

After the meal, there were gifts, and speeches, first of all by the best man, Nathanael.

'Colin,' he turned to look at his brother. 'Do you remember when we were six and eight years of age, playing in the backyard in Munich? Do you remember what you said to me about your future wife?'

Colin nodded and smiled. He remembered.

'We were playing in the backyard in the sandpit, and my brother said to me, 'I hope my future wife likes to make sandcastles.'

Turning to Sophia, Nathanael asked, 'Sophia, do you know how to make a sandcastle?'

She gave a thumbs up.

Nathanael turned back to his brother. 'Congratulations brother, you have married the right woman.'

And so on the speeches went one after another, many jovial, some serious, but all of them wishing well. The last speech came from Colin's minister, the celebrant at their wedding, and a man who had known Colin for many years.

'Colin and Sophia,' he turned to face them. 'I sense that the two of you are well-suited to each other and I'm pleased I was given the opportunity to be a part of your wedding. I also sense that you are not as close to God as others in the church, but I would encourage you, in the same way you have quickly come to know each other, you will find that God can be quickly found too.'

> **Dodo - a Real Delicacy**
>
> The dodo as an animal had gone extinct in 1681, but it had been extinct for 400 years before clever genetic work was able to resuscitate the species in 2089.
>
> The dodo was delicious, more preferred than chicken, but the nature of the animal was that it was unaware, easy to catch, and hard to keep alive.
>
> In the 28th century, an uninhabited and uncivilised planet was chosen for Dodo farming, and named Dodo. A minimal number of species of plants and insects were introduced sufficient for the Dodo to thrive, which it did in the wild. No predators exist in that place, providing an ample and self-sustaining supply of this delicacy.
>
> From time to time, people venture to Dodo with a license to acquire a select number of birds for the purposes of catering.

The time came to depart. Colin took Sophia's hand, and walked her down the short boardwalk onto the small ship waiting for them. They were occupants on a ship that was going to sail to Enaiposha for two weeks. There they would begin married life. Sophia knew they would be on the ship, but she didn't know where the ship was going. That was still a surprise.

As the ship left dock, heading into the sunset, it drew near to the watergate. Sophia's eyes widened, as she started to realise they were going to sail to another planet. As it neared the portal, the engines slowed. The boat began to putt towards the gate, and lining up with the tide, they allowed the ship to drift into the gate. From the shore the boat seemed to disappear inch by inch as it moved into the gateway. At one point it seemed to the observers that half a boat sat on the water. But like the waning of the moon, the vessel progressively disappeared until it was gone.

Once they had passed through the gate, it was a different time of day. The sun wasn't setting, it had in fact set hours earlier, and it was already night. While time was the same everywhere, it was uncommon for the cycle of day and night to match other planets. The weather was cold, and a light wind was blowing. Colin grabbed Sophia and held her, it made her feel a bit warmer, but there was more to the hug than giving her warmth. There was also desire in the hug. .

'It's just us now, wife.'

'I like the sound of you calling me wife.'

While holding her, he turned the two of them around, so that her back was to the ship, and she could see over his shoulder the expanse of the sky, and the black water lapping just below them on the edge of the ship.

'Look at the stars,' he said.

She looked up and saw thousands of stars, but none of them in any pattern of constellations that she recognized. Everything was similar until you really looked, and then it was completely different. There was no Big Bear, no North Star, none of the familiar night patterns. But the stars everywhere filled the sky in a glorious display.

'Wow, there are so many. They are so bright.'

They were bright. The moon on Enaiposha was not out and it made everything darker. There were no other lights near them to dull the sky. It was just them, on the deck of a ship, many light years from Earth.

'Do you see that constellation up there that kind of looks a bit like a kite?' He let go of her and pointed towards the starboard of the ship off into the distance. She looked where he was pointing.

'Yes.'

'In between that bright left star and that star just under it, is Earth.' Colin explained. 'You can't see Earth's sun from here, because it's too dull, but we were there, half an hour ago.'

He paused to let that sink in. The universe was a big place. It was humbling. And, right now in that part of the sky, where that star was, all of their family and friends were packing up from their wedding celebration and going home.'

Sophia looked at her husband, and she loved him.

'Come to our cabin,' she said. And she pulled his hand and led him down the side of the ship toward the stairs, then under the deck to their little room. They were going to go to bed together for the first time, and along with that to begin to explore the joys of being married together.

While they slept that night, the small ship would sail onto places unknown to them. In the morning they would awake to see this whole new world. As yet, not many people from Earth had visited the newly recovered lands of Enaiposha, but that was for tomorrow. Tonight, one more thing had to happen.

'Colin, would you be willing to share your physical senses with me?'

'Yes.' He accepted, 'And Sophia, would you share yours with me too?'

They both were willing, and so mentally they consented to each other, and the two commenced their honeymoon.

The Sharing of Physical Sensation in Marriage

The sharing of physical sensation is most often used in medical circumstances, for measurement of pain, for diagnosis, and triage. Parents can feel what their children feel for example, to know what the problem is in their little body. In marriage it has another more pleasurable benefit.

When a couple wants to be physically intimate with each other, they can go beyond sharing thoughts and emotions, to also share intimate physical sensations. Even though the male and female bodies are not the same, the human brains are similar enough. The mind interface is able to map male to female, and female to male sensation if the participants are willing. When couples are in tune with each other, this has the potential to produce a more intimate sense of belonging, pleasure, and joy. This of course belongs in marriage.

When couples are newly married, there is an aspect of learning how to bring joy and pleasure to each other physically. Each can sense what the other feels and work to please them.

Before the ability to share physical sensations was discovered, the learning process was frustrating for some people, but being able to share physical senses meant that learning became more fun, removed frustration, and helped each to know what was happening to the other, and enjoy it.

CHAPTER THIRTEEN:
THE CATHEDRAL CATHEDRAL

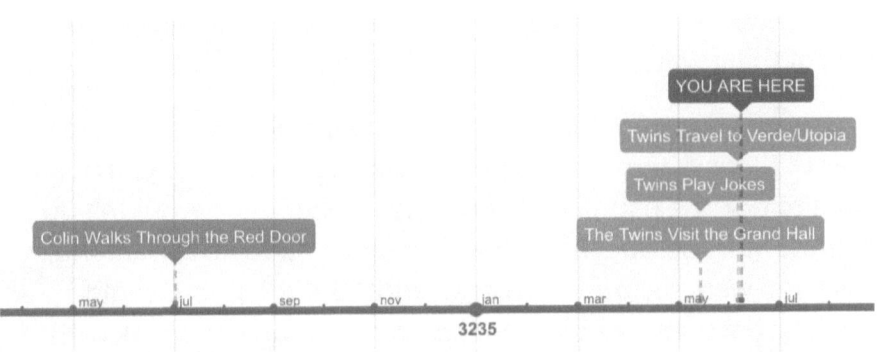

Colin Walks Through the Red Door

YOU ARE HERE

Twins Travel to Verde/Utopia

Twins Play Jokes

The Twins Visit the Grand Hall

may   jul   sep   nov   jan   mar   may   jul

3235

Silas was back on Earth, and he was not doing well. He had a decision to make, and was not finding it easy. Should he go to Verde and join his brother, or should he go back to Utopia? He didn't want to do either. Uncle Terry and Aunt Joy were waiting for him at Verde. Another pair could be organised, and within a few days he would be there. That was what he preferred, out of the two things he didn't want to do.

Or, he could reach his right hand up, and press that little blue button on his left upper arm, and go back to Utopia. This time he knew he would arrive underwater, and being prepared for that in advance, meant he would survive it. He knew he would have to keep a low profile and avoid attention. But he also knew where Nathan's shed was and how to get there. He knew Nathan would want to see him.

His preference was neither. He would rather stay here on Earth and enjoy the summer, but life was not that simple. His parents wanted him on Verde, and it seemed, if his feelings were true, that God wanted him on Utopia. To make the decision more complicated, his parents said that if God wanted him on Utopia, he should go, but if not, he was going to Verde.

The truth was, except for that nagging feeling within him that he was needed on Utopia, the decision was cut and dried. His parents wanted him on Verde, and there was nothing more to it. Except there was.

Where was that nagging feeling coming from? It wasn't his crazy idea to go back there, was it? Why make up something you don't want to do? The nagging thought was pestery, and wouldn't go away. It must be God. And, if God wanted you to do something, then you were supposed to do it. Right? But then, you would think God would be a bit more obvious. Couldn't he speak with a booming voice from heaven or something like that? All these thoughts rattled around within him. He was only sixteen. How could God be wanting something so difficult from someone so young? Finally, he concluded there had to be a way of testing this idea to see if it was God or not.

It wasn't a Sunday, but Silas decided to go to a church. Not to any church, he wanted to go somewhere where he could be thoughtful and spiritual. It wasn't about being there for a meeting, or preaching, or even the singing which he did like sometimes, but to just sit there and pray, mostly to think. He wanted to feel connected to God. There was one obvious place he could go, the Cathedral Cathedral.

There was this thing about thinking. People were always thinking. But a lot of the time their public thoughts were so loud, and they were bombarded with the public thoughts of other people. He knew in the midst of that thought cloud, that God could and did insert his thoughts into the minds of people too, just the same as other people did. It was a matter of finding a quiet place and sifting through the various thoughts to try and figure out what God wanted, what people wanted and what he himself thought. Knowing with clarity what God wanted might help to clear things up.

Then he had another thought. 'Who cares what God wants?'

That obtrusive question came crashing into his mind like a bull slamming into the fence at a rodeo. Where did that come from? He was certain that God did not give him that thought. It must have come from either him or somewhere else. He knew for certain that within himself there was a part of him that wanted to avoid God's will. Deep down, he wanted to do his own thing. That really was a part of who he was. But he also knew better than that too. Another bigger part of him knew that God was important. Being in a quiet place would help sort out all the inner noise.

That morning Silas said goodbye to his parents, and travelled to Alexandria, then to Delhi, then into the Hall of Doors for the second time in his life. He took a few moments to admire the spectacle of being in the Himalayas. Then finally he walked across to the back of the room, and stood before the third door in the middle of the wall. The word CATHEDRAL was written over the door in silver engraved writing.

As he was about to enter a door to a planet he had never visited, he noticed the message in mosaic on the floor just a few feet before the doorway. Christ the Redeemer held out his hands. Jesus was dressed in white, nothing fancy, but somehow had the appearance of being regal and dignified. Under him were written these words.

ALL WHO ENTER INTO CHRIST ARE FOREVER CHANGED.

AS YOU ENTER CATHEDRAL TODAY MAY YOU ENCOUNTER CHRIST.

'What an unusual thing to say,' he thought. He didn't understand what it meant, and within two seconds had stopped thinking about it.

And, even though he didn't understand it, the thought on the floor was significant and true. And though its significance was lost on him, his visit to Cathedral would in fact forever change him.

He scanned his left hand at the entrance.

He got the green light.

And he stepped across the threshold into another world unlike any place he had ever seen before on Earth.

He found himself standing on a path in an elevated position, probably a few kilometres above sea level; he didn't know for sure. Off to the left, the mountain dropped away, and there were views of a tropical fjord below him, and the sea in the distance. To his right the mountain climbed up higher. There were clouds both below and above him. The mountain on his right went into the clouds so that its peak wasn't visible. It was high. But the path ran along the side of this mountain, gently rising as it went.

He had thought that perhaps when he got to Cathedral he would enter another Hall and need to navigate more doors. Standing on this mountain path came as a surprise. He began to climb the path as it went away from the door. He could see in the distance that it wasn't a long path before it reached a structure.

As he walked, little red and blue birds flew across his path. They were fast, and almost flew into him as they zipped by. He didn't know it, but they were crimson rosellas, from Australia.

Australian trees and animals had been used in many places to populate planets

Climbing higher he noticed that the path he walked on was made of evenly-spaced pavers, all of them brown in colour. He noticed a bigger paver than the others which said:

THE HAND OF GOD HAS BEEN ON PEOPLE

FROM THE BEGINNING

He kept walking. After about twenty more metres there was another paver with writing. This time with two names written on it.

ADAM AND EVE

'How strange?' he thought.

Continuing along the path, he came across a third paver with a single name.

ABEL

And further along.

SETH

As he kept walking there were more and more names. He knew some of these names from the Bible, and it seemed to him that each person was someone who had served God in some way.

Further down the path he came to a name he knew for certain.

NOAH

'Why weren't his sons listed too?' he wondered.

As he continued the walk he began to see key figures from the Old Testament such as Abraham, Isaac, Jacob, Moses, Gideon, Samuel, and David. He did know some of these names because he had read the Bible. But as the path continued he came across other more obscure names. He didn't know about them, like Hosea, Zechariah, and Malachi.

With his attention to the path, he had been distracted from the view. Looking up he took in the increasing altitude and clouds now swirling around him. He felt like he was ascending into Heaven. Looking back down at his feet, the path also gave him a sense of God too, of history, that there was a plan, that things had purpose.

As he continued to walk he came across a paver which instead of being brown like the others was white, and bigger.

JESUS CHRIST

OUR GOD

He knew that God not only had a plan; he became a part of the plan.

He kept walking and started to see the names of New Testament figures like Peter, James, John, and the disciples, Matthew and Thomas. Then there were other names such as Paul, Silas, and Barnabus. Silas felt a little kick inside as he saw his name written on the pavement. It wasn't him of course, but he was named after that biblical figure. *His name was on this pavement.*

But then as he continued to walk upwards, a most unexpected thing happened. The path came to an end of Bible names, but the names did not stop. He started to see names of people he had never heard of before.

POLYCARP

And

CLEMENT OF ROME

And

IRENAEUS OF LYON

Who were these people? And what did they do? He made a mental image of these names, so he could learn about them later. As he continued to walk he saw other names like Tertullian, Patrick of Ireland, Augustine, Gregory of Nyssa,

There were a LOT more names coming now than during the Bible period. How could this be? Weren't all of God's best people in the Bible? He had never considered that there might be people as good as the Bible characters, that were not in the Bible.

More names followed

THOMAS AQUINAS

And later

BONIFACE

Silas had never been interested in history, which included church history. He preferred the stories of wars and conquests. He could not have realised how profound and impact these Christian figures had in shaping the course of nations, often without war or conquest.

He walked past more names he didn't recognise like Tyndale, and Luther and Calvin.

Looking just ahead up the hill, something was different. He could see decorations on the path. A cross, and flowers. He came to a name he had not seen or known, and this paver was decorated with bright colourful flowers. Even Jesus' paver was not bright or fancy.

WILLIAM CAREY

What was it about this paver that caused it to be decorated in this way? Who was this person and what did he do? Looking around he saw someone coming down the path from above. Being a weekday, it was quiet on Cathedral, but a few people were to be seen. As they approached, Silas could see it was a woman, and she had a little child with her.

'Excuse me, good afternoon.'

'Hello, how are you?'

'Can you tell me why this name here is decorated?'

'Today is William Carey Memorial Day.'

'Oh.'

'Today is the 9th of June, the day that William Carey died in India, in 1834. Over in the Cathedral, they are remembering him today as the father of modern missions.'

'Missions?' Silas didn't know what that word meant. He should have paid more attention at school. He must have said it aloud because she replied.

'Missions is when we take the good news of Jesus to people who don't have it. William Carey went to India in the late 1700's and was responsible for translating the Bible into many Indian languages.'

As the woman spoke, the little baby sucked its thumb. Silas looked at the little one, and then at the woman, presumably the mother.

'Thank you for explaining,' he said.

The lady looked at him. She examined him.

'You are a little young to be here on your own. Who are you?'

'I'm Silas, I needed to find somewhere to pray.'

'On your own?' she queried.

'My parents don't mind. They sent me to Verde with a translator, but it failed and I went to Utopia instead. I was lucky to get home, but now I feel God wants me to go back to Utopia and I don't want to.'

Even though he didn't know this woman, he found himself telling his whole story of the last few days. It all came out like when you pull the plug in your kitchen sink. She listened intently to it all, before she answered.

'My name is Vicki,' she said. 'Come with me, I'm going to take you to see Pastor Xavier Mendosa. He is my husband.'

And before he knew what was happening, Vicki Mendosa and the baby had turned around and were going back the way they came, taking Silas up the path towards the top of the hill. As they went, they went past more names in the pavers like Wilberforce, Livingstone, Harriet Tubman, and more. He wasn't able to pay attention. Mrs Mendosa was a fit little woman, and almost seemed to pull him along with her. She was strong and determined. The baby made faces at him as they climbed.

They went past more names, Pope John XXIII, Corrie Ten Boom, Billy Graham. Silas recognised Graham; he had heard of the famous evangelist in history classes. They kept walking past many names from the twenty-second and twenty-third centuries when many missionaries had done remarkable things in Asia, especially in India. It felt like they had covered a kilometre, and a thousand years of famous names with it, in just five minutes.

At last they stood at the top of the incline, and before them the view expanded in all directions. Below him Silas was looking down into the biggest, grandest, and most magnificent gorge he had ever seen, but somehow it had also been converted into a building with a glass-like roof and what looked like millions of seats way down below.

They walked into a five-sided arched building. The path came in through one arched opening, and there were four other arched doors which took visitors to different places in Cathedral. Vicki pointed at a door that said 'Administration' and they walked through.

Next they found themselves elsewhere, in another high position and once again with a glorious perspective, but now they were under the glass ceiling and could see what was inside with more clarity. Looking below, Silas could see the architecture of a cathedral. He knew it was the biggest in existence, but it was also somehow natural as well as sculpted by humans. Millions of seats spanned the bottom of the gorge. There was also seating which seemed affixed to the canyon walls. More seating spread into the distance along the gorge floor, but as it reached about a kilometre away, it began to rise also. That seemed to be a human addition to the gorge floor. Through the middle of the Cathedral a river ran, somehow incorporated into the infrastructure of the place. And the entire facility had some kind of climate control, even though it was massive inside. Silas had no words to describe it.

He continued to follow Vicki. They walked through hallways and Silas was soon lost. But even so, he soon found himself in an office, once again overlooking the huge auditorium below.

'Honey, I've brought someone to meet you.'

Xavier Mendosa looked up from his desk. Noticing Silas with his wife and baby, and he was curious.

'Hello. I'm Silas.'

'Nice to meet you.' Xavier stood up and pushed his chair under the desk.

Vicki began to explain. 'Silas has come from Utopia, and is praying about whether to go back or not.'

And just like that, as soon as she mentioned the word Utopia, Xavier Mendosa was all ears.

'Utopia? You were there?'

'I wasn't supposed to go there. There was a glitch with my translator. It is supposed to be paired to go to Verde, but sends me to Utopia instead.' As he said this, Silas pointed to the translator on his upper left arm, with its transporter chip still inserted.

'If I press the light blue button right now, I will be in Utopia.'

'What did you see when you were there?'

'Actually, the strangest thing happened.' Silas paused. 'I arrived under the water, in a lake. I was confused but was able to get to the surface. I don't know how I survived. I tried to return, but I couldn't because my translator was wet, so I had to stay for a few hours.' Silas proceeded to recount what happened to him and how he had met Nathan, and the note he had left for Nathan.

Xavier looked him in the eyes.

'I know this is going to sound a bit direct, but you must go back to Utopia. The Lord is wanting you to go. I know it for certain.'

'How can you know?'

'It was last week that Vicki and I were praying for Utopia. We even had the chapel parishioners praying last week. It was our prayer that God would send someone. Do you know how impossible it is to get there? It has been closed for more than thirty years to all people other than atheists. It's obvious that God has made it possible for you. You are the answer to our prayers.'

'But how could I be the answer to any prayers? I'm just sixteen,' Silas replied.

'Age doesn't matter to God. Jeremiah was just a teenager, and so was Mary, the mother of Jesus.'

'But it was just an accident that I ended up in Utopia.'

'There are no accidents with God,' rebuffed Xavier.

'I nearly died.'

'But you didn't die, He looked after you.'

'I don't want to go,' Silas countered. 'I'm scared.'

It was then that Vicki interrupted.

'Do you remember what today is?'

'William Carey day?'

'Yes, and I think God wants you to do what William Carey did. He went to India despite being uncomfortable and knowing it was dangerous. But he did it because God wanted him to, and knowing his visit would be helpful to people who had never heard of God.'

Silas had a sinking feeling. He felt like he didn't have an answer for these two people. It felt like they were being pushy, but somehow it also felt like God was saying these things, even though it was coming from the mouths of people.

How strange to think that just a few weeks ago Silas was playing pranks on his brother and laughing at the school assembly. And now he was contemplating the will of God calling him to be the first Christian to visit the planet of atheists.

Silas said the first thing that came to his mind.

'I don't want to drown in that lake.'

With that Xavier Mendosa turned his back and walked over to the mantel where he kept a photo of his wife and baby. Next to the photo, lying on its side was a pair of two rings, like rubber bands, both black and circular. But they weren't rubber bands. Picking them up, he brought them back and took a hold of Silas' hand, and placed just one of the rubber circles into his palm.

'This is a flexible breather,' said Xavier. 'I was given this by a generous parishioner here at the Cathedral. This is going to help you more than it helps me.'

Silas looked down at his hand at a plain black circle.

'What is this?'

With his left hand, Xavier held up the other black rubber circle, so it dangled down.

'Watch this,' he said.

Xavier pushed his right hand into the circle. It was tight, but as he wriggled it through it disappeared. Silas could see his arm down to the wrist, but then nothing. Xavier then pushed his arm further and half of his forearm disappeared.

'What? What is happening?'

Xavier smiled the biggest grin as though he was a magician showing children a trick he knew they would never figure out.

'That's not the biggest surprise,' he grinned from ear to ear. 'Look at your palm.'

Silas looked down at his palm where the other ring was, and to his astonishment, Xavier's hand was sticking out of the rubber circle. He felt no weight at all, none more than the weight of a rubber black circle, but Xavier's entire right hand and half of his forearm were sticking up from his palm.

'How exactly?' Silas was confused.

Xavier gave a little chuckle. 'You know what a door is, how you walked through one leaving Earth to come here. Well, these little rubber rings are like tiny circular doors that are connected in space. What goes into one comes out the other.'

'Oh!'

'This is a breathing device. It is designed for going underwater for extended periods of time. If you put one half in your mouth, it is connected to the air in the outer circle, and you can go underwater as long as you need.'

'Oh!'

'Understand?' Xavier asked.

'Not yet.'

'You can put this in your mouth, and when you translate to Utopia, it won't matter if you are underwater in a lake, you'll be able to breathe like normal. I'll leave the other half right up there on my mantel. You'll be in Utopia, but you'll be breathing the air from the Cathedral.'

'OH,' now he understood.

Xavier smiled at him, 'I want you to have this. It was given to me, but I've never used it, but I know that the person who gave it to me would love nothing better than hearing it was used to help bring the gospel to Utopia.'

And with that it seemed to Silas that his question about whether to go or not had been answered. He had come to Cathedral with uncertainty, hoping for an answer. He had found one. He didn't even get to sit in the Cathedral and sift through thoughts. There was nothing to do, but to summon up his bravery, and do what God was saying. It was time to go.

CHAPTER FOURTEEN:
A UTOPIAN LIFE

Colin and Sophia stood in the Great Hall of Doors before the portal to Utopia, which had been opened for them. While they hadn't been married long, and their engagement was even shorter, the plan to live on the atheist planet had in a short amount of time, had taken root in their minds. With Sophia's inheritance money from her deceased grandfather, they soon paid for and organised their move to the atheist planet.

A small group of family and friends were there to say goodbye, in this case a permanent goodbye. Colin's parents were there, Gary stoic and upright, Collen with a tear in each eye knew that this would be the last time they would see their son. Colin's brother Nathanael hugged him goodbye, and whispered as he did, 'Never forget that God is there on Utopia too.' Colin ignored that.

Bridie was there to say goodbye to them too, but she had decided to follow them as well, and would be coming behind them at a later date. She wasn't sad for them, but excited.

After final hugs, they each scanned their left hand, then turned their back on their loved ones and stepped through the door into a whole new chapter of their lives. Not only would their futures be different, but their children would never meet their parents and friends back on Earth. It was a decision with long-reaching consequences.

As they stepped through the doorframe, the Grand Hall was gone, with its elaborate colours and all its people. They were now in a plain white circular room with two doors before them. One door on the left was purple, and the other on the right was red. An official, dressed in purple stood before them.

'Welcome.'

'Hello.' It felt formal.

'In a few minutes we will admit you to Utopia. There you will be assigned an assistant to take you to your dwelling and acquaint you with your new surroundings.'

They nodded.

'Before we proceed, there are some procedural things that must be done. First as you are aware, Utopia is an exclusive planet, limited by non-adherence to religion and faith. Here on Utopia we follow three founding principles, the three rules. Are you familiar with these rules?'

'Yes,' said Colin. They both nodded again.

'I must state the rules and you must agree before you can proceed.'

'We understand,' said Sophia.

The man in purple then began to speak in even more formal language.

'All citizens of Utopia agree to abide by the founding principles, otherwise known as the Three Rules.

Rule 1: All inhabitants of Utopia on immigration agree to leave behind all religious beliefs of any kind. They will not pray, or practice any type of spirituality. They will not possess any religious literature.

Rule 2: No inhabitant of Utopia, children included, may speak the following words I am about to state once, and once only: God, Jesus, or Christ. These words will not be spoken here by myself again, or by yourself from this point onwards.

Rule 3: All inhabitants of Utopia are required to immediately report any suspicion that Rule 1 or 2 have been broken. If they do not, they will be considered a collaborator.'

Colin and Sophia listened along as he read his legalese. They had no intention of being religious or talking about God. They also couldn't imagine anyone else doing it either on a planet exclusively for atheists. They did not realise how hard these rules would be to keep.

The purple official continued talking.

'The punishment for the breaking of the founding principles is eviction from the planet, and permanent banishment.'

He paused.

'Colin do you agree to bind yourself to the founding rules?

'Yes.'

'Sophia do you agree to bind yourself to the founding rules?'

'Yes.'

There was no need to sign anything, their voices had been recorded. Their identity was clear. They had agreed.

"Congratulations,' said the official. 'Welcome to Utopia. You may now step through the purple door.'

'Excuse me,' Colin interrupted, 'What is the red door for?'

'The red door is the door of exclusion. If you did not agree with the founding rules, you could not enter the purple door, and you would exit by the red door.'

'Where does the red door go?' Colin wanted to know.

The official replied, 'I am unaware of where the red door leads, but you can be assured it takes you away from Utopia.'

They both took one look at the red door, and then turned to the left and approached the purple door. Sophia stepped through first, and Colin followed.

They were now Utopians.

After stepping through the door they found themselves in a courtyard. It was unlike so many of the other transit spaces elsewhere in the galaxy. It didn't have the lounges, the shops, the crowds of milling people. It was just them in an elegant courtyard, terracotta tiling on the floor, and surrounded with lovely gardens. Standing before them was a lifelike figure, a young lady dressed in formal attire, wearing a light purple suit, and with long dark hair. She seemed to be maybe about twenty years of age.

'Hello,' she said. 'My name is Aña, and I am your personal assistant on Utopia.'

As Aña spoke, she sounded like a real person, but there was something just a bit proper about her cadence and tone. She also stood straight, almost like she was a member of some royal family.

Sophia interrupted her. 'Are you real?'

'I am real,' replied Aña, 'But if you mean am I human, no, I am not a human. However, you will find me to be useful, and more helpful than many humans can be. Do you have any more questions?'

'I have a lot of questions,' said Colin.

'Would you like to discuss the questions now, or would you like to see your home first?'

'The home first,' replied Colin. Sophia thoughtfully agreed.

'Certainly,' replied the robot. 'Follow me.' She walked no more than about twenty metres to what looked like a lift. The doors opened and she walked in. Colin and Sophia followed. Once inside she spoke.

'Your house number is 7349,' she advised them. 'This is a multi-door traveller and will open in your house.' Two seconds later, just like she said, the doors on the 'lift' opened, and they walked out into a living room.'

'This is your home,' said the human robot. 'Welcome.'

'Can anyone do that?' asked Sophia. 'I mean can any person just come into our house.'

'Most certainly not,' replied Aña. 'You will fin d that on Utopia everything is customised to you. The multi-door traveller recognises you, and would not allow you to enter into the home of any other person, And likewise, nobody else will be able to enter your home. You must be with the other person, or have their thought permission to be able to enter their home.'

'Does the multi-door thing actually travel?'

'Not at all,' replied Aña. 'It reprograms the doorframe of the traveller to the doorframe you need to walk through. There are hundreds of these multi-door travellers all over Utopia, and thousands of doors they can connect to.'

As if to illustrate, Aña stopped and pointed back towards the front door of the home, which they had just entered through. 'You may reopen the door and look,' she said. 'What do you see?'

Colin started walking towards the door. Aña interrupted him.

'You don't need to physically open the door, just think the door open. It's just like deciding to move your arms or legs. Try it now.'

Colin looked at Sophia, hoping she would try it first.

She looked at the door and wanted it open, and it opened. They looked outside and noticed that the lift they had come through to arrive here, was not there.

'Where did it go?' asked Colin.

'It didn't go anywhere,' replied Aña. 'The truth is that it was never there. Rather it was only the two doorframes that connected to each other. The nature of the multi-door travel system on Utopia is that you can move anywhere you want, by walking through your door and thinking to go where you want.'

Neither of them said anything. They were still trying to understand what had just been explained. Aña, taking their silence as permission to proceed, kept talking.

'We don't need the door anymore for now, that was just a demonstration,' she said. Then the front door closed on its own. Colin knew that he hadn't been thinking about closing the door. He looked at Sophia and she hadn't either. It must have been Aña.

'Notice your house,' she said, 'with its clean walls and floor and comfortable furniture. Every single thing can be controlled by your thoughts and your wishes. If you wish to have blue walls today, think about it and have it.'

As she said that, the walls turned blue.

Sophia giggled, 'We'll have to take turns choosing what colours the walls will be.'

Aña kept talking. 'Most things in your home can be changed by your thoughts. Food can be prepared that way also. Temperature can be adjusted, music can play, video can play. In fact, video can play on your screen, on your wall, or just in your mind's eye. It is all up to you. You can also choose a wide range of video or music, almost anything that has ever existed with the exception of religious themes.'

'Of course,' said Colin. They weren't going to miss that.

'I do have a question,' said Sophia.

Aña stood waiting, 'Yes, please speak.'

'If this house can do so many things on its own, and the mutli-door thing can take us so many places by itself, why do we need to have a personal assistant like you?'

'Good question,' Aña wasn't offended at all. 'There are many things I can do that the house cannot do. For example, I can wash dishes for you, clean, and take things to other people, making deliveries. I can watch children for you after they are born, including taking them to school. I can also be their teacher if they are sick and cannot go to school. I can also be your teacher. I have been programmed with tertiary level information in 39 fields of academics. I am also trained as a doctor, and can attend to all sickness, and medical emergencies in your home. If you are unwell

I can also diagnose the situation and manage the house if you are not capable of doing so. If I am not here because you have sent me on a task, I remain aware of your needs and can organise other help for you.'

After having said all of that, Colin half expected Aña would need to take a breath, but she didn't.

'I am programmed to be able to help you with many things, more than I have outlined. Please ask at any time how I can help you.'

Sophia looked at Aña impressed, but then giggled again. 'I have another question. I hope it's not dumb. That's a lovely business suit you are wearing. Do you get yourself dressed in the morning?'

'Yes I do. I have a full cupboard of clothing in your home and can wash my own clothes and dress myself, unless you have a preference for what I wear. For special occasions I like to match the clothes that you will be wearing.'

It all seemed too good to be true, and they were still standing in the first room of the home, the living room.

'Come with me now,' the robot said, 'And I will show you the other hemisphere of your house.'

They began walking out of the living room. Adjacent to the living room was a kitchen and dining room with spacious cooking and food storage areas, but they were heading for a hallway. Walking past several doors, which they were to see later on, they came to a thicker doorframe at the end of the hallway.

'This looks like a normal door,' said the assistant. 'But you are going to walk through to the other hemisphere of your house. The other side of your house is on the other side of the planet. This side is always day. The sun never goes down on the dayside. But the other side of the planet is permanently night and the sun never comes up. The nightside of the planet is where you sleep, and is where you will find your bedrooms.'

As they walked through the mid hall doorframe it became dark. But no sooner were they there than the lights came on.

'Congratulations,' said Aña, 'you wanted the lights to come on, and they have come on. You are a fast learner. Sometimes you will want the lights to stay off, perhaps if you have sleeping children or something, and you control them exactly the same way.'

Leading them into the first big room:

'This is your together bedroom,' she said. 'You also have your own individual bedrooms nearby. Each bedroom has its own bathroom, a space ceiling where you can see the stars, but also a ceiling mounted television which can appear if required. All windows can block out light; this is not to stop light coming in, of which there is little, but to stop you being seen from outside. Each room is temperature adjustable, weather adjustable, mood adjustable, and each bed is also height, softness, and angle adjustable.'

With each room, and each feature, Colin and Sophia felt more and more overwhelmed with how wonderful everything was. This really was Utopia.

They hadn't even made it to the second room, when Sophia looked at Colin and said, 'We should start a family.' She was only saying it half seriously but there was something about this house that made it feel safe, like it was the perfect place to raise a child.

Colin looked at her, 'I like the idea,' he said. 'You don't mean right this minute do you?'

'No,' laughed Sophia. 'I'm just happy. Everything feels just right.'

But time would show that there were some things that in fact were not right at all.

CHAPTER FIFTEEN:
DOUBLE TROUBLE

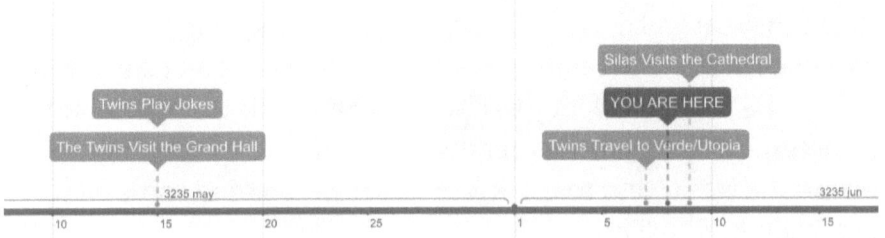

Many years earlier, Bridie had moved to Utopia, following her friend Sophia. After moving she had met the fabulous Nathan and they had met, fallen in love and married. Today, she was sitting on the lounge wondering what Nathan was doing?

It was one of their days off. Many people on Utopia worked; some needed to, some didn't, but those who did only worked about three days a week. Despite being bright as midday, which of course it always was on the bright side of the planet, it was the equivalent of evening time, and that day they had agreed to have dinner together.

Bridie had an idea, a moonlight meal, which meant they would take their food through the bedrooms, and out their back door to the nightside. They didn't always have a moon out, but the stars were always brilliant because of the blackout blinds on every single house in Utopia. No light ever escaped, and millions of stars were visible. On a cloudless night, they could identify Verde shining brightly just as Venus shines for Earth. Being outside on the dark side was perfect for a quiet evening together.

'Nathan,' Bridie tried to get his attention with a thought. 'Are you far away?'

There was no answer. Where was he?

'Nathan, are you nearby?'

Still no answer.

He often went walking, or fishing, or geocaching in the early part of each day, but rarely was he out later in the day. Like many people, he had a tendency to get absorbed in his thoughts, and sometimes didn't notice other thoughts that were there. He didn't realise she was trying to think him down. Bridie tried something old-fashioned, yelling.

'Nathan, Where are you?' Her voice echoed through the house.

Still no answer.

Starting to get a little bothered, her chair stood her up automatically as her mind wanted her to rise. Their furniture, synchronised with their thoughts, often helped them out. But she wasn't feeling helped. Walking from the lounge to the hall, she crossed the doorline into the bedroom part of the house. She was now on the darkside of the planet. Lights came on automatically as she walked into each room. Nathan was nowhere to be seen.

Was he already outside? Had he anticipated her idea?
No, not there.

Retracing her steps, she crossed back over the doorline and was now back on the light side of the planet, still in the same house. She then walked into Nathan's office but he wasn't there.

Maybe the shed? She walked through the connection door taking her to the woods.

'Nathan, are you in here?'

The place was a schmozzle, with things piled everywhere. It was like Nathan himself. Looking across the room she noticed that one of his posters had fallen off the wall. And, there appeared to be writing on the back of it. How unusual.

She walked over to take a closer look, and noticed that it did indeed have writing, but it wasn't an official notice, rather it was handwritten. Actually, to be more accurate it was scratched in by hand. She picked it up.

Nathan, my translator is working now. I must go. I might come back and see you again in a few days if my parents let me. Silas.

As she read those words, all feelings of frustration were gone. Instead, they were pushed out by anxiety and panic which flooded in. She knew that their lives were at risk. Had Nathan been talking to an outsider? Who was this Silas? Why was Silas leaving notes in their shed? Was this why Nathan left every morning to go outdoors? There were so many questions. Where was he now?

Taking a few deep breaths to calm herself, she tried to think it through. Should she ignore it and hope it went away? Should she confront him? Should she report him now? Should she talk to him and then report him, but give him a chance to escape? It was overwhelming.

'Sophia, are you free?' Her thoughts went to her friend. Unlike Nathan, Sophia replied straight away.

'Yes, I'm here.'

'I just found a note to Nathan in his shed.'

'A note in his shed! Who wrote it? What does it say?'

'The what isn't anything, but the who is an outsider.'

'How do you know it's from an outsider?'

'He says he translated here, and will come back in a few days if his parents let him.'

Sophia was silent as she did some of the other kind of thinking.

'What should I do Sophia? Should I pretend I don't know?'

In that moment Sophia's heart sank. It had been five months since her own husband had said the dreaded word that had him evicted from the planet. Her son, as little as he was, had followed her husband just two months ago, and she was now alone. She dreaded the thought that she would lose any more friends, especially her closest friend.

'You have to report him Bridie. I'm so sorry. If you don't report him, you will both be evicted. We'll never see each other again.'

The advice Sophia gave was true, but also motivated in part by her own interest. Bridie sensed that as well. They both knew it. If Bridie didn't report and they were both evicted, at least they were together. But if she did report, she might spend the rest of her life alone, without her husband. At some basic level it was a choice between her friend Sophie and her new husband Nathan. Or at least that's how it seemed. She didn't know which way to lean. Or what to do? Her husband was a priority, but she had known Sophia most of her life and the thought of never seeing her again was troubling.

'Don't leave me?' Sophia pleaded.

'How would I leave you?'

'If you don't report it, you'll both end up being taken away, and then I'll be on my own here in this wretched place, stuck like a bird in a fancy cage.'

Bridie had always been a stickler for the rules. She had chided and admonished Sophia all through their teenage years about doing the right thing, but now she was looking for a way to bend the Utopian system. There was no way of getting around the rule that everything must be reported, immediately.

'I know what to do,' Sophia thought.

'What?'

'Get rid of the evidence that an outsider was here. Get rid of the note. Then have Nathan report that he had seen someone in his shed. Then neither of you will be evicted, just the outsider only.'

'That is a good idea.' Relief was dripping all over her facial expression, not that Sophia could see it, but she felt it somehow. Bridie was relieved at an idea that seemed would work.

'Talk tomorrow?'

'Ok, talk tomorrow.'

Bridie immediately took the poster with the scratched message and put it back up on the wall. For now that would cover up the message, and nobody would think of pulling it down. Later they could work out where to dispose of it.

It was not long until Nathan arrived back.

'I've been looking for you,' he asked. 'What are you doing in my shed?'

'Same thing, looking for you. Where were you?' Bridie asked vocally.

'Down at the lake.'

'What were you doing there?'

'Fishing.'

'Fishing after lunch?' she queried.

'Yes.'

'Did you catch anything? Or maybe see anyone? Maybe even someone called **Silas**?' She emphasized the name.

'How do you know about Silas?'

'Who is Silas?' questioned Bridie.

'I don't know who he is, but he is young, just a teenager. When I was fishing earlier today before lunch, there was this boy swimming in the lake. He thought he was on Verde, and was shocked to realise he wasn't.'

'And?'

'He tried to translate back, but his translator wouldn't work. He said his name was Silas. I was worried he would get arrested, so I brought him to the shed to hide for a bit.'

'But what about us? Didn't you think we might get arrested? Why didn't you report him?'

'I'm not like you,' Nathan was starting to get edgy. 'I haven't lived on Earth and met thousands of other people like you. You would be interested too if you were me.'

'So where is he now?'

'I thought he was here. It was only a few hours ago I brought him here.' Nathan looked puzzled and confused. 'How do you know about Silas?'

'The other side of that poster explains it all.' She pointed at the nearby art hanging on the wall.

Nathan walked across, took it down, flipped it over and examined it.

'Oh, he's gone.'

'Yes, and you have to report him,' said Bridie. 'You have to pretend to know nothing about who he is. You must not admit to bringing him here, or talking to him, or telling me anything either. We don't know anything. Just report him, and we'll all be fine.'

'But what if he comes back in a few days?'

'Not our problem. Do you want to be evicted?'

'No,' he paused, 'Well sort of, maybe. Hmm, no, not really.' He kept talking as his mind considered the possibilities.

'OK, report him, right now.' Bridie was demanding. She wanted an outcome, and wanted to know they were going to be safe.

Nathan looked at her.

'Right now,' she demanded.

'OK,' he gave in.

At that moment, it looked like he was doing nothing, but he was in fact reporting. Sending a public thought to the reporting system wasn't complicated. It was a matter of willing the communication just as any other thought-based communication would work.

And within about five hundred seconds, three figures in purple arrived, and all five of them were standing in Nathan's shed. The leading figure began a conversation.

'You are reporting an outsider, is that correct?'

'Yes.'

'Where did you see him?'

'By the lake.'

'Which lake?'

'Lake Sound, just out this door and about two kilometres down the path.' Nathan pointed out the door in the direction of the lake.'

'Why did you come here before reporting? Why didn't you report immediately?'

It was in that exact moment that Nathan knew he was in trouble. He should have gone back to the lake and stood on the shore before making his report. It was an error of significant consequences. Bridie sensed it too. All incidents had to be reported promptly.

'He wanted to ask me what to do?' Bridie jumped in, anxious to save her husband.

'So you know about it too?' The leading figure in purple queried. He looked at her, 'Why did you not report your husband straight away?'

And it was at that moment that Bridie knew she was in trouble too. If only she had not insisted that they report the incident 'right now.' If only they had taken some time to work out their story.

Before they knew it, three other figures in purple had arrived, making six in total. Both Nathan and Bridie were gagged with jawlocks, and bound with thought cuffs, and both of their thought processors disabled. Then they were taken away as helpless as baby animals.

A few minutes after that, both Nathan and Bridie passed through the red door and were gone from Planet No-X.

CHAPTER SIXTEEN:
BACK TO DANGER

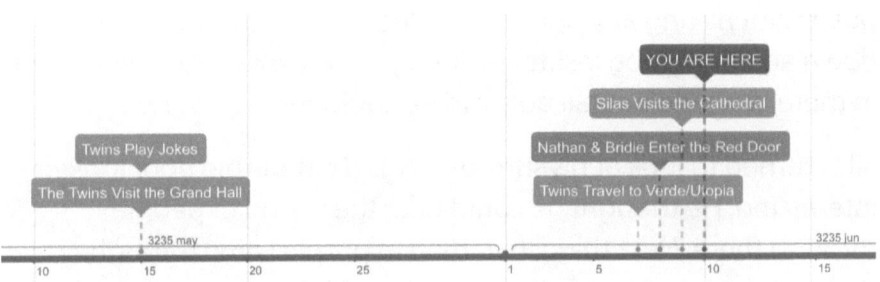

This time Silas knew that he was heading into danger. He said goodbye to his parents, and they bowed their heads for a prayer. There was a possibility he might not see them again, and they committed his future into the hands of God. Then he inserted the rubber breather into his mouth, knowing that in a minute he would be at the bottom of that lake again. Taking a big breath of Cathedral air through the breather, he waved at his parents, and then reached up his right hand and pressed the little blue button.

Blink. He was gone.

Last time Silas had translated to Utopia he had the shock of his life when he found himself underwater. This time even though he was ready for that, once again he was shocked by what happened. In fact, he might have been even more surprised than last time, because when he arrived in Utopia, he was in fact NOT at the bottom of a lake.

He was standing at a place that Colin, or Bridie, or Nathan would have recognised, but he had never been there before. He was in a white circular room, with a red door before him, and a purple door to the side. It was plain and empty. Where was this place? He had no idea. He didn't even know if he was on Utopia.

He reached into his mouth and removed the rubber breather. It was obvious he had no need for that now. He didn't want to throw it away, it had been given at significant expense. Where could he put it? Not having any pockets, he decided to push the breather down against his leg inside the lining of his exoskeleton. Squished in there, it would not fall out, and he could retrieve it later.

Silas turned to look at his surroundings. That purple door looked interesting. He thought he could hear the sound of people through there. Next thing, two men in purple came through that purple door. He saw them coming maybe a microsecond before they saw him. For the briefest of moments, he wondered why there were purple doors and purple people, but he didn't have time to think about it because once they saw him, many things happened.

The two purple men grabbed him, and one of the men spoke. 'Are you Silas?'

'Yes, I am.'

'What are you doing here?'

'I came to visit a friend.'

'What is your friend's name?'

Silas didn't know if he should tell the truth, or tell a lie. He knew that telling the truth was the right thing to do, and that lying was forbidden by the Lord. But on the other hand, what if by telling the truth, it led to the death of his friend?

'Um, can I ask a question first?'

The two purple figures stopped and looked at each other. They must have been communicating behind his back, via their thoughts. He didn't know what they were thinking to each other.

'You can ask a question,' the first purple figure said.

'Where am I?' asked Silas.

'You are on the planet Utopia?'

'Oh,' Silas did his best to act surprised. He wanted them to think he didn't realise where he was.

'How did I get here?' He asked another question.

'We said you could ask one question, but now you are asking another question.' A demanding voice came from one of the purple figures. Then, despite his grumpiness, he proceeded to answer the question.

'The fact is, we had a report about you. We then investigated the situation and learned that you have been here before, and you arrived last time in a lake. This morning we put divers into the lake and retrieved half of a translator pair, which we believe is yours.'

Reaching down to the carpet, the second of the purple men opened a translator pouch stitched into the carpet, and pulled out the half and showed him. It was half of a translator pair, and contained a purple label.

'A few hours ago, this was in Lake Sound, but now it is here. And strangely, you are here too. If we were to open your translator activator on your arm, we would find that these two pairs match. Would I be right?'

The third official reached out and took a hold of the strap on Silas' upper left arm. That strap contained the activator, the little blue button, the device that controlled his coming and going. Silas had been unable to reach for it while the two burly men held him, but now the device was taken off him. The official looked at the half that was in the device. It also had a purple label, just like the other half that was originally in the bottom of the lake, but was now in the white room.

'This chip was used many years ago by terraformer workers on Utopia,' the official spoke calmly. 'How did you get it?'

'I don't know.' Silas answered. He had no clue how he ended up with the wrong pair.

'A likely story.' the official replied. 'It seems to me that you have tried to bring religion to our planet. You have broken our rules and will have to pay for your indiscretion.'

If Silas had been able to see through the official's mirror mask, he would have noticed an evil smile, a grin of delight, coming from the face of someone who can't wait to catch someone, or jail someone, or punish someone.

At that point two more purple officials came into the room. Now there were four of them, and one of him. He contemplated making a run. He might have been able to break free of them and get away before when there were only two, but it seemed almost impossible now.

One of the new purple men must have been a senior official, because he took over the conversation from the previous purple guy.

'Who was your friend?'

Silas bowed his head, not in prayer, but in shame. 'It was someone called Nathan. I met him at the lake. I was hoping to see him again.'

'You'll never see him again,' laughed the leading purple official. 'We've taken care of that man.' He seemed happy about it,

'And guess what?' The senior official asked a taunting question.

Silas didn't like playing these games, but he knew he
had best reply.

'What?'

'There's another reason why you will never see him again too.' The
senior officer waited again for a reply.

'Why?'

'Because see that red door, over there. You are about to walk
through it, and when you do, it will be all over for you too.'

The four purple men started laughing. They thought that last
comment was funny. Silas decided he was not going though
that red door, but it was then that he discovered why there were
four of them.

Taking an arm or a leg each, all four picked him up and walked him
over to the red door. Then standing him up, they opened the door
and pushed him in. There was nothing he could do to resist. He
wasn't strong enough.

CHAPTER SEVENTEEN:
TROUBLE

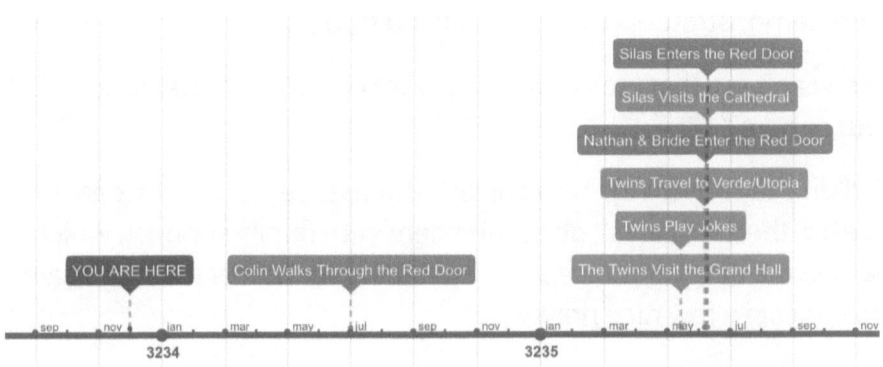

For Colin and Sophia, their attempts to start a family had been frustrating. Sophia had been pregnant many times, but it took six years to keep the baby past the magical first trimester. At that point, Sophia did nothing but sit or walk slowly as though any tiny bump might terminate that little life. It was physically exhausting for her, and emotionally exhausting for them both. After years of trying, their little baby was born in their seventh year. But other things were taking their toll too.

Maybe it is because when things are consistently good, you come to not appreciate them as much. Or maybe it was because there were genuine problems to be complained about, but either way, Sophia was not happy, and Colin was even more agitated.

'The health system here on Utopia stinks,' grumbled Colin to Sophia one morning. By the 'health system' he meant their assistant Aña who was in all ways amazing, but could do nothing for conception, and did not have the power to keep a baby in the womb. By this point, they had a five year old son, Gregory, but had failed miserably trying four years for another child. Frustration was mounting. Would they ever get number two?

'If we were on Earth, I would be talking to my parents and asking them to…..' he held his hands together in a prayer-like manner and demonstrated as if he was talking to God.

'You can't say that,' said Sophia. 'Do you want to get us kicked out of here?'

'I didn't say anything,' he retorted. 'But maybe it's a good idea if we do, then we can all go somewhere with family support, which would include a few nice ……' he did the motion of praying again to indicate a few nice prayers.

'Aña might see you. Stop it.' Sophia meant it.

They had also learned that as wonderful as Aña was, and despite being a most amazing humanoid, she was also a reporting facility. She noticed everything they said and did. There was no privacy. Not only that, every house had a humanoid. They were not all called Aña, but they all had one. There were also public servants humanoids located all over the planet, and they all "talked" to one another. Colin and Sophia had learned to be careful what they said, not only at home, but everywhere. The walls had ears.

One day, Colin and Sophia had decided to make a cheese and meat platter for a snack. Little Gregory loved cheese. Sophia had called to him to come to the table.

'Come look at all these cheeses,' she yelled.

A moment later purple officials had arrived at the door assuming she had said 'Jesus' instead of 'cheeses'. It was a misunderstanding, but it highlighted that they had no privacy, and the frailty of their position.

After that, Colin had commented, 'It's like we are birds in a gilded cage.'

'Don't be silly,' Sophia replied.

'What's a gilded cage?' asked Gregory.

'It's a fancy jail,' Colin told him.

Sophia thought he was speaking nonsense, and Gregory didn't understand it. They weren't in jail; they were free. But it wasn't full freedom, because what they could speak, believe, and even think were controlled.

The straw that broke the camel's back however was the thing that happened next.

It was December the 1st, and Christmas was just over three weeks away, except that it wasn't. Before moving to Utopia, nobody had informed Colin and Sophia that there would be no Christmas. If they thought about it in advance they might have realised. The name of it was a giveaway, **Christ**-mas. But, there was to be no hint of anything that was a reminder of Jesus, of God, of spiritual stories, Bible stories, scripture lessons, nothing at all.

The founders of Utopia had thought it through. They realised that atheist governments of the past had attempted to remove religion, in particular Christianity, with a full frontal attack. The communist regimes of the twentieth century had arrested and killed ministers, and closed churches, but they had failed. Every overt thing they did was like a seed planted that resulted in more of what they hated, not less. Like blowing a dandelion flower to get rid of it creates even more dandelions. But Utopia had noted these failures and its method was to go quiet. By avoiding anything spiritual, by not talking about it, the idea was to create an environment for children growing up where they never heard of it, and within a generation, the entire culture would be purged of such things.

So, no Christmas.

The first year in Utopia, it was disappointing to realise. As December rolled around, they automatically expected something 'Christmassy' to happen, but nothing happened. It was as if nobody knew anything about it. Colin wanted to ask someone, but knew bringing up the topic of the birth of Jesus was going to be hard to do without being evicted. He brought it up with Sophia.

'Do you remember what happens at this time of year on Earth?'

'Yes.'

'Do you think it will happen here too?'

'No, I don't think it will.'

'Aren't you sad about that?'

'A little.'

It didn't affect her like it did Colin. She had grown up with so few family around. But for Colin, Christmas was a time of extended family gatherings, gift giving and a lot of personal joy. He knew the Bible stories, not that he believed them, but there was something about hearing them every year, and singing Christmas Carols. One song by Andy Williams summarised it nicely in a line… 'It's the most wonderful time of the year'.

Colin got over it that year. And the next. And the next.

Finally Gregory was born, and the little boy didn't know what he was missing. But this year he was five. He started school, and there was an itch in Colin that had to be scratched. Even if it wasn't officially for Christmas, Colin HAD to buy his wife and his son a gift.

And so, he went shopping.

Sophia always said that shopping on Utopia was one of the more disappointing aspects of living there. Whatever they wanted arrived at the house without any effort. It took away the process of going somewhere, admiring the merchandise, feeling it, smelling it, and making a selection. That was what made shopping fun. So yes, there were shops, though nothing like the old-fashioned places which stored things you could look at. They were virtual stores with virtual goods. It was from these stores that real things eventuated, and quickly too. It was amazing, but Colin did not go shopping at these stores. No, he went shopping in the twilight zone.

The twilight zone was the region on the planet between the day that ended and where the night started. Because the planet was locked and didn't rotate, this zone of semi-darkness never moved. The twilight zone was 'shady' not because it was in the shade, but because under the semi-awareness of most Utopians, was an actual shop. It was like the black market that used to exist back on Earth in the twentieth century.

Back on Earth, to buy things you were not supposed to buy, you went to the black market. The black market wasn't physically a place, but it was a concept. It was the idea of buying something illegal. On Utopia, it wasn't that the items themselves were illegal, but that the store itself was illegal. It was a place for barter, trading and selling, and was itself an unsanctioned mode of transaction.

To make it more illegal, it was well-known that the rats brought things to sell, and also purchased and sold things there too. Items traded here did not sell with Utopian currency, or with Valens, but often with gold or silver itself.

And so Colin decided he wanted to go shopping to get his wife and son presents, not for any reason except that he loved them. The fact that it was December was apparently, 'a coincidence'.

The market was situated in a valley between two mountains, in a spot located in semi-dark shadows. If needed, the rats could grab their wares and exit to the rear, gone into the night without a trace. Any Utopians who were there could claim to be doing nothing wrong without the presence of the recently departed rats.

Colin browsed the tables and found a whistle carved out of timber, a perfect gift for Gregory. Kids loved things like that. And given that a rat had made it, there was nothing like it anywhere on Utopia, and probably beyond. Colin also saw a hand made bowl out of wood too. Sophia would love that. It was hard to find such genuine 'earthy' artifacts like these. They would be one-of-a-kind gifts.

After he purchased these gifts, he turned to make his way back home. Seeing another Utopian, they walked together.

'Hi I'm Colin,'

'Ivan. What brings you to the market today?'

'I wanted to buy gifts for my wife and son. And you?'

'Just curious. My first time.'

'Did you buy anything?' Colin queried.

'Not this time. How about you?'

Colin showed Ivan the two gifts he had bought.

'Back on Earth we used to always give gifts at this time of year, so I just wanted to do that too, not for any reason, you know, just to give gifts.'

They continued to talk. Ivan seemed friendly.

But when Colin arrived at the front door of his home, two men in purple were waiting for him.

'Before you enter your home, we understand you have illegal merchandise,' said the first man in purple.

'Illegal merchandise?' Colin was confused.

'You purchased gifts, did you not?'

'Yes.' Colin produced the two items and showed them. 'It's just a wooden bowl and a whistle.'

The two men took the items from Colin, and informed him not to speak of these items to anyone, because the circumstances of their purchase was in contravention of the religious code of ethics on Utopia. Then they were gone, and so was the whistle, and so was the bowl.

Colin was dumbfounded. Ivan was a snitch. How dare he? But even more annoying was the loss of his gifts! How could they justify such a thing?

When he entered his house that day, he was determined he was going to take his wife and son. They were going to leave this planet through the red door and go back to Earth. He was going to convince Sophia they had to leave. It was clear in his mind. They had to get out of this place, and they would.

CHAPTER EIGHTEEN:
HALLWAY OF DOOM

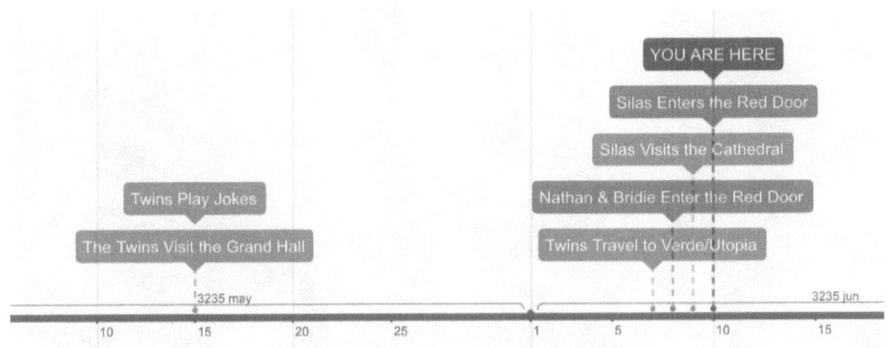

Having just been forced through the red door, Silas stood before an imposing sight.

Before him was a long dimly-lit hallway which stretched at least one hundred and fifty metres. The end was just visible, and appeared to be another doorway of some type. He walked forwards about three steps. Along both sides of the walkway, every two metres or so, was a blue dot of light. On the ceiling above were also equally-spaced circular patterns of the same blue dots of light. Everything was precise, and the walkway was straight and long, with no curves, bends, or changes in colour, hue or texture of any kind. The floor was a walkway of black steel grates about fifty centimetres above the floor. The ceiling itself was black, apart from the blue dots of light. There were no windows, and didn't appear to be anything else in the tunnel except the red door he had just exited, and the dark-coloured door far ahead. Otherwise everything was dark.

Silas turned around to look behind him. The red door that he had just walked through was still there, but now seemed dark, almost black, an effect of the blue light in the tunnel. He turned back and thought he might try to test its permeability. It had an opaque white-coloured almost fog-like appearance. He moved his hand into the fog, but it felt solid, like glass. He pushed against it. No good, it was strong.

The door was most certainly a one-way door as they had said in the other room. Nobody was getting back into that other place from here. He turned back to the hallway which seemed his last remaining option.

As he approached the other end, he could see the other door clearer now. It was also blackish in colour. Maybe it was also red. The blue light made it hard to tell. It was identical to the first door, except minus the fog. He wondered if it was also a one-way door.

If so, he wouldn't see the fog on this side, but it would be too late to know until he had walked through.

He contemplated the long hallway with two doors. Perhaps it was a kind of double protection against people trying to get back into Utopia. The more he thought, a conviction strengthened in him. This door was a one-way door too. Why such an extreme measure? Why were they so determined to be separated from everyone else in the stellarverse? Why two one-way doors?

He knew what he had to do. It was an age-old trick, well at least as old as the invention of one-way doors. He needed a piece of string, or something thin and long. Until the space between the doorframe had been emptied, the one-way part of the door would not activate, so if you walked halfway through you could still go back. You could even walk all the way through but leave your hand extended back in the doorframe. You could see one side and still change your mind and go back. But once you were all the way through, that was it, there was no going back. And so the string trick had been invented.

One way portals were not common because they were time-consuming and expensive to build, and there wasn't much need for a one-way door. Sometimes a door like this would be used in the military for training, or in custom mazes at theme-parks, but most people did not encounter one anytime. But Silas knew of the string trick from stories.

As you walk through this type of door, you tape a piece of string to one side of the door, walk through, and then tape it on the other side and it keeps the door open. Or, if you don't have tape, a long piece of string could work by just laying it on the floor and pulling it into the threshhold as you walked through. Of course you had to leave it so it lay in the doorway. The danger was that anyone could pull the string from either side and the door would close, leaving you on the wrong side, unable to get back.

He needed a piece of string.

But there was nothing he could use in that long thin dark hall. He tried pulling on a wire that held up the walkway, but without tools, it would not be possible to make use of that. One thing was certain, there was no way he was going through that second door until he had a way of coming back. He knew within himself that he had to take this precaution.

Many years earlier his father Jonathan had taught him not to ignore inner impulses. 'Often that is how the Holy Spirit will speak to you,' he had said. Silas thought that this must he case at least some of the time, but he also knew his own human impulses overpowered anything God might want to say. Silas, like most people tended to be more 'earthly' and less 'heavenly' and hadn't trained himself to be sensitive to God's often gentle suggestions.

As Silas looked at the second door, he didn't know if it was a feeling from God, or just his own intuition. Maybe it was both. No matter which, he needed something long enough to lay through the door. He reached down to feel for a belt, but he never wore one normally, and he didn't have one on today. That was pointless. He had no shoelaces, and like many people, he wore rip-proof clothing, so there was no chance of tearing a strip off his clothing.

Turning back to look down the long hall again towards the first door, he had an idea. Was there anything under the flooring? Maybe someone had dropped something and it fell through as they had walked along. It was unlikely, but it was possible. He knelt down to try to look through the walkway, and noticed that the sections of flooring clipped together. They were solid when joined, but could be independently lifted. So, lifting the panel closest to him, he stared into the dark underfloor. He couldn't see down there. There was nothing to do, except to get down into the space and crawl along and feel. With reluctance, he climbed down into the subfloor.

Feeling his way, he crawled along the low area. After a few metres, he bumped his head on a metallic cross beam. It was unexpected and painful. It took him a moment to recover and catch his breath. He didn't know it yet, but it left a nasty egg just above his hairline. He crawled for what felt like an hour, and all the while came to know when to expect another beam. About every three metres, the space would tighten where a cross beam existed. He would lower himself onto his stomach and wriggle through before being able to proceed.

It wasn't as dusty as he expected, maybe because this hallway was only accessed by two doors, and they didn't open often. That was something to be grateful for. Eventually he came to the end of the tunnel and he could see above him the foggy mist in the midst of the first doorframe. Its light was minimal, but after having adjusted to the dark of the tunnel, it was relatively bright. Turning around he noticed a steel cross beam and scrawled on it were the words 'Hallway of Doom… Ha Ha.'

What type of joke was that? Or was it a joke? Who would even write such a sadistic thing?

He had little time to think about the meaning of what he had just read when there was a clicking noise. The door above opened. He heard voices. Through the red door came two figures, wearing purple, but it appeared like dark clothing. It was difficult for Silas to see who they were, even though they were not wearing their masks. They might have been the same people who had sent him through the portal just a few hours ago. They laid a light plastic rod in the doorway to keep it open and then turned on a switch near the door. At once the entire tunnel was lit up in brilliant lights.

All the blue dots on the side walls illuminated such that if anyone had been in the tunnel they would have been seen in an instant.

Despite the fact that the hall was now flooded with lights, they didn't see Silas. They were in fact standing right above him, unaware of his presence. Had they looked down and through the floor they would have seen him straight away.

'He's not here. Looks like he did go through the second door.' said the first man.

'I'm glad we didn't have to shoot him,' said the other.

'Weird how we didn't get the signal that the door had been opened,' said the first.

The two figures were standing right above where Silas was laying, with their gaze down the tunnel.

'A glitch I suppose.' The second said.

'Well that's that then.'

'Isn't it risky sending him so soon after sending that other one yesterday?'

'There's no way they can escape from the other end. Don't worry about it.'

'It makes me uncomfortable that we had to do this check. The least they could have done is have some cameras installed.'

'Don't you get it? The point is not knowing what happens.'

'Why are we even checking if we don't want to know what happens?'

The question lingered in the air. It was a good question. It shocked Silas who as he lay under the floor was trying to get a grasp on what this conversation meant. But before he realised, both dark figures had exited back through the first red door. As he lifted his eyes he could see the fog was once again in place. He was trapped in the hall again.

Lifting the floor panel above him, he clambered back onto the walkway reeling with the information he had learned. He reached out and turned on the switch and was grateful to now be able to see easily. He walked slowly back down towards the second door peering into the floor all the way.

What was on the other side of that second door? And why didn't they want to see what happened? Why did they want to make sure he had gone through it? Now he was certain he had to keep that one-way door open.

With the help of the lighting he checked each and every section of flooring a second time, this time visually, but the room was empty, clean, and sanitary. There was nothing in here that would help him at all.

As he neared the other end, he considered his personal inventory. He had a breathing gateway in his shoe pocket, but apart from that nothing, other than his clothing.

Clothing?

He thought about that for a moment. He had an idea.

Maybe it was a heavenly impulses, but where it came from didn't matter right now. He had a shirt; he would use that. A smile spread across his face as he removed his shirt. Standing shirtless before the second door, he laid his shirt into the doorway to keep the door open, and stepped across the threshold into the room on the other side.

CHAPTER NINETEEN:
SORROW OF A LITTLE SIZE

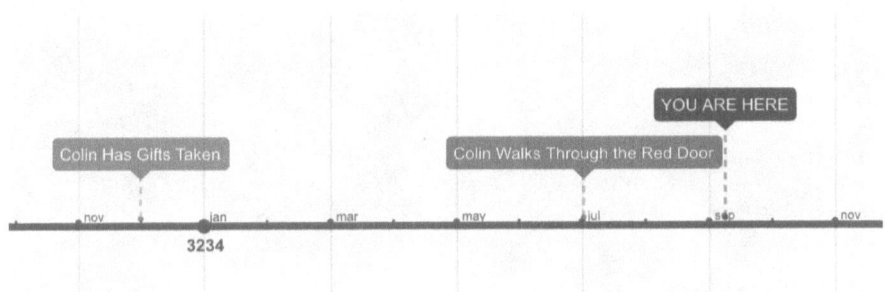

Gregory Philips was five years old when his daddy, Colin, had been taken away. Greg was now six. Normally a birthday would be a joyous occasion for a little boy, but without his father it just wasn't. Those two months since his daddy left, had been full of tough times.

On this particular day, Greg was at school on Utopia. There were several schools in Utopia to choose from. Colin and Sophia had chosen a stream with emphasis on Science and Maths. Their background working for ICE helped make that decision. Utopia would need good scientists and engineers in the years ahead.

It was lunch break, and Greg was playing outside with his friend Markus. They were at the playground, a feature of childhood anywhere in the universe. Today they were having races down the slide.

'Hey Markus, how long does it take you to go down the slide?'

Greg jumped into the entrance of the first slide and started counting.

'One, two, three, four, five, six, seven, eight. Eight seconds. I bet you can't beat eight seconds.'

Markus replied. 'I can beat you easy.'

'Show me.'

Markus climbed up the steps to the same slide that Greg had just used. He reached out and grabbed a handle each side of the slide, and pulled himself in, feet first.

Greg started counting.

'One, two, three, four, five, six, seven, eight, nine, ten.'

Markus appeared at the end of the slide.

'Ten seconds,' said Greg, informing Markus of his time.

'Was not, you counted fast.'

'I counted the same as for me.'

'I counted too, and I got seven seconds.'

'Liar, you always want to win.'

Markus was about to punch Greg, when he stopped. He remembered what his mum said at home. 'Don't hit your friends.' But he still wanted to win the argument.

'My dad can beat your dad down the slide.'

Greg was not to be outdone.

'If my dad was still alive he would beat your dad in a fight.'

Markus paused. 'Is your dad dead?'

'Yes.'

'What happened to him?'

'He said a word and then the purple police took him away.'

'What word did he say?'

'He said "Jesus".'

'Jesus. What is a Jesus?'

'I don't know, I never heard of a Jesus before.'

'Why would they take him away for saying that?'

'I don't know. My mum said it was a bad word. She said don't say it.'

It was right at that moment that their conversation around the word Jesus was overheard. Firstly because that word was *always* heard on Utopia, but secondly because their teacher had walked into the playground at that moment. She had no choice but to report it. If she didn't, it would be her that would be in trouble.

Within minutes the figures in purple had arrived, and had taken into custody two little boys. They were removed from civilization, and sent through the red door, deported from Utopia.

Markus was terrified, and he screamed as he was taken away, at least until he was jawlocked. Gregory was terrified too, but he also thought that perhaps he might see his dad. He hoped he would. He was scared about never seeing his mum again.

Later that day Sophia received a short little message.

'We regret to inform you that Gregory Philips has been deported for talking to children in his class about unspeakable things.'

It was as if someone had plunged a knife into her heart. The sorrow came because of a little person, but it was not a little sorrow.

CHAPTER TWENTY:
TEN SECONDS OF TERROR

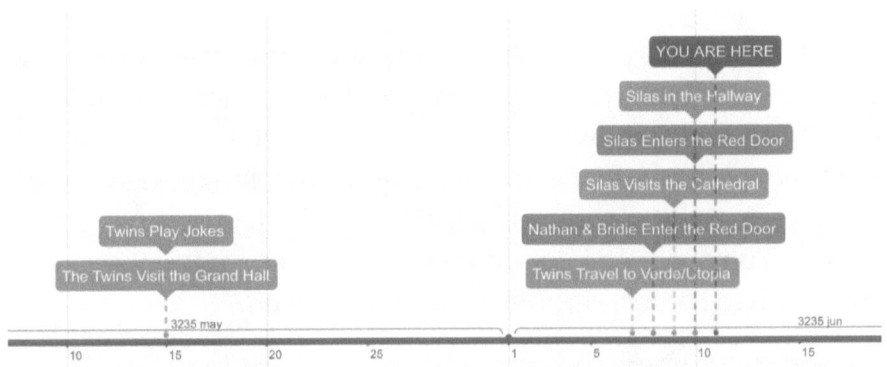

Judson had been on Verde now for four days, and had settled into a work routine. He had a hunch he was doing more chores than he might have if Silas had been there to help, but it wasn't as bad as he thought. The company of friendly Uncle Terry and lovely Aunt Joy made it pleasant.

The day and night were all out of sync with the calendar, so that took some getting used to. Days here were shorter than actual calendar days so sleeping was weird. The first night on Verde the sun came up at 8300 metric seconds, which was about 2am in the old Earth time. The morning after that while he was trying to sleep the sun came up even earlier at 4150 seconds and the next night it came up in the middle of the night. It was one of a few things he had to get used to. It meant that some 'days' they got up and worked in the night hours, or partially in night hours.

After a few of those Verde days, Judson had got used to the notorious Verde gravity. His muscles had gone through the sore stage and started to strengthen, and he began to feel nimble and recovered his ease of mobility, or at least most of it. Also, without all the electronic connectivity and the absence of thought servers and screens, he was amazed at how clear his mind felt. He felt alive.

Then there came a perfect day for exploring. The weather was good, the daylight was lined up with his free time after his chores were done, and there was a whole planet, (apart from near the construction zone), that was more or less unexplored. There were entire parts, most of them in fact, where no human had ever set foot. Judson packed a bag, with plenty of water, some light-weight energy bites, some fruit, and was about to set off.

'Do you know where you are going?' It was Uncle Terry.

'No, but that's part of the fun.'

'How will you get back?'

'The same way I left of course.'

'Sure, but how will you know which way is back?'

Judson thought about that. It seemed like a dumb question.

'I'll watch where I'm going, and then return the same way,' he said.

'A long time ago on Earth,' started Terry, 'there were explorers, and some of them got lost, and even died because of that. People now tend to forget about that because navigation has been controlled by satellites for so long. But trust me, when you get out there in the vegetation, or if you go into a forest, everything will look the same and you can forget which way you came. It's called disorientation.'

'It can't be that hard?' Judson sounded incredulous.

Terry looked at him and shook his head. 'I tell you what,' he said. 'Take this little black director tag and put it in your bag. If you don't come home, I'll know which direction you are, and will come looking for you.'

Judson said nothing.

'Deal?' said Terry.

'OK. Deal,' said a confident Judson.

'Sundown in four hours,' said Terry. 'Take a light in case you need it on the way home. See you then.'

'Bye Uncle Terry.'

And off he set.

Judson had gone no more than perhaps a kilometre when he reached the end of the main part of town. It was colloquially called Verde City, even though only two thousand people lived there. Most people on Verde lived in this one spot, leaving an entire planet to discover. His friends at school were going to be jealous. He made a mental note to try and take thought pictures that he could share with them later.

> **Director Magnets**
>
> Director magnets were a type of entangled magnet that had a special compass that went with them. Instead of the compass pointing to north as most would, or to the magnetic north of whatever planet it was on, this compass was entangled to the specific magnet and would point to wherever that was. If Judson was lost, Terry would follow the arrow and find him.

As he left the edge of town, houses and buildings thinned and there was grass, a lot of grass. On Earth it would have been called jungle grass, but here it was taller and thicker. There were trees too, but all of them were small to medium in size because none of them had been planted more than fifty years ago. There were none of the large established oaks, or pines, or gums you might see on Earth. Verde city didn't have proper streets, with any road surfacing; everything was dirt paths. Now the path leaving town thinned to several tracks, like car tyre tracks, but bigger. He followed the tracks through the tall grass. He couldn't see anywhere except down the path. The grass on either side was higher than he was. Looking at the tracks he concluded they were caused by large trucks or something like that.

'I can see why they call it Verde,' he thought to himself. Everything was so green and lush, or as they would say in English, it was verdant. He had never seen so much grass in all his life. On the first day he had arrived he had asked Uncle Terry about the grass.

'Why doesn't anyone mow the grass?'

'It grows back.' The answer was obvious. But now he could see the real reason why. The grass had taken over the planet like a virus. It looked nice, but it was also everywhere. It was going to make it hard to explore because he couldn't see anything. He had no idea where the horizon was, or even any mountains, because he had to get higher somehow to see over the top of the grass. He followed the path for ten minutes. He chuckled to himself as he thought about Uncle Terry's warning about getting lost. There was no way he was getting disoriented. He only had to turn around and follow the path back.

After another kilometre he came to a place where some large construction machines and vehicles were parked. They looked like they had not been driven in a long time. On the left was a large scraping machine, and behind it was a digging machine with a huge scoop. On the right there were two large trucks with tippers that had once carried dirt. In between the machines was, of course, grass. If the machinery wasn't so tall he would not have even known it was there.

The machinery looked as if it had at first been painted red, but the colours had dulled with the sun and time, and had started to show signs of rust. On the side of the vehicles was written in bold black writing the word 'Terrecom'. With it was the Terrecom logo, a planet with a butterfly imposed on it. He remembered that company from his history subjects at school; it was famous because Nick Jones had worked there when he terraformed six planets. It was amazing to see some of that machinery right here.

He pushed his way through the grass to the tipper trucks and took a closer look. The front wheel was higher than his head. Stairs ran up the side, over the wheel guard of the truck to the cabin, where the driver would sit. He climbed up and stood on a small ledge. Now at last he could see beyond the grass, and what he saw was what he expected to see, but was also surprising. He saw mile upon mile of grass as far as the eye could see. It reminded him of desert photos he had seen of the Sahara, except instead of undulating brown dunes, it was both flat and undulating green. There was a difference though. When the wind blew, the entire sea of green moved with it.

The path kept going through the grass. As he studied the layout he noticed other paths too, in fact at least a dozen. In the distance he spotted another clump of machinery, and a large white square object. Was it a building? Was it something else? It was too far away to know. He doubted he would get that far today with just three hours of sunlight left.

Turning to look at the cabin of the large truck he was standing on, he tried lifting the latch to the cabin door. It opened. He didn't expect that. Climbing inside, he sat in the chair. He felt big, and special. Would it start? There was only one way to know. Give it a try.

'Start,' thought Judson to the machine. Nothing happened. Then he remembered this planet didn't operate with thought servers.

'Start.' This time he said it verbally to the machine, but it didn't respond either.

'How do you start this thing?' he said, still talking.

Now he actually looked at the dashboard. It was primitive. Then he remembered the famous quote from Nick Jones that they had learned in school, 'The simpler something is, the less can go wrong.' Nick had always advocated that when terraforming, the use of basic reliable machines was better.

He noticed a key.

A key! Since when did machines have keys? It must have been more than a thousand years since machines had used keys. He had heard about it at school, but he couldn't believe his eyes.

He turned the key. He heard a click, but nothing more. Apparently he wasn't going to be driving any trucks today. That didn't matter. He didn't know how to drive anyway. Nobody drove anymore, not to get around.

He was about to exit the truck, when he saw a sign above the window. 'Battery must be enabled before starting the vehicle.' Looking back to the dash he found the battery button, a simple on and off switch. He turned it to 'on'. He tried the key again. This time the truck came alive.

This wasn't a diesel truck. It was an electric machine, and like all motorised machinery it ran on small nuclear engines the size of a football. Batteries had been known to last for centuries, but even so Judson didn't really think the truck would start.

Now, how to actually drive it?

There were no instructions, but there was a lever sitting in 'Park.' He moved it to a spot called 'Drive'. That seemed straightforward. At once it began to roll forward. The steering wheel was easy to figure out, but how did you make it go faster, and even more importantly, how did you slow it down when you needed to?

He didn't have time to think about that because the truck had already rolled about twenty metres and was picking up speed. The grass didn't matter at all because the wheels just drove right over the top of everything. He couldn't see through the grass properly. What if there was a crevice, or a huge hole, or a big bump or something hiding in the grass? It was a risk.

He discovered the pedals, and with that started to realise with increased speed, he could cover some distance in this thing. Now he could really explore the planet. Turning the wheel he aimed for that large square white object he could see in the distance. How far away might it be? Ten kilometres? It was hard to tell, but with this truck, it wouldn't matter; he would be there in no time at all.

He had long left the truck path he originally started walking down. Now he was driving by faith through the long grass, trusting that under it was solid ground. And so far, so good. The square white object was drawing closer to him.

He started to contemplate the object. How big was it? It seemed perhaps about twenty metres in height and large. What was it? He still didn't know. He looked at the pile of machinery that was nearby. Now that he was closer, he could tell it wasn't vehicles or machines at all, like he first assumed, but a series of pipes, and electrical components, almost like an electrical substation, but they were not close to the white object. There was maybe a kilometre or more separating them.

And it was then that the strangest thing of all happened. The big white square changed shape.

It was as though the white square was a set of double doors that opened in the middle, except instead of opening in, or opening out, they both dropped into the ground, and disappeared. It was remarkable how fast that happened. What was left in its place was a white frame, around the outside of where the white square used to be. It was like a window open, and without curtains. Now, he could see right into some other place. Looking through or into the white frame, Judson could see what looked like a huge block of concrete almost as big as the square frame. Around it some blue sky could be seen.

All this took place in less than a second, but it was then that the scariest thing that had ever happened in Judson's life occurred. The truck that he was driving dramatically increased in speed, then lifted off the ground and started flying through the air faster than any speed it was capable of being driven. If Judson had accelerated to full speed and had driven up a jump ramp and become airborne, the truck would not be travelling as fast through the air as it now was. Some unknown force had grabbed the truck and either sucked it through the air, or thrown it through the air at hundreds of kilometres per hour straight toward that white frame that stood against the sky.

It was as if a huge but invisible vacuum cleaner had come down from the sky and been pointed at his vehicle and whoosh, he was being sucked into the air at speed

The truck didn't elevate more than a few metres above the ground, and had only been airborne for about five or six seconds when the next thing happened.

The white square that had disappeared into the ground suddenly reappeared, and the white frame filled in again. With that, the powerful source of energy immediately ceased and the strong gravity of Verde pulled the truck back to the ground. Like a plane, the wheels landed first, but the truck was not directly front on; it had spun sideways in the air. On impact, all four wheels sheared right off, and the truck tipped over as the ground caused its speed to slow. Sliding through the grass on its side, it started to lose momentum as part of its shell, its ladder and undercarriage were twisted, broke loose, and started to tear away from the cabin. The machine became an instant wreck, although miraculously the cabin itself stayed intact.

Judson screamed. Sliding at speed in the cab of a tipped sideways truck, he could see nothing now except grass zooming by at speed. But the speed did slow. Dirt piled up against the front and side of the slowing metallic wreck. Finally the truck, and he with it, came to a resting place. He lay there for a moment breathing in deep breaths, and collecting his thoughts. What had just happened? What was the white square, and what was it doing? None of it made sense.

As he lay there, he began to feel pain in his body. His right shoulder had smashed into glass somewhere and was feeling raw. There were fragments of glass stuck into his chest, and even though he was wearing a rip-proof shirt, about a dozen pieces of glass had become embedded, shirt included, into his flesh. HIs right leg also felt sore, and he wondered if he had broken it. How ironic? It was because of him, just a few weeks ago, that Silas had broken his leg. Perhaps he was getting back what he deserved.

He pulled himself out the side window, and tried to stand to his feet. He found he could stand, although his leg was tender. Gingerly, he pulled himself along the side of the mangled pile of steel, and looked back where the truck had come from. Just a minute or so ago he had been driving in this direction, but now there was a huge gash in the grass, as if a giant animal had dug a burrow, leaving a trail of mud and dirt of large dimensions. He could find his way home by following the path he had just made. But would he be able to walk that far? He doubted it,

He hobbled to the other side of the truck and from there he had a good view of the big white square. He must have been no more than fifty or eighty metres away from it now. He decided to investigate. At some point Terry would come and look for him. It was turning dark and they would soon be missing him. Being near a large white object would make it easy to find him.

Half limping, half walking, he made his way toward the white thing. A rudimentary perimeter fence enclosed it. It would not have kept anyone out who wanted to break in, but it served as a warning. He saw a sign, and drawing closer he read:

> **'DANGER'**
> All metallic objects must be kept
> two kilometres from The Stay.

He wondered what The Stay was, and what was so dangerous about metallic objects. Why did they have to be kept away? He had just been driving in a big metal object not so long ago. Perhaps it was possible that whatever The Stay did, and whatever danger it provided, he had just been through an experience of that, in the big red metal truck. He wished someone had warned him. Why didn't Uncle Terry say something?

He looked back at the truck. It was clearly ruined and would never drive again. He looked back at the white object. Something was happening. He heard a whirring noise, like an engine or something with a motor was starting up. Was The Stay about to do its thing again? Looking up he saw the white metal doors like parts swinging open. Yes it was happening again..

Turning back he saw that the truck that he thought would never move again was starting to move through the grass. Coming towards him it began picking up speed. Next, it started to lift off the ground like it did the first time. If he stayed right where he was, he knew that within the blink of an eye, he would be crushed by the flying monster. What should he do? Without time to think, he threw himself onto the ground. The truck zipped over his head and a millisecond later he heard the sound of smashing metal. The white doors to The Stay were snapped off in their downward position in the ground, and the big white frame was bent backwards. The red truck was half embedded into the opening.

Whatever The Stay was, it too was now destroyed.

Judson tried to stand up and discovered his leg was in pain. This time, he really had broken his right leg.

CHAPTER TWENTY ONE:

THE ROOM AT THE END OF THE HALLWAY

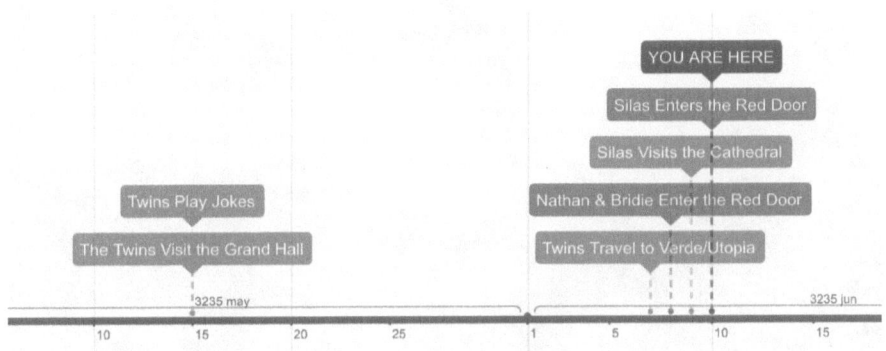

As he walked through the second door at the end of the hallway, Silas entered into a small octagonal room about five metres wide. It had a series of circular windows on most of the octagonal sides, but not on the right side, and not where the door was where he had entered. The room was brightly lit, more than the hallway had been, but this time in white light, so that the colours could be seen: red carpet, white ceiling, and old-fashioned peach coloured wall panelling. The windows looked into space. The room was floating somewhere isolated from any planet. Wherever they were it was on its own.

A one seat lounge chair was placed to the left side of the room, but it was facing away from him towards the windows looking outwards. The room was empty, but the chair was positioned as if someone was sitting in it looking at the view of space. To the right side was a small old looking kitchenette built into the wall. How long had it been there? The room was semi-luxurious and seemed designed for living in. There was a refrigerator. He opened it and saw what seemed to be food supplies inside. Was there a bathroom? He couldn't tell, but there might be something like that in a cupboard door next to the kitchenette. The room looked self-contained and comfortable.

Turning around, he looked back towards the door he had just exited. Above the door was a sign. It was strange, or at least it gave a strange feeling.

> WELCOME TO THE END OF THE HALLWAY.
> ENJOY YOUR STAY.
> WHEN YOU ARE READY,
> LEAVE THE WAY YOU CAME

But the words 'the hallway' had been crossed out and replaced with scribble. Instead it read, 'your life.' So the sign now looked like this:

What did that all mean? He didn't know. Was there really only one door in and out of this room? He had just come through what he believed was a one-way door into the hallway. Could he go back? How would going back in there do anything?

Noticing graffiti on the wall beside the door, he went closer to read. He saw the name of someone written there... Colin Philips.

Next to his name were markings which appeared to be like someone in prison, counting the number of days of their stay. Next to Colin were seven marks, so he must have been in this room for a week. But where did he go? Where was he now? How long ago had he been here?

Next to Colin's name was something else written in tiny writing. He moved his head within inches of the wall to read it. It was barely legible..

'Remember me Lord.' That's what it said. Why had he written that? It made no sense.

There were other names, more people he didn't know, and it seemed each of them did what Colin had done, counting the number of days they had been in the room. Some of them like Colin, had also written comments, not all of them in miniscule script. A woman called Suzy Samuels had written in big bold writing, 'PLANET OF LIES!!!'

Like graffiti often is, it was mesmerizing. As Silas read, he came to a name ... 'Nathan Bingham'. Was that the man he met at the lake? He wondered what had happened to Nathan. 'I hope he is safe,' thought Silas. He noticed a few marks next to Nathan's name. He didn't last long here, whoever he was.

Then, unexpectedly, Silas heard a noise coming from the lounge. It was the sound of deep breathing. He wasn't alone. He had been convinced the room was empty, but apparently it wasn't. Who or what was that?

He listened for a moment and realised what it was. Someone was sleeping on the lounge. He had assumed when he entered that nobody was present. It seemed unlikely that anyone would be. And the lounge, facing outward, hadn't moved when he arrived. Something was there.

He edged towards the lounge and looked over the top, trying to be quiet. Whoever it was might be dangerous. He had to be careful. But as soon as he saw a first glimpse of who it was. And, he knew they were not dangerous at all.

'NATHAN!' He yelled out his name before he could think.

Nathan jumped up out of the lounge, startled.

'You are here.' Silas grinned the biggest grin. He was glad to see him.

Nathan didn't smile.

'Silas, I'm glad to see you too, but I wish you had never come here.'

'Why?'

'This is the room we get sent to die.'

'How?' Silas felt his stomach tighten.

Nathan pointed at the door. He was gathering his thoughts.

'The door you just came through is a double one-way door. You come in from that hallway, but when you leave it takes you somewhere else to die, somewhere in remote space, I don't know where, but everyone who leaves this room dies.'

'Why do they leave?'

'I don't know,' said Nathan. He looked thoughtful. He looked sad. 'My wife came here with me a few days ago. She left straight away.'

'Bridie?'

'I don't want to talk about it.'

The look on Silas' face in that moment completed its journey from joy, when he had realised Nathan was still there, to horror, knowing they were going to die, to sadness, the saddest he had ever been. It was because of him that Nathan had lost his wife, and Nathan didn't want to talk about it. It was all his fault.

'I'm sorry,' he said quietly.

'Me too,' said Nathan. He wasn't bitter or angry.

Silas wanted to evaporate into the floor, or at least change the subject as fast as possible.

'How long have you been here?'

'A few days.'

'Is the food good?'

'Actually it is good. They look after us well here.'

'Why do they take care of you when they want you to die?' Silas paused, then added another question. How do you actually know you are here to die?

'I think I know why,' said Nathan, 'They don't want to be blamed for murdering anyone. So if we leave, it is our choice. But there is nothing to do here, and people don't last long. They go mad. They decide to risk leaving. That's what Bridie did.'

'I'm sorry, it is all my fault.'

'It's her fault,' said Nathan thinking of his wife. Then, Nathan looked at Silas, as if he was looking at him for the first time since he had arrived. His face changed and displayed a perplexed expression.

'Where is your shirt?'

It was then that Silas remembered the hallway door and how he had left it ajar with his shirt.

'Oohh. It's not all bad news,' Silas said thinking as he spoke. 'The hallway door hasn't closed yet. I used my shirt to keep it open.'

Now it was Nathan's turn to get excited.

'Show me.'

Together they walked to the door and it was slightly ajar, with the sleeve of Silas' shirt sticking through. Nathan reached out and slowly pushed the door, and there before them was the hallway.

CHAPTER TWENTY TWO:
THE REAL NICK JONES

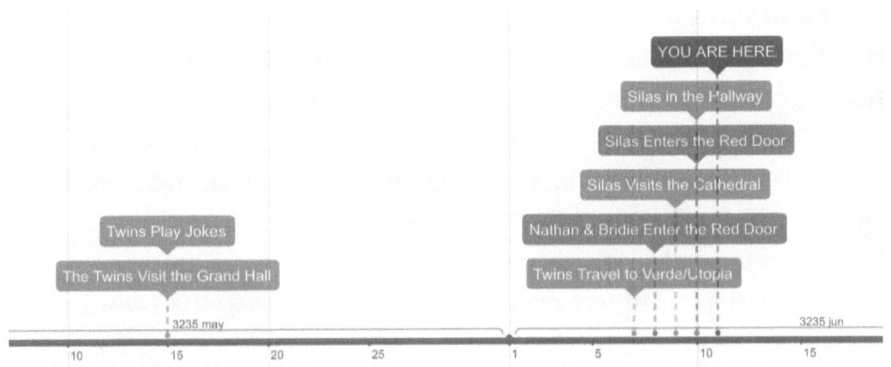

The sun had gone down and Judson had not returned home. Terry looked across at Joy, who had been either his girlfriend and then wife most of his entire life. She read his thoughts. It wasn't because they could share thoughts on Verde, because they couldn't. It was just that they had known each other a long time.

'You knew this would happen,' she said with a smile.

'I'll get organised and go find him.'

Neither of them were worried about Judson because they knew Verde well. It was a safe planet. There was no crime; after all almost nobody lived on Verde, and they were all people of sincere faith and good morals. There were no predators, and no venomous animals either, for none had ever been introduced, and there was no need for them, at least not at this point. Not only were there no dangerous animals, there were no dangerous people. Terry and

Joy knew every single person who lived there, all two thousand of them. There was just one danger. The worst thing that could happen was that Judson might get disoriented and need to be found. So, it was time to go find him.

Terry had a small vehicle, something like an all terrain golf buggy, but a bit more substantial and solid. It had a large screen on the front and sides that came about halfway up. That was to keep the giant grass out of the vehicle. Terry climbed in, mounted his director compass onto a special holder on the dashboard of the vehicle, turned the switch from off to on, and began to drive. LIke the other vehicles on Verde, it was electric, powered by a tiny nuclear engine, with energy to last a thousand years. It never needed to be charged. What a nuisance it would be to have to charge a vehicle every night like they did in the twenty-first century.

Terry drove through town to where the buildings finished and the grass began. He had the choice of two paths. The first path went right, which was the path Judson had taken earlier, but he didn't know that. He took the path to the left because it seemed closer to the angle the director compass was pointing at. Terry hated driving through the grass, and knew he would have to do that at some point, but he hoped he might get close to Judson using roads alone. Of course they were not roads like the paved roads elsewhere on the other planets, but for Verde they were major transit routes.

Driving down the path he noticed the angle on the director compass shifting to his right. At some point he would have to go into the grass. He can't have walked this far surely? He approached a T-intersection. Terry knew all these roads well, having driven them hundreds of times, especially when working as part of the team that terraformed Utopia. He knew the road to the left would take him to a forest where they were growing timber for the future of Verde. But he also knew the road to the right would take him to The Stay. What was Judson doing out near The Stay? How did he ever get this far?

He turned right and started making his way down the road toward The Stay. The director compass in the front of the buggy swung around and lined up with the route he was driving. Judson had to be in front of him somewhere.

As he drew closer to The Stay, the white object started to grow in his vision, but something was wrong, it didn't seem square. It was hard to see in the dark, so he couldn't observe it properly. He kept driving and passed a sign next to the road which read:

> **DANGER:**
> Metal Objects not to be
> brought past this point.

Two bright red and yellow markers stood either side of the road indicating that he was crossing over the warning point the sign spoke of. Terry knew the warning, and understood it well. He looked at his watch, then sped past the two posts. He was aware that he was driving a metallic object into the two kilometre zone. He knew that there was danger to his buggy and his life. He had been here many times both with vehicles and without. But he also knew something else, which made it safe, at least for the moment. He knew something Judson had not known. He pressed on.

As he drew closer to The Stay, the floodlights on the front of the buggy lit up the perimeter fence, and there was Judson sitting on the ground. He lifted his hand to shield his eyes from the beam. Through the shadow created on his face by his hand he could see, although only just. It was the silhouette of a man approaching.

'Uncle Terry?' Judson tried to get to his feet.

'Judson, what is happening?'

'I broke my leg, and I broke the white thing behind me. You won't believe what happened Uncle Terry.'

Uncle Terry lifted his eyes and looked past Judson. Although it was dark, he could make out The Stay, but it didn't look the same as when he had last looked at it many months ago. Instead of a big white square filling the sky above them, with closed white doors, the doors were down in the ground, unable to close. The frame was no longer a big square. Nothing fitted together. The wreckage of a Red Terrecom truck was laying in the opening and shards of steel and concrete lay on the ground.

'I might believe it,' he replied.

'I found this old abandoned truck, and it still worked. And I saw this big white square, and I started driving towards it, and then I was exploring when all of a sud..'

'Stop talking!!'

Terry was stern. He held his finger to his lips to indicate silence. His command came quickly, and forcefully. 'Walk with me.'

He must have forgotten that Judson had broken a leg because Terry grabbed him by the hand, and without saying a word, pulled him up and started walking to the buggy.

'Oh, oh, slower.'

Terry looked down at his leg, and noticing the swelling he let him go. Judson tried to stand there. It was hard without anything to lean on. Retrieving the buggy, Terry brought it over, and stopping right next to Judson, allowed him to collapse into the passenger chair. He then lifted his foot into the buggy. Then he drove with increasing speed away from The Stay. After a minute they passed the two warning posts on the sides of the road.

'Why?' Terry pressed him, ignoring his question back in reply. 'Why did you drive it?'

The question that Terry had just asked was a good question, and it now occurred to Judson that it was a question he should have asked himself just a few hours ago.

'Uh,' he didn't know what to say. 'I thought it was junk,' he answered.

'IT WAS JUNK!' Terry snapped back.

Judson didn't understand, but it didn't stop him from making a silly reply.

'Well it's definitely junk now,' he said, resigning himself to the fact that he had to tell Terry at some point.

'I know,' said Terry. 'The broken truck is a problem, but the real problem is the broken Stay.'

'Uncle Terry, I'm sorry. I don't know what is happening, but I nearly died. That truck went flying in the air all by itself.'

'That's why there are warning signs to keep people away.'

'I never saw any warning signs.'

Terry sighed. It was as though he wanted to say something, but decided not to.

'What is The Stay, Uncle Terry? What does it do?'

No answer came. Judson didn't know if Terry didn't want to answer, or was too deep in thought.

They drove along in silence. Awkward silence.

After a few minutes, Terry did speak, slowly. It was as if he was thinking about every single word that he spoke, making sure he didn't say anything wrong.

'The white square thing is The Stay. Or at least it was The Stay.' He paused before continuing. 'There is one person on this planet that has authority over The Stay, and that is Nick Jones, the architect of planets.'

Judson's ears pricked up.

'Nick Jones? Do you mean THE Nick Jones? The famous Nick Jones?'

'Yes.'

Suddenly Judson had forgotten his pain, his broken leg, the glass in his chest. To think that the architect of planets was living right here on Verde as one of the two thousand inhabitants. What a thrilling idea. Maybe he would get to meet him?

And at that exact moment, Terry had a feeling of dread sweep over him. If he could have gone back in time and changed the last two minutes of conversation, he most certainly would have done so. And the next few things Judson said proved his fear to be true.

'Do you know where he lives?'

'Yes, I know where everyone lives.'

'Can we go see him?'

It was apparent that Terry did not want Judson to talk to Nick Jones, but it was also apparent that he felt he had no choice but to answer the way he did.

'Yes.' It was a sobre reply. 'I'll take you there now.'

The drive back to town was not far in the buggy, but it was quiet the rest of the way. Terry didn't want to say anything. Judson felt like he had pushed him to do something he didn't want, which was the case. On top of that, every little bump was painful. Judson wondered if they would be able to fix his leg, or if his time on Verde was done.

As they drove into the small town of about four or five hundred houses, Judson could tell they were driving down the same road that they lived on. To think that Nick Jones lived so close to them, was a mind-blowing thought. But as they drove down the street Terry turned and parked right in front of his and Aunty Joy's house. Judson was confused.

'Did you forget to go to Nick Jones' house?'

'No Judson, this is Nick Jones' house?'

Judson looked at his Uncle and in that moment one thing suddenly became clear. His Uncle WAS Nick Jones.

CHAPTER TWENTY THREE:
MESSAGE ON THE MANTEL

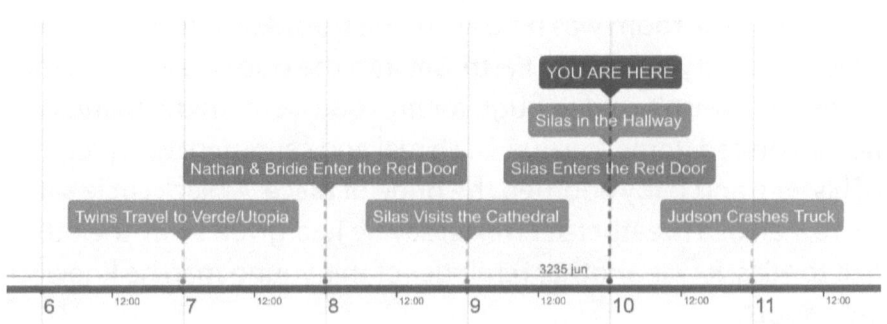

Xavier Mendosa stood looking out the window at the Cathedral Cathedral far below him. It was a magnificent building, and he felt proud. It wasn't personal pride as though this fantastic building was there because of him, rather it was a pride in the accomplishments of what many people had done together. Mixed into that was gratitude to God for how everything had worked out.

People often came to pray, and looking down at them from his office with its full-length glass windows, it provided a unique vantage point. People often appeared as dots below him. He didn't know who they were, but he would often pray for people who came to the Cathedral.

His thoughts flashed back to when young Silas Jones had been in his office. He had come to the Cathedral seeking God too. He remembered how he felt an inexplicable feeling that Silas was the answer to his prayer for Utopia.

He pondered. How was young Silas doing? It had been more than a whole day since he had consulted with him, and given him the flexible breather to use. Had it been helpful? How had things turned out for him? How would he find out?

He turned back to his office with its magnificent bookshelves, thick deep green carpet and large brown leather lounge chairs. In the back of the room was his desk made from Australian Silky Oak timbers, a rarity outside of Earth. Set into the bookshelves was the fireplace. It wasn't cold enough for fire today, but on the mantel he had placed items of value, both real and sentimental. A picture of his wife and baby adorned the pride of place. A black circle sat there, half of a breather set. Yesterday he had given away the other half to Silas. It was another reminder of this young man he knew so little about.

He had spent many hours in this office praying for people, and preparing sermons for his unique and large congregation. As he stood there, he cast his eyes to the mantel where the breather was sitting, his thoughts still on Silas. He noticed something odd about it. It was white, or no, something light coloured was with it. He hadn't put that there.

Walking over to take a closer look, he noticed a leaf under the breather. Yes, an actual leaf, from an actual tree. How did that get here? There were few trees on Cathedral, and none anywhere near the Cathedral itself. Then he realised. The leaf had come through the breather. This leaf was from Utopia.

He picked it up to examine it. It was a eucalyptus leaf, which like his desk had also come from an Australian tree. Many of these eucalypts, commonly called gum trees, had been planted on other planets because of how well they adapted. It looked like a normal leaf. Turning it over, he noticed the other side. Something was scratched into the leaf. It was a word. Just one single word.

'PRAY'

Pray?

He looked down at the one-word message. Is that really what it said? What did it mean? Who was asking him to pray? Was it a message from Silas? What was happening in the other place? Was this a prayer request from Utopia?

He knew that if this was a genuine request for prayer, it must be the first time anyone on Utopia had ever wanted that. What should he do with it?

All those questions ran through his mind, and he didn't have answers for any of them, but he could do the one thing the message said to do, and that was to pray. In fact, he could do even better than that, he could get a lot of other people praying with him too.

*****

Later that same day a small crowd of about twenty five thousand people gathered for vespers. Or, at least it was small relative to usual crowds at the Cathedral. The auditorium felt so empty on an occasion like this, as they closed the day with prayers. Vespers was not always at night as it would be on Earth, but tonight it was actually dark.

'Today I received a message from a young friend.' Reverend Xavier Mendosa spoke. Vespers according to the normal liturgy didn't contain a message, but tonight was going to be different.

'Silas Jones is a young man who somehow found his way onto the Planet Utopia. It was a quirk of fate, perhaps God intended it, and it may even have been an answer to the prayers we prayed right here in the Cathedral on William Carey Memorial Day. His experiences there left him troubled about the souls on that planet.

He felt compelled to return, but he also felt the danger associated with going back. He didn't know what to do.'

He paused to allow those assembled a minute to grasp what was happening.

'Our Lord and Saviour found himself in that situation at Gethsemane. He knew he was soon to die in a painful manner by crucifixion. He didn't want to experience that, but at the same time He felt called to surrender. He gave up his personal rights and put the needs of all humanity first. And we are all grateful that He did.'

'In a similar way just a few days ago, young Silas Jones surrendered too, not knowing what would happen. He took his future in his hands and went to Utopia. He decided to God first, and what he wanted for the sake of others.'

Not a noise came from the crowd. It was pure silence as every soul listened. Everyone knew so little about Utopia, and the idea that it might be dangerous was new to many of them.

'Today I received one word from him, the shortest message I have ever received in this life. It said "pray."' He continued. 'We don't know the situation, or the need, but can I ask you to pray for Silas Jones? Pray for Utopia, and pray that somehow God will open a way into that planet for the gospel.'

And that night, twenty five thousand people prayed for Silas Jones. They didn't know what words to say, but God felt their feelings for him, and they felt God's feelings for him too. Those prayers did something.

CHAPTER TWENTY FOUR:

A DIFFICULT CONVERSATION

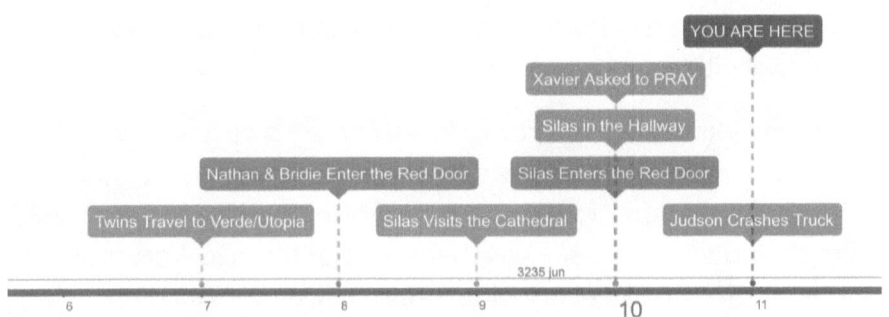

The first thing that needed to happen was tending to Judson's broken leg. Judson had half hopped, half been carried into the house, which he was still shocked to realise belonged to the famous Nick Jones, his actual Uncle. He couldn't believe it.

Then, just like when he first arrived on Verde, Judson sat at the table with his Uncle and Aunty, except this time his foot was placed up on an adjacent chair, and they waited while the doctor was on his way.

Just four days ago, Judson had arrived to start his summer holidays expecting a few dull months of chores, but his brother had mysteriously failed to arrive. Somehow Silas had been translated to Utopia instead. And, something about that Utopia visit had changed him. He returned back to Earth after just a few hours away as an emotionally different person. He carried a burden, a sense of obligation. He said he felt God was asking him to do something. It didn't sound like the Silas he knew who loved joking and being silly. Silas had then returned to Utopia, and as far as they knew, that was where he was now. There was no way of communicating with him. They just had to hope for the best.

But here on Verde, Judson's own experiences were unexpected too. He knew things he didn't know before, and things that his brother on Utopia was still to find out. This last week felt like a lifetime, and like his brother, he was now carrying his own worries, and along with them, a broken leg.

There was a knock on the door. He was pretty sure it was the doctor, but nobody could see who it was. That was something old-fashioned about Verde, and sort of nice; you had to actually go to the door to see who was there, and let them in. You couldn't just think them in like everywhere else. Nick got up and let the doctor in.

'Nicholas, good to see you. I hear you have a young patient.'

'I do. Right over there.' He pointed.

They walked into the dining room.

'Young man I'd ask you to stand and give me a good strong hand shake, but I guess you had better stay seated. Now what is your name?'

'Judson Jones.'

'I see, and what have you done to yourself?'

'I broke my leg tonight.'

'Hmmm yes. Now how did you do that?' The doctor started to loosen his shoe. The swelling was evident above the shoe, but once the shoe and sock were removed he knew there would be bruising.

Judson didn't know if he was allowed to say. He looked at Uncle Nick who nodded.

'I was driving and crashed.'

'Driving?' It was a question, a reply, and a statement all in one word. But it was followed by a real question.

'What were you driving?' He peeled off Judson's socks while asking. 'It was one of those red trucks.'

The doctor looked across to Nick to see his reaction. Nick gave a slow shake of his head. Then he said something.

'He didn't know it would drive.'

Now the doctor asked Nick a question. 'Why didn't you tell him not to touch them?' All the while he was holding Judson's foot and examining the bruising.

'You know,' said Nick, 'the agreement I made back then.'

'Oh yes, the agreement.' The doctor appeared to remember some long-forgotten fact. 'It was such a weird thing that they wanted, wasn't it?'

Nick nodded, and had more to say. 'My nephew here, not only crashed the truck, he drove it into the exclusion zone while the gate was opened.'

'Oh,'

'And the truck has destroyed The Stay. It is now stuck in the open position.'

'OH.'

The room was silent for a moment as the doctor digested that information.

The doctor turned to Judson, 'Young man, there is bad news, good news, and there is also some extremely bad news. The bad news and good news are about your leg, and as a doctor I can tell you about that. But the extremely bad news is something your uncle here should tell you.' The doctor's voice slowed and deepened, 'HOWEVER, I'm am sure your uncle won't tell you the extremely bad news, because he isn't allowed to. So I am going to tell you that too.'

Judson felt sick.

'The bad news is, you have a broken fibula. There are two bones in your leg, and the fibula is the thinner one. The good news is that we can put a cast on, give you some crutches, and you will start healing. You'll be as good as new in five or six weeks. You won't have one of those fancy casts like you might have had on Earth, but it will do the same job.'

Judson nodded. He understood. Only a few weeks ago his brother had been through the same thing in Port Sudan. And of course he was given a fancy exoskeleton, which he was probably still wearing right now.

'What about the extremely bad news?' Judson did not want to know, but he had to find out.

The doctor was a kind man, who had a wise face with some wrinkles, but was not overly grey-haired. He was no older than 120 years of age, or at least that was how it seemed. He looked at Judson and smiled.

'Sit here for two minutes young man, while I go and get supplies. I need water, plaster and linen. I'm going to make you a cast, and as I apply it to your leg, you will hear about the extremely bad thing that has happened.'

Judson couldn't wait those two minutes. He knew that somehow The Stay was important. He had destroyed it. Whatever it was doing, it had stopped doing. He couldn't imagine what it was needed for. He looked at his uncle. His head was down in his hands. Aunty Joy, who was really Aunty Jay, was rubbing his back. They both knew what was so bad. Why couldn't they just tell him?.

The doctor returned with an armful of supplies and set to work in a cheerful and light-hearted manner. You would not have known that he was about to share something that would darken the hearts of every single human on Verde, once they found out.

'A long time ago,' the doctor started working and started talking at the same time. 'Your Uncle Nick was given the job of terraforming Utopia. They wanted to stop the planet from spinning so it would face the sun all of the time, and your uncle figured out how to do it. He designed The Stay.'

Nick interrupted, 'there's are eight of them.'

'Oh yes, there are eight of them, positioned in various places, and they are all different colours. The one near us is the white one.'

The doctor started washing Judson's foot with antiseptic liquid and wiping it down.

'The Stays are powerful superconductors, the most powerful magnets ever built. They are built into gates that connect this planet to Utopia. At first they were used to slow down Utopia and stop its rotation. But now, twenty times a day, every five thousand seconds, the gates open, and the magnets turn on. As the power surges through them they work to keep Utopia in place. Without them, Utopia would start rotating again.'

'So is Utopia going to start spinning again?'

'Not at all,' said Nick.

'I thought you didn't want to talk about this?' queried the doctor.

'Sorry, you're right. Yes, I don't.'

The doctor continued, 'There are other Stays, and they will keep the other planet still, so we don't have to worry about that part.'

Nick nodded to confirm that fact.

'No it is something else that is very bad, but let me go back to the story.'

The doctor finished cleaning the leg and wiped it dry with a fresh towel. Medical supplies were not common on Verde, so ordinary things were used.

'So your uncle built The Stays, and succeeded in slowing the other planet down. But it was then that a strange thing started. Utopia started spinning again. Every day it would pick up some movement. After just one day it was not noticeable, but after a few days it started to build momentum. If it was allowed to continue, within a few months it would return to how it was before.'

'The Stays were supposed to be temporary, but now everyone realised they needed to be permanent. That's why we call them stays. They help Utopia 'Stay' in place.'

As Judson was being worked on, he still didn't understand what was the problem. If the other seven could keep the planet in place, why was it very bad if one of them had been broken?

'The problem started years ago when your uncle signed a terreformation contract with Utopia. They wanted a planet that would be totally isolated from the rest of the galaxy, and your uncle agreed to give them that. But now, with eight Stays being needed to hold the planet in place, and opening twenty times a day, Utopia wasn't isolated; it was connected. Or at least connected to one planet.'

'The officials of Utopia demanded that they had the right to own Verde as well, so that they could be totally isolated. But everyone on Verde disagreed. This was their home now. So there was an argument. In the end it was your Uncle Nick who settled the argument by making an agreement with them.'

'An agreement?'

'Yes, an agreement. Your Uncle Nick proposed that Verde be closed to visitors, and he promised that nobody would cross into Utopia. Everyone who was here had been a part of the terraformation project. He proposed that in exchange, those who wanted could stay here and develop the planet in their own time, but without physical contact with the rest of the galaxy.'

'And?'

'And Utopia agreed, but they wanted a few more things. First they made Nick promise that he would not talk about the connection between Utopia and Verde. His fame as a terraformer meant that people want interviews. He promised he would not talk about it. As you can see, he is a man of honour because he won't even tell his own nephew.'

'What else did they want?'

'They also wanted us to promise to keep The Stays functional, but otherwise to leave them alone.'

'So what is the bad news?'

The doctor had started layering the linen. He was enjoying himself. It was hard to believe he was about to share some of the worst news that would ever be heard on Verde.

'Well, the fact is that not only is your leg broken, and not only is The Stay broken, but the agreement that your Uncle Nick made with Utopia has been broken too.'

'Huh?'

'Your uncle promised The Stays would keep functioning, but one isn't. So according to the agreement, everyone on Verde must leave.'

'Leave?'

'Yes, your Uncle made that agreement on behalf of us all. There are two thousand people here who have made homes and lives in this place. Some of them have nice houses. All of us will have to go.'

Judson felt his stomach tightening.

'Surely you don't all have to leave?'

The doctor looked across to Nick. who looked back.

'I'm afraid we have no choice,' said the doctor.

'Why aren't you angry?' asked Judson.

'What difference will that make?' replied the doctor.

The doctor finished wrapping up Judson's foot and packed up his equipment. Holding onto the table, Judson was able to stand and shake the doctor's hand.

'Thank you,' he said to the doctor, 'for wrapping my cast.'

'I've enjoyed living on Verde. And I enjoyed meeting you tonight. But now I must say good night.'

And with that, the doctor was gone. Nick looked sad. Jay looked sympathetic. Judson felt horrible.

In one day, he had managed to break a truck, break a leg, break The Stay, and break his uncle's agreement. Now, every single person on this planet would have to leave. Where would they go? Would they blame him? What would happen to him? It was a day he wished he could start over again.

CHAPTER TWENTY FIVE:

ESCAPE

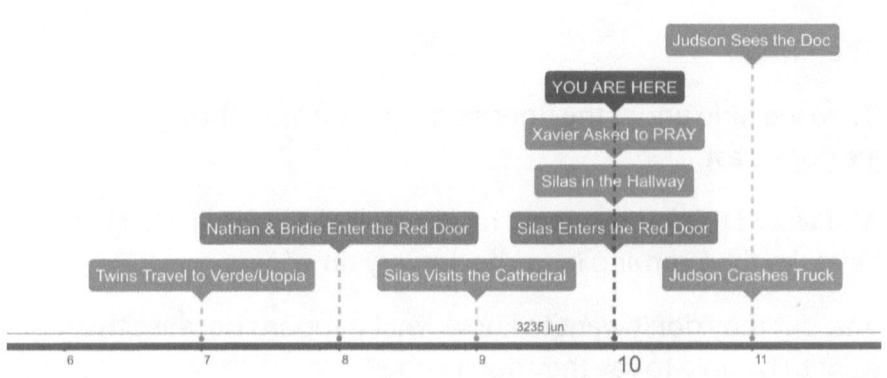

Nathan and Silas pushed the door open until the hallway was fully visible, still brightly lit before them both.

'Let's go back into the hallway,' said Nathan. 'And then shut the door. They will think you are now in the room.'

'How do you know that?'

'They have a sensor in the door, so they know when it opens and closes.'

'But they already think I'm in the room,' said Silas. 'They came to check on me, but I was hiding under the flooring.

'Oh,' said Nathan. 'That means, they will assume one of us has just left the room then.'

They both stood there for a moment contemplating that thought. And then they realised something. It was possible that at any minute, the purple figures might come through that door to check again, just like they did earlier for Silas.

'I know,' said Silas, 'let us quickly open the door and shut it again. Then they will think that *both* of us have left the room, and they will definitely come to check.'

'Then what?'

'Then we hide under the floor, and jump up after they are gone past.'

'You would think they would have installed a camera. That would be easier than coming in to check every time.'

'Yes, but they don't want to know what happens because they want to be able to say they don't know.'

'But they do know when they come to check.'

'Of course, but they would technically be telling the truth.' Silas had them figured out. They wanted to feel like they were innocent, even though they were guilty as hell.

'It's lying,' said Nathan, annoyed.

They both stood in the dark hallway looking at the door. Nathan reached out, and opened it again, but they both remained where they were in the dark hall. Then he closed the door.

'That's it,' he said. 'Now they think both of us have left the room.'

'Now, follow me,' said Silas. At that moment he turned and started running down the tunnel. Speed mattered. Nathan followed not far behind.

Reaching the far end, he first turned off the hallway lights, to return the hall to how it was when the purple officials left. Everything went dark. Then, he bent down and pulled up one of the flooring grates. He had been in there before, and knew the quickest way to open it up. There was ample space for the both of them under the floor.

'You crawl in here, and I'll jump in behind you, and then we wait.'

'For them to come?' asked Nathan.

'Yes, and when they walk past us to the other end, we jump up as quietly as we can, and exit the door.'

'Then we lock them in,' said Nathan with a look of satisfied revenge on his face.

Silas was horrified, 'You can't lock them in.'

'They did it to us.'

'But they will die.'

'Maybe.' Nathan didn't care. If they sent him to die, he would do it back. It was one or the other in his mind.

They both climbed down under the flooring, and Silas pulled the grate over the top of them. And just like they suspected, they didn't have to wait long.

About ten minutes later there was a click as the first door to the hallway opened above them. Two officials in purple came through the door, but this time they were not wearing their mirror masks and their faces could be seen, at least briefly. Nathan looked at them but did not recognise them. He had never seen them before. There were more than 50,000 people living on Utopia. He didn't know them all. Maybe that was why. The door closed and the room was dark again.

But then he turned on the lights and flooded the hallway. Both of the escapees hiding under the floor hoped they would not look down. They didn't, rather they started walking the length of the hall.

The first official spoke. 'That last guy didn't take long to leave.'

'Strange how both of them left the room about the same time.'

'Do you have your neutralizer?'

'Yes.'

As they walked overhead and beyond, they chatted the whole way down the tunnel.

'When you step in the door, you look left, I will look right. If anything is there, neutralize it?'

'OK.'

Their footsteps on metal could be heard getting further and further away. Silas carefully started lifting the metal grate above him. Hopefully they could be quiet and would not attract attention that far down the hall. By this point their voices were muffled and were nearing the far end.

'Go, go, go,' whispered Nathan.

Silas jumped up first, his feet landing on the metal walkway, making a slight noise, a shuffle and a bump. It wasn't loud enough to be heard. Nathan jumped up next. He was heavier and if he had not slipped over he would probably have been able to avoid detection. But he did of course slip.

When he fell, his body, larger than Silas', slammed into the metal grates and created a large metallic gong followed by a series of echoes that reverberated down the hallway. The purple officials had disappeared into the room. Nathan picked himself up off the flooring. They both looked down the long hall hoping upon hope that they had not been noticed. But they had been.

The door at the far end swung back open, and two men in purple emerged. Silas and Nathan turned to run. Only a few steps and they would be out of here. The purple officials both produced something that looked like a small gun, and both started firing.

Silas was the first through the door, and he stood to the side to wait for Nathan. Where was he? He had been just behind him. Silas looked back into the tunnel to see Nathan lying on the floor as if dead.

'Help me,' he pleaded. 'I've been shot.'

So he wasn't dead.

Silas reached to the side and turned off the light switch. How unusual to have a light switch here on a planet controlled by thought. The tunnel was dark again. That might help a little.

He then grabbed Nathan by the arms and pulled. Meanwhile the sound of shots came repeatedly from the two purple officials who drew closer. Silas pulled Nathan with all his might, and was able to get half of him through the door.

More shots. The officials were closing the gap, just fifty metres away now.

Silas grabbed Nathan and pulled again. He slid through the door and Silas dropped him on the floor.

'Shut it,' yelled Nathan. He could not move, but his voice worked just fine, even at volume.

Silas hesitated.

The officials were now just fifteen metres away. They would be here in seconds.

'NOW!'

Silas kicked the door with all his might, and it slammed closed. The tunnel was gone from sight and the two officials were no longer heard or seen. Silas crashed on the floor next to Nathan.

'That was close,' he said.

They were lying on the floor of the round white room with the red door. It was the same room that Colin had walked out of voluntarily believing he was going to a better place. It was that same red door that little Gregory had been forced through while he screamed for his mummy. It was that same door that Nathan and Bridie had walked through together resigned to a future somewhere else, not knowing it was to lead to their separation and her death. There were two other doors in the room, the white door that came from Earth, and the purple door to Utopia. Silas lay on the floor looking around him.

'I can't move my arms or legs,' said Nathan. 'I feel numb all over.'

'Is it permanent?'

'I don't know, but we can't stay here. What if they have a way to get back out? We better hurry.'

Silas stood up and went to the white door and pushed it. It would not open. They were not going out that way. They would have to go through the purple door. He took a hold of Nathan's arms and started dragging him again.

'Oww.'

'What?'

'That hurts.'

'I didn't pull you differently than before,' stated Silas. He lifted Nathan's shirt to see if there was a wound, but everything looked normal.

'You don't seem to be injured.'

'Owww,' Nathan started moaning. He then started writhing on the ground.

Silas looked at him as he twisted in pain on the ground. He felt helpless, with no clue what to do about it. Then he realised, 'he is actually moving.'

Over the next few minutes, Nathan's pain reached a crescendo, and then began to diminish. After that, Nathan was exhausted, but was pain free. He seemed to have fallen asleep.

'Nathan,' Silas whispered.

'Nathan, are you OK?'

'Nathan, Nathan.' He tried again. Silas stopped calling not sure what to do.

Then Nathan responded with a faint voice, 'I feel exhausted.'

'You need to get up. You must get up now.'

'Help me.'

Silas helped Nathan who struggled to his feet. He was weak, and dizzy, but he was alive and the pain had mostly departed. They staggered through the purple door into the terracotta greeting room. When Colin and Sophia had arrived on Utopia it was in this room that they met their friendly robot helper. Now the room was deserted. Not a soul was there. That was fortunate.

Nathan knew where to go.

'We have to get to the dark side. Nobody will find us there.'

'Which way?'

'To the construction zone,' he spoke weakly, and pointed
to their left.

They walked out the door, and in the distance, perhaps no more
than two kilometres away, was a series of new buildings. It was
going to be a long walk for a weak Nathan.

'Why are we going there?' asked Silas

'Those houses are empty,' said Nathan. 'But the doors to the dark
side work. We are going to get into one of those houses, and then
cross over to the dark side of the planet.'

'Then what?'

'I don't know.' Nathan didn't have any knowledge of the nightside
of the planet, nor did he have the energy to think about it.

They staggered towards the newly-built homes. Nobody realised
they had escaped yet, and nobody as yet realised the purple
officials were trapped. It was a lucky break, but it wasn't going to
last for long.

CHAPTER TWENTY SIX:

MEETING AT THE PETREA

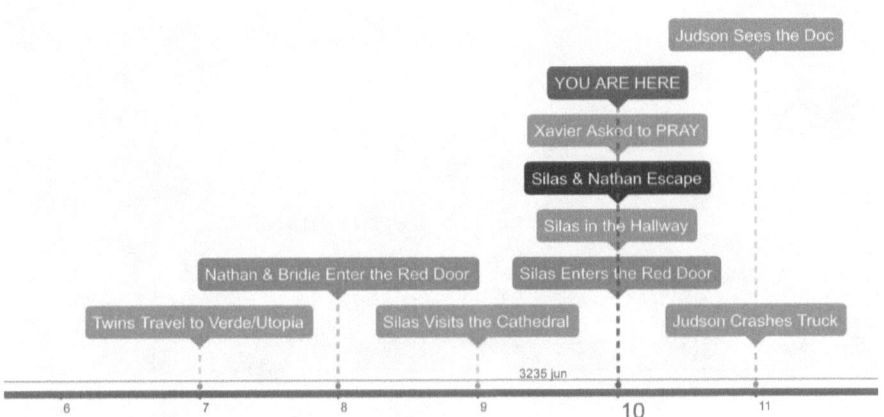

If you looked down from above, the Petrea was a large sort of star-shaped auditorium, purple in colour. Each wing was like a petal, elongated and visually resembling an unusual piece of architecture, like a flower with five leaves. Each of the petals was a wing that adjoined a central five-sided stage in the middle, and each wing could seat four thousand people. The entire building held twenty thousand but because of its unique design, gave the feeling of a smaller building to the inhabitants. It felt more intimate, when in fact it could host a significant crowd.

Inside the building, in the centre of the petals, the stage was set low into the ground, so that all five wings were like grandstands that sloped down. This inside looked different to the outside. The stage was shaped like a pentagon, and trimmed with gold and purple, the colours of Utopia. The pentagon slowly rotated so that over the duration of ten minutes, the stage had moved to face each of the five sides. Five large viewing screens placed above the five wings always allowed audiences a close view of what was happening from the stage, no matter which way the stage was facing.

On this occasion the Petrea was filled. Not a seat was spare. But even so, far more than twenty thousand had joined, because the majority of Utopians were present in their thoughts A buzz filled the air, with the sound of loud and expectant chatter taking place, the sound of thousands of Utopians talking. There was a genuine amount of curiosity as to why this meeting had been called.

Sophia was there. She, like others, was curious about the reason for the meeting. In her twelve years on Utopia, just a handful of official meetings had occurred. Most often the Petrea was used for entertainment. Human interest got the better of her.

A chime interrupted the silence, a sombre note, the indication that the gathering was about to commence.

Shanti Combollino, the chair of the Board of Utopia, shifted onto the stage, and held up her hands. As she did so, the electric wall behind her flashed three times in a vibrant succession of colours, a visual indication designed to make sure she had the attention of every Utopian. Music began playing in the background, an ominous tone, in a minor key.

'Utopian Citizens,' she commenced. 'Today you have been summoned because the foundation of our beautiful society has been challenged by a religious incursion.'

The crowd was quiet.

'A few days ago, an illegal shift occurred bringing to our peaceful planet the first person of religion. Because we are such a tolerant society, we could have allowed him to leave in peace. But when he became aware that this was the only place in the galaxy with no religion, he became intent on changing that.'

Sophia knew this had something to do with her friends Bridie and Nathan. She started trembling in her seat. Her muscles began to shake as she lost control of them. She was anxious.

'Show the photo,' Shanti declared.

Onto the five large screens at the centre of the Petrea an image appeared. It was a picture of someone that none of them had seen before. It was a picture of a young sixteen year old male, with a red shirt. It was Silas Jones.

'This man arrived on our calm and undisturbed planet, bringing with him chaos and disturbance. Not content to leave us alone, he persuaded two others from Utopia to join him in his mission to evangelize. Some of you know of whom I refer.'

Another photo went up on the five big screens. It was a photo of Nathan and Bridie Bingham. Sophia gasped.

'These are the accomplices,' said Shanti. 'Fortunately, we have been able to arrest the woman, Bridie Bingham.'

There was silence.

'She has been deported from Utopia.'

Sophia sat there listening. She knew it.

'As for the man on your screen, Nathan Bingham, he has escaped with the suspect, Silas Jones, and they have gone to live with those despicable people in darkness.'

Shanti kept talking. 'These people live in caves on the dark side, stealing from us when our backs are turned. They are rats.'

And then, as if to emphasize, she yelled. 'RATS!!'

With that emphasis, the music swelled to a crescendo. Everything she said was compelling. Not a single Utopian disagreed, except one.

Sophia.

Sophia knew that something was wrong. Shanti wasn't telling the whole truth. Had Nathan and Silas really escaped leaving Bridie behind? That didn't seem possible. She had talked to Bridie and they had made a plan to avoid trouble and not help Silas. What was really happening?

Shanti stood on stage and waited for the music to die down.

'As a peaceful planet, the time has come to make a most difficult decision. We must decide what to do about both the young men Silas Jones and Nathan Bingham. And we must decide what to do about the rats. And,' she continued, 'we do have options.'

'Firstly we could take a military approach to the rats and these two young men they are now harbouring. While we are peaceful by nature, at times peace requires war to maintain the peace. The history of humanity has shown this to be true. We could send in soldiers and destroy them. The first option is war.'

That first option was a shocking thought. It was contrary to the way of life that had existed, not just on Utopia since its founding, but in the entire galaxy. War in human history was historical, and humanity in general was peaceful.

'Or,' she continued, 'there is a second option. We could just send in soldiers to kill the two young men themselves. While weapons are not seen in public often, we possess weapons of destruction and can take care of the matter discreetly. The second possibility is a raid.'

'There is a third option,' continued Shanti. 'We proceed to capture the two young men with the help of our officials, and we put them on trial. At that point we kill them with a lethal dose of digitalis, and we publicise the execution to the rest of the galaxy. In this way, not only will we deal with the problem here, but we warn the rest of the galaxy about how serious we are when it comes to religion.'

Shanti seemed pleased with this third option, and she beamed as she explained it. But the third option was also hard to swallow. The idea of publicising an execution was strange as well. These were the types of things that rebel groups and governments did back in the barbaric second millennium. Should Utopia really revert to those types of behaviours? Also, everyone knew that capital punishment had started to wane as a practice of governments on Earth over a thousand years earlier. By the twenty-second century it was thoroughly abolished. The idea of killing someone, endorsed by the government, made everyone feel uneasy.

'There is also a fourth option. We could do nothing. They have escaped to the side of darkness and left our civilization. We can hope that they keep their religion to themselves over there and nothing further happens. But let me warn you, that is not how these proselytizers think. They WILL come back and try to convert us to their religion.'

The feeling in the room was that the crowd didn't like the last option either, but Sophia did. For the first time in her life, she thought that maybe people of religion weren't that bad after all. She remembered her husband's parents, Gary and Colleen. They were good people, and they didn't try to push religion, or at least not a lot.

Shanti kept talking, 'A difficult decision is before us. As Chair of the Board of Utopia, I can assure you that the Board is capable of making such a decision like this. But we have decided to let the good and peaceful people of Utopia make the decision for us. We want you to share the weightiness of the choices, to consider each option with its potential benefits and disadvantages, and to come to your own sense of what should be done.'

Shanti paused, and looked up the rows of seating into the crowd.

'Soon, you shall vote and we will have an answer.'

The large assembled crowd was quiet as they contemplated all that they had been told. Normally the Board made major decisions, but something about this felt bigger than even the Board. .

Shanti kept talking. 'Before we vote, I would like to invite a dear old friend, whom many of you will know to speak.' As she said this, Arthur Christmas appeared on stage as he shifted in. Arthur was indeed well-known, now an aged fig ure standing before the audience, but an atheist of long standing, and known all around the galaxy long before Utopia even existed.

'When I was young, living on Planet Earth, you could not escape the constant talk of religion.' His raspy voice echoed out into the halls. 'It was religion here, and religion there. It was religion everywherrrre.' His old voice trilled on the letter r. 'There was no escape, and they wanted you to bow to their opinions.' His voice slowed slightly. 'It was too heavy a weight to bear.'

'Soon it became clear to me that we needed our own place in the universe free from these pests, and the idea of Utopia was born. It took a long time to build this planet, during which time those moronic people of religion helped us with the construction phase. There were simply too many morons, and too few people of sense for it to be any other way. We paid them for their help of course, but when the last one had left, we closed the door to religion once and for all. And now, we are trying to forget all of that. Leave it in the past I say.'

Arthur looked up at his audience. 'Now do you suppose we want to start allowing these fiends back into our beautiful planet?'

He answered his own question, with strength in his voice, and a sense of moral rightness.

'Not at all. We shall give no allowance to them. So whatever decision we make today, it does in fact require making a choice which is difficult, but necessary.'

He continued.

'There is a choice between war, a raid, a public execution, or to ignore it and hope it goes away. Let me tell you, that I will not be voting to do nothing.'

He had one more comment.

'I know that for many of you, none of the four options are palatable, but the fourth option of doing nothing is also a choice which cannot be abided. So it has come down to this. You must choose between four things, none of which we would normally want to decide between. But one of them MUST be chosen.' He looked at the crowd, and said one last thing. 'Choose wisely.'

After his rousing words, they voted.

Each citizen in the Petrea, and those mentally present on Utopia who were elsewhere, each cast their decision via a thought. Sophia voted for option number four. She didn't like the idea that her friend's husband, Nathan, might be killed by her choice.

After that the votes were electronically tallied, a process that lasted a mere twenty seconds.

Shanti once again stood before the gathering.

'Fellow citizens of Utopia. I congratulate you for making a difficult choice. In the days to come, after we have apprehended the two suspects, there will be public executions in Utopia for the first time.'

CHAPTER TWENTY SEVEN:
THE RATS

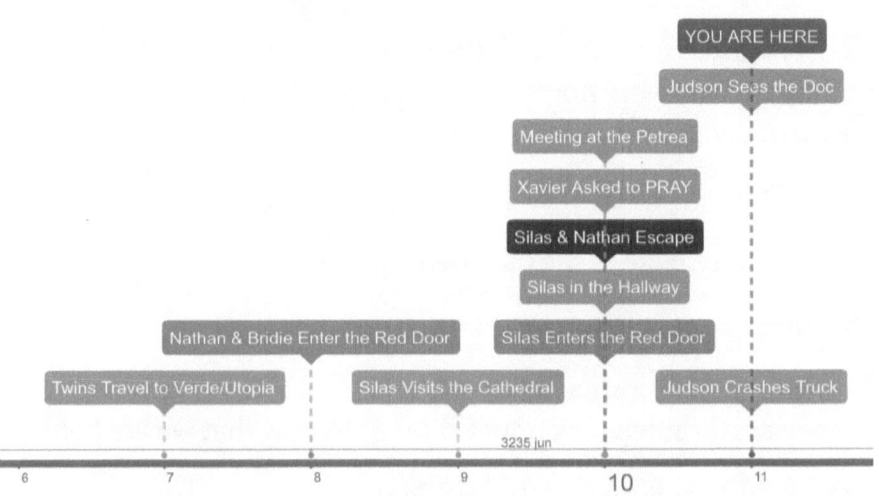

Nathan and Silas entered the construction zone. There were many homes in various states of completion. Finding one that looked finished, but still unoccupied, they smashed a side window, and entered the house. It was a clean home, but empty, ready for someone to move into.

'This way,' said Nathan.

'How do you know where to go?'

'All these houses have the same basic plan. The hallway is north-south, in line with the light-dark hemispheres on the planet. We want to get to the dark hemisphere. They won't find us there.'

Nathan continued to comment as they walked along, and Silas listened, learning many interesting things about Utopia.

Each of the Utopian houses were large and luxurious, but they all had the same pattern of a hallway connecting the daylight side of the house to another construction on the dark side of the planet where the bedrooms were located. The hall was what connected them.

As they walked down the hall they ported to the other side of Utopia. They were now in the other half of the house and it was now dark.

'Why is it dark?' asked Silas.

'It's because we are in the dark hemisphere now.'

'Will these lights turn on by themselves?'

'Yes, they would normally. But you and I had our thought processors disabled. The house does not know that we are here.'

'Let me find the light switch,' said Silas.

'Don't touch it.'

'Why?'

'If you turn on the lights, people in other nearby houses will see that someone is here in this house. The lights are visible from outside. We don't want anyone to know where we are. Wait until your eyes adjust. We will find the back door and go out from there.'

After about fifty seconds their pupils had dilated and they started to see the outline of everything. It was also a bright moon outside and some of the light filtered in through the windows.

Making their way to the end of the hall, with bedroom doors on each side, they came to an entertainment room.

'This is where people relax at night,' said Nathan. 'They watch television in this room. The back door should be here somewhere.' And just like he said, there it was.

They opened the back door. There was a noticeable drop in temperature, maybe twenty degrees difference from the light side.

'That's cold,' said Silas.

'This side never gets the sun.'

'What do we do?'

'We need to find somewhere to hide.'

'Won't we shiver all night?'

Nathan shut the back door again to keep out the cold. He looked around the entertainment room. It was already filled with basic furniture, including a lounge which extended to a bed. He had an idea.

'Help me get this bed out?'

'What for?'

'For the blankets,' said Nathan.

They unfolded the bed, and just as Nathan thought, there were sheets and a blanket and pillows built into it. They stripped the bed of its linen. Nathan wrapped both the fitted and the top sheet around him. Silas wrapped the blanket around himself too. They both took a pillow, and headed for the back door.

Opening a second time, they paused to look at the landscape. Nobody seemed to be moving around out there. They stepped out of the house.

'Let's leave the door unlocked,' suggested Silas. 'What if we want to come back? We might be able to get water here if we need it.'

So leaving the house unlocked they made their way into the black side of the planet.

The dark hemisphere had few buildings. Most of the houses they could see were bunched together in groups. There were no streets between them, or much in the way of any other facilities. All of those things were located on the light hemisphere. As they left the area near the houses they began to walk across a vast flat area of sand, like what the Sahara desert in North Africa was like. Thankfully it was night, and the temperatures were not scorching. After a while their body temperature began to heat up, and Nathan removed the sheets, and Silas did likewise with the blanket. Their body movement alone was sufficient to keep them warm. They continued to walk.

After a few kilometres they came to an escarpment, a kind of rocky ridge that ran along the edge of the sand. They started to skirt their way along the side of it. Finally, they came to a cave. Standing at the entrance of the cave they looked out upon the Utopian night. It was an interesting sight. In the distance they could see the glimmer of the twilight zone, the part of the planet where the daytime and the nightime are in a state of permanent half and half. Above them the moon in all its brightness was shining.

Turning back, it was warmer inside the cave, which would help them once their bodies started to cool down. They made their way inside, and sat down on the sand to have a rest. Soon weariness overcame them, and they lay down, and fell asleep.

Sometime later Silas woke up. Where was he? That's right, he was on Utopia, in a cave. What time was it? He didn't know for he had never used a watch; he had always consulted his thought chip, but it had been disabled. Was it really still night time?

'Nathan, are you awake?'

'I am now,' he said with a grin. Silas couldn't see the grin.

'Why is it still night?'

'It's always night on this side of the planet.'

'Should it actually be night time right now?'

'I don't know that either,' Nathan laughed. 'The other side of the planet is always day, and this side is always night. We sleep when we get tired here.'

'How do we know when it's the next day?'

Nathan laughed again. 'You are not used to how this works are you? We have to use calendars and watches on Utopia to know the day or time. But because we don't have our thought sensors working right now, we have no way of knowing what day it is, or what time it is.'

Silas walked to the entrance of the cave and looked out. It was the same view as the night before except for one thing. The moon was not there anymore.

As he stood at the mouth looking out, he noticed a small red light in the distance. What was that? Could it be a fire?

'NATHAN!!'

Nathan was by his side in just a few seconds.

'Shhhh!! We don't want people to hear us.'

'Look, a red light,' Silas pointed into the distance.

'I see it.'

'What is it?'

'I don't know.'

'Do you think it is people?'

'Maybe.'

'Is it safe?'

'Probably not.'

They sat back down on the sand. Should they go to the light, or should they stay? It was impossible to know what was the safe decision. One thing was certain. They wouldn't be able to stay in this cave forever.

Nobody talked. They lay there. Silas started thinking about all the events that had happened since he came back to Utopia. It had been such a blur. No sooner had he been back than he had been grabbed and shoved through the red door. He barely had time to think. Then just a few hours later they had escaped from the end of the hallway, and now they were somewhere on the dark hemisphere of Utopia, in a place without food or water.

Two things stuck in Silas' mind. The first was the writing on the wall in that far room at the end of the galaxy.

'Nathan, did you know a man name Colin?' Silas remembered that someone called Colin had spent seven days in that room and had written *'remember me Lord,'* on the wall next to his name.

'Yes, he was the husband of my wife's best friend.'

'Why was he in the room?'

'He came from Earth, and left it behind to live here with his wife. But something went wrong in his mind, and he wanted to go back. He said the unmentionable word.'

'The unmentionable word?'

'You know, the word nobody is allowed to say.'

'No, I don't know about that. What word is it?'

'Well, I'm not allowed to say it.'

'Why not, what will happen if you do?'

Nathan suddenly had a funny feeling come all over him. Up until this point in his life, he knew that if he said the name 'Jesus', it would result in consequences. But now, since he already faced those consequences, it would make no difference at all if he said 'Jesus'. He could even say it a thousand times and it would make no difference.

'Jesus, Jesus Jesus, JESUS, JESUS, **JESUS.'** Nathan yelled out the name of Jesus a bunch of times. That felt good. He looked at Silas, 'I never thought that saying the unmentionable word would make me feel so good.'

One thing was for sure, just a minute earlier, Nathan was telling Silas to be quiet because people might hear him. But now, he was yelling 'Jesus' at the top of his lungs.

Silas looked back completely confused. 'Why is 'Jesus' an unmentionable word?'

'You know, this is the atheist planet. This is Planet No-X. X is Jesus. We don't have Jesus here.'

'Ohh, I didn't know you weren't allowed to even mention Jesus.'

'Well it makes no difference now,' said Nathan.

Silas had another question. 'Did you see what Colin wrote on the wall next to his name?'

'Yes.'

'What do you think about it?' Silas queried.

'I think he converted back to God before he left that room.'

'Why would he do that?'

'He knew about God growing up, and it gave him comfort, and he wanted comfort because he was all alone.'

'Do you think it was a real conversion?'

'Of course not,' Nathan replied. 'He was sincere, but he was sincerely mistaken. There isn't any God.'

'How do you know?' Silas asked.

'I just know. Anyone can tell by looking around, there is no God. It would be more obvious if he was really here.'

'It's obvious to me that He is there,' rebuffed Silas.

'You are delusional,' said Nathan. 'I like you a lot, but that is not logical.'

'The issue isn't about logic.'

'What is it then?'

'It's about being able to see. And you can't see it, because you're blind.'

Nathan was stunned. Here they were in a precarious survival situation, which literally was all Silas' fault, and he had the nerve to tell him that he was blind.

'I don't mean to hurt your feelings.' Silas sensed he had said something wrong, and tried to retrieve the situation.

'Well that does hurt my feelings.'

'Have you ever met an actual blind person?' asked Silas.

'There haven't been blind people for hundreds of years.'

'But you've read about them right?'

'Yes.'

'Was it their fault that they were blind?'

'No.'

'It's not your fault if God isn't obvious to you. There are other eyes that see Him. I don't mean your eyeballs, but I mean there is an awareness that turns on when you place your trust in Him.'

Nathan looked at Silas with a semi-skeptical expression.

'I can't explain it really,' said Silas. 'I'm just a teenager, but I know that when I decided to hand my life over to God to trust Him, I became a lot more aware of Him after that. It's not your fault you don't feel Him, because that part of you doesn't work. But if you want it to, you can ask God to turn it on.'

Nathan was stunned. Nobody had ever said anything like that to him before. Of course he did live on an atheist planet where discussing God was illegal, so naturally he never heard anything said about God before. But at the same time, he actually didn't care that much. It was up to God to prove himself, not up to him to figure it out.

'If God is real, he should be able to help us right now,' said Nathan.

And THAT was when Silas decided to mention the second thing that was on his mind.

Reaching down inside his exoskeleton leg cast, Silas pulled out a rubber breather. He held it up and showed it to Nathan.

'Do you know what this is?'

'No.'

'It's a tiny portable doorway to Cathedral planet. Pastor Xavier Mendosa gave it to me.'

Nathan's eyes widened.

'We can't travel through it, but we could use this somehow to communicate with people in other places.'

Looking around the cave, Silas noticed a handful of leaves that had blown in, probably from the twilight zone. Taking one of them, he used a button on his shirt to scratch one word into the leaf… PRAY. He then pushed the leaf into the breather and it was gone.

'I've just asked my friends on Cathedral to pray for us,' said Silas.

'That won't do any good,' said Nathan.

'How about we wait and see.'

They sat there another hour, and then Nathan jumped to his feet.

'You know what, we may as well go to that light. There's nothing to lose. There is no food here, and no water here, and if we stay here we will die. If we go to the red light, we might die too, but we might not.'

Silas stood up. Apart from the sheet and blanket, they had no possessions to gather, so they started walking out of the cave and across the sandy valley towards the mountains on the other side.

It was a good thing it was night because walking through this landscape in the day would have been unbearable. As it was, walking in the night was not easy either. The stars looked completely unfamiliar, and if it weren't for the central point of the red light, they could have lost their sense of direction.

The red light grew in size as they drew closer. It was in fact a fire. That was a good sign. They kept walking until they were perhaps four hundred metres from what seemed like a camp with maybe a dozen people.

Suddenly Silas felt pain in his back. A man grabbed him from behind and held something sharp against him.

'Who are you?' the voice demanded.

Silas saw out of the corner of his eye that Nathan had also been grabbed by another man, holding a knife to his throat.

'I'm Silas Jones,' he said, 'and this is Nathan Bingham.'

'What are you doing here?'

'We are hoping to find somewhere safe to live. We escaped from deportation.'

The man holding Silas released his grip.

'You are deportees?'

'Yes.'

'What for?'

'I came to this planet by mistake. I didn't know it was Utopia. And he…' Silas nodded in Nathan's direction, 'he didn't report me properly and we were both deported.'

Nathan was about to jump in and tell the part about Silas leaving and coming back, when he decided to bite his tongue.

The man who had been holding Silas spat on the ground. 'Utopia is run by donkeys,' he said. 'They don't think about what they do, and they make dumb decisions that affect everyone. That's why we live over here.'

Now Nathan jumped in. 'Who are you people?'

The man holding Nathan whispered right into his ear.

'We are dark Utopians.'

'Dark utopians?' Nathan repeated it as a question. He had never heard that name before.

The first man spoke. 'You might have heard us called by another name. The Rats. We are the rats.'

Nathan relaxed. They would be safe after all.

''My name is Ronain, and this is Olsen,' said the first man. 'Welcome to the Dark Side,'

CHAPTER TWENTY EIGHT:
SOMEONE SETS A MOUSETRAP

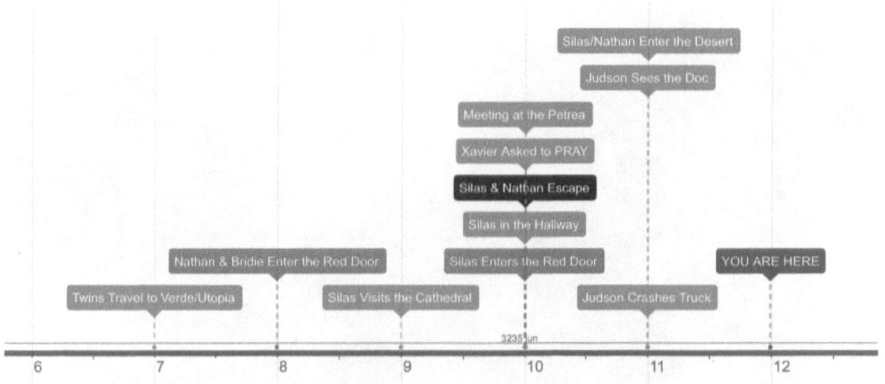

Shanti Combollino stood at the door to the Utopian board room. She had called a meeting.

The Board met inside the tallest structure on Utopia, the Stately Building. It was both stately in appearance, and the main decision-making centre of governance for the state of Utopia. But actually it was only three storeys high. Located away from the other buildings, it stood by itself out in the countryside. It was the equivalent of Parliament House, but nobody could access it except for board members. There were no doors to this building. Access was via translator chips alone. And so it was that whenever a meeting was required, each of the board members would arrive on the lower levels and make their way up to the seats of power.

The Board room contained light purple carpet and a white table with twelve white chairs, five on each side and one on each end.

The walls were made of glass to maximize the view of the nearby manicured grass and hillsides. A lake was visible in the distance.

One by one the Utopian Board arrived and took their seats until they were all present.

'Members of the Board, good day.' Shanti began to address the decision makers. 'You are already aware that we have the support of Utopian citizens to pursue a process of public execution in the case of the two runaways,' she stated. 'The days ahead of us are going to be historic for this planet, and will help to establish a solid foundation of ongoing atheism.'

A number of both key atheists with historic significance to Utopia were on the Board, as well as some new and younger prominent atheists. Richard Heibermann was there. It was his idea fifty years earlier that had brought Utopia to reality. His friend Arthur Christmas was there too. He had always been a loyal and ardent supporter of atheism. Among the younger atheists was Clare Coolidge, a lawyer with tremendous rhetorical talent.

Shanti continued to address the Board.

'Ironically and sadly, you may not be aware that a majority of citizens actually voted for option four, to do nothing.' She paused and let that sink in. 'It was a good thing we had decided in advance what we wanted the outcome to be.'

'The public execution is necessary,' interjected Arthur. 'It sets a standard out there in the galaxy, but it also does the same here on Utopia. Everyone will assume that the majority of others want it this way. So we, the Board, must enforce what the people think everyone wants.'

'Yes,' said Shanti, 'But we have to catch those pests. Today's meeting is to decide on the best course of action. How are we going to do it?'

'Do we know where they are?' asked Arthur.

'Our officials followed their footprints yesterday to a cave,' replied Shanti.

'Why didn't you arrest them?'

'They were no longer there. We cannot have missed them by more than a few hours. They left in the direction of the Rat's camp.'

'Why didn't we keep following?' Arthur Christmas continued to ply questions, not being combative, but inquisitive.

'We don't want to aggravate the Rats,' said Shanti. 'The Rats know the land better than us, they have weapons, and there are more than fifty of them. Plus it is our policy to be peaceful to all those who are peaceful to us.'

'Will the Rats kill the runners?' another Board member interjected.

'It's not likely.'

'Why do you think not?'

'The runners will tell whatever story they want to hear, and they will be believed.' After she answered that last question, Shanti looked around at all the faces. 'But the situation is actually good.' She grinned. ' We KNOW where they are.' She emphasized her words. We could kidnap them anytime we want.'

'I thought you didn't want to aggravate the Rats.' The voice came from Richard Heibermann himself, the father of Utopia.'

'Richard you are right. We don't want to stir up trouble. What do you propose?'

Richard thought about it for a moment. Over the years, he had come up with many effective ideas for atheism in general, and Utopia in particular.

'How about we give the two fugitives a reason to come to us?' he proposed.

'What type of reason?' Shanti quizzed back.

'What about food and supplies? We could tempt them with those,' suggested Richard. 'Everyone needs food and supplies.'

'Yes they do,' answered Shanti, 'but the Rats already have supplies, plus, that type of bait would attract not just the two, but a whole group. It wouldn't achieve our purpose.'

It was at this point that Clare Coolidge, the youngest of the Board members spoke. She had been sitting up at the far end of the table listening.

'I understand that Nathan Bingham's wife had a close friendship with Sophie Philips.'

'That is true,' Shanti confirmed.

'So, we let Sophie appear to need to talk with Nathan and Silas, and let them come to her.'

'It's an interesting idea,' replied Richard, 'but isn't sending a message our problem. How is Sophia going to let them know she needs to talk? There isn't any way of communicating between these groups.'

Now it was Shanti's turn to jump back into the conversation. 'Actually that's not true,' she paused as if she was combing through the files in her mind trying to remember something she had heard long ago. 'I understand that the Rats communicate in the orchards.'

'The orchards?' quizzed Clare.

'Yes. The orchards contain an excess of fruit, and the Rats come every few weeks to raid the trees. They have been doing it for years. We could leave a note in the orchard for them. Something basic. They will see it.'

And so, a note was left in the orchard, in an attempt to lure Nathan and Silas to come to the light side to see Sophia. The note was simple. It said, *'Nathan and Silas, we must talk, Sophia.'* They would certainly hear of it, and when they came, the purple men would be waiting for them.

A mousetrap had been set.

CHAPTER TWENTY NINE:

EXECUTION

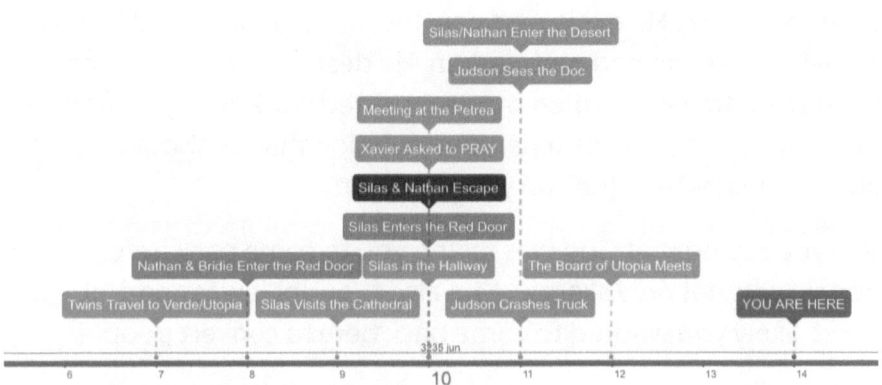

Ronain, Olsen and the other Rats guided Silas and Nathan to the fire, and they took a seat. Not long after that, they were eating some type of stew, and there was water to drink. Soon they were refreshed. It was a good feeling, and they started to relax. They were safe, and right there next to the fire, they both fell into a deep sleep. .

Sometime later, maybe the next day, or maybe even two days later, it was hard to tell, they awoke. The fire was still going. It was hard getting used to the idea that it was always night. It was so strange waking up in the morning having a feeling that it ought to be daytime, but it was wasn't.

Seeing them awake, a number of the other Rats gathered around the fire with them. Ronain sat down next to Silas and stared at him.

He was just a boy. Alright, he was a teenage boy, but he hardly looked like a threat to anyone.

'How did you get to Utopia?' he pressed. 'We want to know.'

Silas didn't want to tell the whole story again, but there didn't seem a way to avoid it. He told them of his brother Judson and their practical jokes. He told them of the discipline their father tried to enforce. He explained how his translator dumped him in the lake where he had met Nathan. He described how he left as soon as his translator dried out and started working again. Finally, he came to describe his sense of conviction that he should return, and that was where the story broke down.

'Are you saying that God was telling you to come back here?' Ronain was not only skeptical, he also thought it was comical. 'More likely you wanted to come back here to convert people.'

'Not at all,' said Silas. 'I was scared of coming back, but the feeling that I was supposed to wouldn't go away.'

'I don't believe you kid.' It was Olsen talking this time. 'You're lying. God doesn't give people feelings.'

Silas looked at Olsen. 'Have you ever done something you knew was wrong, and then felt guilty? Where did that feeling come from?'

'From my conscience.'

'Yes, but who gave you that conscience.'

Olsen grinned a cheeky grin, 'I see the game you are playing boy. Clever.'

Ronain slapped him on the back, kind of like a huge love pat. 'It's going to be good having some different conversations around here. We might not believe in God, but we sure don't have a problem talking about it.'

Just then into the camp came running some of the other Rats.

'Boss, boss, we got news.'

Ronain turned around to see two men, dressed in similar clothes to himself, wearing long pants, and long shirts, all dark colours with a cloth over their heads like a bedraggled tea-towel, but sufficient to cover most of their face, but not the eyes. It was clothing designed to stop people who might identify them, and had the double benefit of keeping them warm on the cool, dark side of the planet.

'What is it?'

'There was a note in the orchard?'

'A note? What did it say?'

'It said "Nathan & Silas, we must talk," by someone called Sophia.'

Ronain turned back to Nathan and Silas. 'Do you know someone called Sophia?'

'I do,' said Nathan.

'Does she know you are here?'

'I don't think so,' Nathan answered. 'She was my wife's friend, but we were taken away so quickly we never had the time to tell anyone.'

'Boss,' it was the other of the two Rats who had returned. 'There was also a big meeting at the Petrea the day before yesterday. Everyone was there. They told everyone to watch out for the deportees.'

'Who told you?'

'We saw a notice with a picture of those two,' and the man pointed at Silas and Nathan.'

Ronain turned back, 'You are wanted men. But you are safe here with us. Otherwise it is through the red door with you both.' He chuckled at what he said.

Silas was about to interrupt and tell them that they had already been through the red door, when Nathan spoke. 'What do you suppose Sophia wants to tell us?'

'Probably about the meeting that happened I would say,' Ronain answered the question automatically.

'But I feel that we should go and see what she has to say.' Nathan pushed a little more. 'What do you think Silas?'

Silas nodded. 'I want to go.'

Olsen spoke up, 'You realise it could be a trick, to try and catch you. And if they get you, it's through the red door you go.'

This time Silas didn't hesitate. 'We already went through the red door. We are not scared.'

Nathan jumped up, 'Speak for yourself. I don't want to go back through that door again.'

And in that moment every single rat eye was on them.

'You have been through the red door? Tell us about the red door,' pressed Ronain. 'What is on the other side?'

Silas looked at Nathan. 'You tell them,' he said. And so Nathan began by telling his story of how he and Bridie had been deported, of how they had encountered the black hallway, and then the room at the end. He told them how Bridie had refused to play their game and had immediately left the room going to her death. He then told of how not long later Silas had joined him.

Silas then joined in, telling them of his hunch about the door, and how he had kept it open with his shirt. He told how they had escaped the hall by dragging a motionless Nathan out of the door, and made it to the dark side through one of the newly-built homes in the construction zone.

After all had been told, there was silence as everyone digested all that had been shared.

A woman spoke. 'I'm Corella,' she said. 'And I'm glad you made it here. I'm sorry for how the people of Utopia have treated you, and I want you to know that we are not like them. We will look after you.' She seemed to care.

She continued, 'But I am disturbed. Why is this planet killing people? It was never the purpose of Utopia to kill. It was never like this in the beginning. Atheists were always peaceful people.'

She then looked at Nathan and Silas, 'I must say, that if your friend Sophia wants to see you, there must be a good reason for it. You must go, but not alone. We must go with you.' The other Rats concurred. Ronain nodded in approval.

'Get your things men, we will be on our way,' he said.

Nathan explained to Ronain where Sophia's house existed on the light side, and from that information they plotted a path to the dark half of her house. The plan was to knock on the door and hope she would hear. They should be able to get her attention and speak to her without venturing into the light half of the planet and being seen.

And so it was about two hours later that Silas and Nathan stood at the back door to Sophia's home. Ronain and the band of Rats stood back in the darkness where they could not be observed.

KNOCK KNOCK. Nathan rapped on the door.

He waited a minute. Nobody came.

KNOCK KNOCK. This time a little louder. It wasn't customary for people to have guests at their back doors. He was about to knock a third time, when the door opened a tiny crack. It was Sophia.

'Sophia,' Nathan whispered.

'Nathan, what are you doing?'

'We saw your note in the orchard?'

Sophia stepped outside, shutting the door behind her. She looked at Nathan, and then noticed Silas in the dark next to him.

'I didn't leave a note,' she said.

'It said you wanted to talk.'

'I didn't leave any note,' she said again. At that moment, she had that same feeling she had before, when her husband had been taken away. She knew something bad was about to happen.'

And right at that moment Sophia's back door opened again, and through it came the men in purple. Not two of them. Not three or four. Twenty of them came through the door. They were not taking chances.

Before Sophia had time to think, they had seized Nathan and Silas, and also seized her too. They took all three of them back through the door into the house. The door was closed and locked behind them. Ronain and the Rats looked on helplessly from far away in the night. There was nothing they could do; the distance was too great.

Inside, the men in purple let Sophia go. They didn't need her; they had what they had come for. Taking the two men, they left through her front door and were gone. Sophia was left standing in shock. She would later describe this as one of the worst moments in her life.

The men in purple took Nathan and Silas to the containment room, where they were both locked into beds, shackled by the arms, legs and neck, and those locks were closed by thoughts. It was not going to be possible for them to escape.

They were left alone next to each other, shackled.

'Silas.'

'Yes Nathan.'

'I'm not afraid of dying.'

'Why?'

'Remember back at the fire, you said you weren't scared of the red door, and I said "speak for yourself."'

'Yes.'

'I thought about what you said, and I realised it must be God giving you the courage.'

'He is.'

'As we were being carried here just now I said a prayer.'

'Oh.'

'I asked God to give me those eyes you talked about.'

'What happened?'

'I don't know how exactly, but something changed.' Nathan smiled. He couldn't move his head at all. It was shackled straight, so that while he was laying on his back, he could only look at the ceiling. But he could smile. 'I feel warm. I feel light. I'm not scared.'

Silas smiled.

'I'm happy for you Nathan.'

'Not as happy as me.'

Next, four men in purple came into the room. Taking the shackled prison beds, they started wheeling them down a long hallway.

'We are taking you men to the Petrea,' one of the purple officials said. 'And then you are going to be executed.' His voice was deep, serious, but also matter of fact. He didn't sound like he cared even one little bit.

Silas felt strange. He hadn't actually expected to die, but on the other hand, he hadn't expected Nathan to find the Lord. He didn't know what to say. He wasn't concerned about what would happen after he died, but he also hadn't wanted to go to Heaven so soon.

After a few minutes they were presented on stage. A huge crowd of people was gathered in the Petrea to witness the first public executions on Utopia. The two men, shackled, lay there on their backs, while thousands of atheists looked at them. Some looked with sympathy, others looked with anger, and still others with confusion. Finally Shanti Combollino, the Chair of the Board, arrived on stage and stood next to them.

'Men and Women of Utopia. Fellow Atheists.' She started her formal address.

'A few days ago we were gathered in a similar manner to discuss what to do with these profligate runaways, these purveyors of religion.' She paused for effect. 'And it was you, the good people of Utopia who voted. You decided that we should hold a public execution for the benefit of the future of our planet.'

'Now, in accordance with your wishes, I have invited our public servants to come with two syringes. Two fatal doses of digitalis, to send these men to their right and fitting end.'

Silas tried to look sideways at Nathan. He couldn't really see him. He could see two purple officials approaching. One was carrying a tray and some medical instruments.

'Nathan, I'm sorry that my arrival on this planet has brought you death.'

'Silas, I have never felt more alive than I do right now.' He couldn't explain it, but it was like he was brand new. He felt light and wonderful all over, but not in the same way as when people modified their mindchip to make happy feelings. It felt deeper than that.

But regardless of how he felt, the two people in purple approached. One of them, a woman, appeared to be a medical officer. The other, a man, held the stainless steel tray containing the two syringes and a bottle of purple liquid, with a label that read 'digitalis.'

The woman opened the little bottle, and filled the first syringe. She then turned to Nathan, and pushed the thin needle into his upper right arm. A crowd of thousands watched on. None had seen an execution before. Nathan lay there in full view, unable to move because of the shackles, but his lips made a whispering motion, barely audible.

'Thank you for helping me to see Jesus.'

Silas tried to whisper back, but found he was unable. Overcome with emotion, a strange mixture of gratitude to God, and anxiety at what was happening. He couldn't say anything.

Nathan started to feel light headed and it was hard for him to concentrate. Within a few seconds he had lost consciousness. The poison was quick to start working.

From the crowd's perspective it was anticlimactic.

The woman then turned to Silas. Drawing the second syringe and filling it with the deadly purple liquid, she pushed the needle into his left upper arm. The syringe punctured the same place where the translator pair had been strapped to him just a few days earlier. She pushed the needle and the purple poison started its work on him too.

Within minutes their hearts had stopped pumping, and their bodies became lifeless.

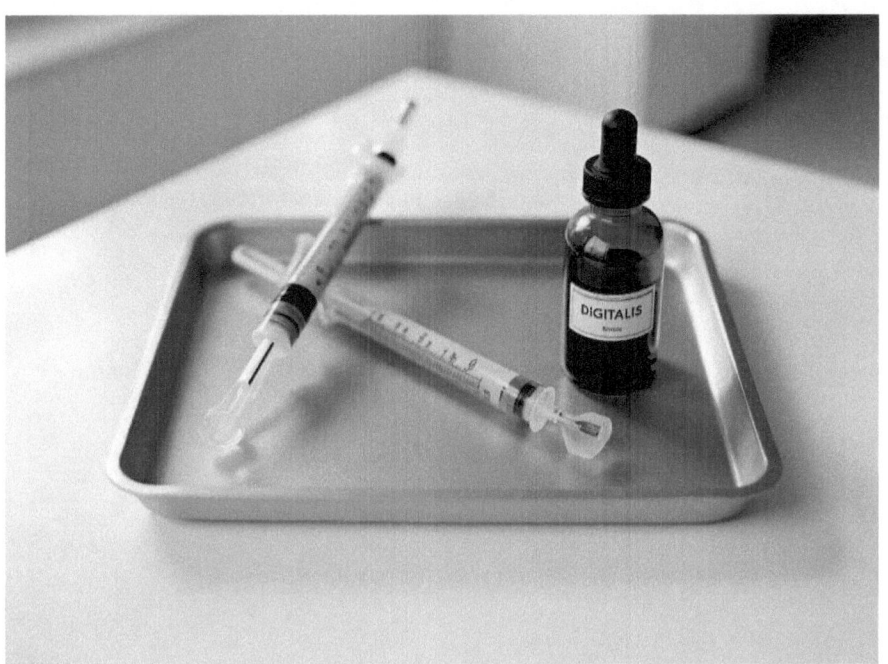

CHAPTER THIRTY:

PLANET NO-X NO-MORE

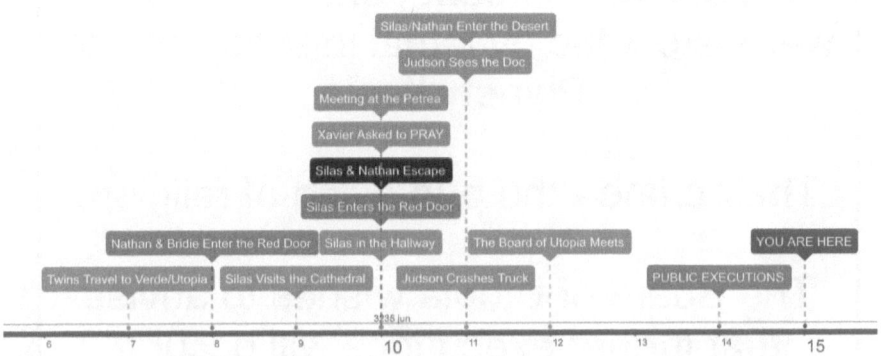

An hour after the executions of Silas and Nathan, the Board of Utopia published a press release for dispersal to ICE, the Interstellar Communications Exchange, the very same place that Colin and Sophia had worked just twelve years earlier.

PRESS RELEASE

DOUBLE PUBLIC EXECUTION

On the 14th of June, 3235, two men were executed by lethal injection on the Planet Utopia.

Their crime - the purveying of religion.

The Board of Utopia wishes to advise that further executions will occur if similar situations arise in the future.

News from Utopia was not common, and would normally have received a great amount of press interest regardless of what it was, but this particular press release went viral. News of it reached the majority of the galaxy swiftly, in just hours. People were in shock. There hadn't been public executions for more than five hundred years. It wasn't civilized. Many could not believe that such a thing could happen in modern society.

It was this shock that the Board of Utopia had hoped to cultivate. They knew the news would spread, and they wanted it to. They needed to set a cultural boundary for their planet and their future civilization. It must be unambiguously atheistic.

But there was a side-effect of this news too, something the Board of Utopia were not able to foresee, and indeed they were not capable of seeing it. Rather than put fear into the hearts of the people who heard it, it encouraged them.

All around the galaxy, hundreds of millions, maybe even billions of Christians on Earth, on Kepler, on Kepler 2, on Barnard, on every inhabited planet, all began to pray for Utopia to change. Virtually the entire galaxy cared, and their prayers showed it. Rather than being disheartened by the news, they realised God was doing something on Utopia, and they prayed to speed it along. Whatever God was up to, they wanted it to succeed.

Something had become clear in the minds of Christians everywhere. Silas and his friend Nathan had become seeds. And those seeds now planted, and watered by the prayers of billions, would produce something. Time would show what.

-- -- --

One person who heard the news was Xavier Mendosa, the pastor of the Cathedral Cathedral parish. He was the one who had given the rubber breather to Silas, and had received a request to pray, written on a leaf, that had come through that tiniest of portals. The other half of that breather still sat in his office on the mantel, now a momento.

Xavier sat with his wife Vicki, and they prayed their own prayer. It was a prayer of gratitude, that God had received unto himself the soul of this dear young man and his friend. What they learned in the press release was *very* encouraging. There was *another* man that was executed. Silas had clearly been having an effect of some type. Who was this other man? They knew nothing of him? Was he a Utopian? It seemed he might have been. It was clear that God *had* done something as a result of their prayers. There was momentum for more.

Xavier over the months to come would lead his entire congregation of more than twenty million people in consistent prayers for Utopia. There was a groundswell of believing that something miraculous was not only possible, but likely to happen.

-- -- --

Jonathan and Connie Jones heard the news too. It was not news they wanted to hear, but they knew there was a distinct possibility of a bad outcome when they had given Silas permission to go back to Utopia.

Jonathan took a hold of his wife's hand, and they sat together in their lounge room in Port Sudan. They too prayed. It was a sad prayer, but a grateful prayer at the same time.

'Lord, we thank you for giving us our precious son Silas, and for the sixteen years we had with him. Thank you for the joy he gave us, and even for the pranks and the silly things he did. Thank you that his life counted for something. Our prayer is that his life will not have been wasted, but will make a difference.'

As they prayed, tears flowed. Silas was not replaceable, but they also knew they had not actually lost him. He would not come to them, but one day, they would go to him.

-- -- --

News travelled more slowly to Verde, but it did get there late that evening. After Nick and Jay heard what happened, they sat Judson down, and passed it on as gently as they could. There was no sadder news he could have heard. He went to his room and cried.

'Boys don't cry,' he thought to himself. But he couldn't stop.

Laying on his bed that night he thought about many things. He couldn't avoid thinking about them. He thought about the joke Silas played on him that day at school. He thought how stupid he was to have reacted so impulsively. If he had controlled himself, they would not have been sent to visit Uncle Nick, and Silas would not be dead right now. But he also thought of how his brother had changed. It was his brother's choice to go back to Utopia, and he had nothing to do with that. He admired Silas for his courage. He missed Silas. How he wished he could have his silly joke-playing brother back. He wished for and missed many things about him.

The next morning when he awoke he felt numb, as if he was dreaming. It couldn't be real. But it was real. Uncle Nick gave him space and didn't ask him to come for breakfast. He lay in bed for hours and didn't help with any tasks that morning.

At lunch time, there was a knock on the door. It was Aunty Jay.

'Judson, are you OK?'

Judson stirred in his bed, and rolled over to look at the door.

'I guess,' he replied. 'I'm just sad.'

'You are supposed to feel sad,' she answered. 'Your brother died. How else would you feel?'

There was something about her statement of the obvious that helped. She was right. This was how he was supposed to feel. He didn't feel less sad, but there was a spark of something that lifted him in those words.

'Would you like some milk?' Aunty Jay asked.

'Yes,' he answered.

Aunty Jay left and returned with a cup of milk and a banana. Even more than the food, her thoughtfulness was soothing.

As the day went on, he got out of bed and even helped a little. He even did the dishes that evening after dinner. However, he went to bed early. It was better to be asleep than awake, because at least he didn't feel anything when he was sleeping. You do dream when you are asleep though.

That night he dreamt of Silas. Silas was on Utopia and he was looking right at Judson and he reached out his hand.

'Come and join me here,' he said. 'We need you.'

When he woke up the next morning, the dream loomed large in his thoughts. Was his brother actually calling to him to come? Did that mean his brother was alive?

He needed to take his mind off everything that had happened. And as it turned out, Uncle Nick wanted his help, and sat him down for a chat.

'Judson I need to talk to you about some changes taking place on Verde in the next little while.' Uncle Nick sounded very formal.

'What is it?' Judson truly wanted to know.

'It has to do with the broken agreement with Utopia.'

'Oh.'

'The day after tomorrow, the Board of Utopia is sending a small militia to guard The Stay.'

'Why do they want to do that?'

'It's because they now know that the two planets are connected all the time. With The Stay open, it means anyone could come and go between the planets, and of course they don't want that to happen.'

Judson thought of his dream. If he was going to join Silas on Utopia it would have to be today, or otherwise he would never get the chance. He pushed that thought away, and tried to focus on what Uncle Nick was saying.

'The bigger problem is that everyone on Verde has been given thirty days to leave.' Uncle Nick spoke matter-of-factly, not betraying a hint of emotion.

"Thirty days!' Judson couldn't believe it. 'That's only one month. How can you move an entire planet's worth of people and things in just one month?'

'I don't think we can,' replied Uncle Nick. 'We will only take the most important things. A lot of things will be left behind.'

Judson looked into his Uncle's eyes. Did he detect a hint of sadness? He knew he was to blame. Why did he have to ruin everything?

Uncle Nick kept talking. 'Can you help Aunty Jay and I to start packing?'

In that moment it was as if an entire lifetime of thoughts, feelings, and decisions swirled around him. Everything was coming to a head right at this moment. He could say yes to help his Uncle, but then would have to say no to the dream he had about Utopia. But if he said yes to the dream, he would leave his Uncle without help. It was just a dream after all, and dreams are often nothing more than nonsense. But this dream didn't seem like nonsense. It was different to all the other dreams he had ever had. It felt so normal, so undreamlike.

'I had a dream,' he finally blurted out. 'Silas told me I am needed on Utopia.'

Nick stared at Judson as if he couldn't believe what he was hearing. He said nothing for a brief minute, then he called out.

'JAY!'

Aunty Jay came running. 'What is it?'

'What were you saying to me this morning about your dreams?'

Aunty Jay looked a little embarrassed. 'Well,' she started. 'I had this weird little dream last night. I hate to mention it. But I dreamt that you,' and she pointed at Judson, 'you went into The Stay.'

'Go on,' said Nick, 'there was more, wasn't there?'

'Yes,' she replied. 'We tried to stop you, but you told us to let you go.'

The three of them sat there silent, deep in thought. Finally Nick spoke.

'Sounds like you won't be helping us, instead we need to be helping you. If you are going to Utopia, we need to get you ready immediately. We have one day. Let us get a buggy together for you, I have maps of Utopia, and we have Bibles. There will also be food and blankets too. You will need whatever we can get our hands on.'

And so the three of them worked to get Judson ready. Uncle Nick proved to be the perfect person to help pack for Utopia. He knew everything about the planet. And in a few hours, Judson was packed up.

He gave Aunty Joy a big squeeze, and this time Uncle Nick also offered a hug. It was a fond farewell, nobody knowing if they would see each other again. Judson already knew where The Stay was, so he started the buggy, and as he drove away, he waved goodbye.

-- -- --

Sophia was not able to bear the thought that her best friend's husband had died because of her. She couldn't believe that they had used her as bait. She didn't go to the execution. She hadn't voted for it anyway, and there was no joy in it.

She went to the back half of her house, and turned off her mindchip. She didn't want any of the infrastructure to know what she was thinking, and definitely not Aña. She sat all alone in her lounge, in the dark with the lights out, and her thoughts turned to God. It was her very own husband Colin who had suggested praying when they couldn't get pregnant. It had seemed so childish at the time, but it didn't seem so dumb anymore.

She thought she might try praying something. But what to pray? And how do you pray? She didn't know any of those things. So she just thought to God like she would have done to her helper Aña. She hoped that would work.

She thought, 'God if you really are here, like people say you are, then you will know what I'm thinking right now.'

She didn't feel anything. But she kept her thinking going.

'Show me a sign or something,' she thought. 'Show me what to do.'

Sitting in the back of her home, she remembered the moment not long ago when she heard a knock at the back door. She had opened it to see Nathan there with his friend Silas. And she remembered that there were other people there as well, in the distant darkness, too far away to help. Who were those other people? Were they rats? She didn't know. The purple police had intervened too quickly and she never found out.

She stood up and took a few steps to the back door. Opening it, she looked outside, just like she did the day before. Nobody was there. She didn't expect anyone would still be there. She was about to close the door again, when she noticed something glowing in the distance. It was a light, although very dull, about one hundred metres away in some rocks.

Leaving the back door unlocked, she walked to where the glow appeared to be coming from, and noticed it was a flashlight, laying in the rocks. It was still turned on. One of those people must have dropped it. Picking it up, she noticed it had a name written on it.

Ronain

Who was Ronain? She looked into the darkness and thought of the rats that lived out there somewhere. She didn't know any of them personally. But they seemed to do just fine. They didn't have a problem surviving in the dark. It occurred to her that Nathan and Silas had come from the dark side. They must have had help from the rats. At that moment, she knew something. She had to find this Ronain, and talk to him. He would be able to tell her about Nathan and Silas.

She set off into the darkness, not knowing where she was going. No matter what, she was going to find those rats.

At another point in life she might have thought this was an incredibly foolish thing to do. Who just walks into the darkness without knowing where they are going? Who goes looking for someone on the basis of a first name only? It's true, it was a little foolish, but she wasn't at another point in her life, she was at this point. And this moment made her decision seem like the right one.

As she walked through the night, Sophie tried to walk in a straight direction, but it was hard to remember which direction that was. It was also a good thing it stayed night on the dark side, because it meant it also stayed cool. Her body didn't overheat, and it meant that she was able to walk many kilometres without much fatigue.

After walking for a few hours, she noticed a buggy approaching. It was a sand buggy, or something like that, an all terrain vehicle.

It was driven by a man, but she couldn't see him properly. As he drew closer, the lights from the buggy shone directly into her eyes, blinding her. She lifted up her hands to shield her eyes from the light.

The buggy slowed down and pulled next to her. Her eyes started to adjust. Whoever the driver was, he was not afraid of her at all. A young man, maybe about the age of sixteen looked across at her.

'Do you need help?' he asked.

His face came into focus. Sophia looked back at the driver and gasped, 'It's YOU.'

'I don't know who you are,' he replied.

'You're alive,' she shrieked. 'I thought they killed you.'

Sophia opened the door, and without asking, climbed into the buggy next to Judson. As yet she did not know that Silas had a twin. And Judson did not know who she was, but he realised in that moment, she thought he was Silas.

'I'm coming with you,' she said.

So Judson took her with him.

Following the map that Nick had laid out for him, he navigated toward some caves in the mountains, where he would set up camp. He had just met his first Utopian. Whoever she was, he hoped she would be able to help him, and he hoped he could help her too.

THE END

If you have enjoyed this book, would you give a review to help others enjoy it too: Please scan the code below.

Scan me

Epilogue

The story of Planet No-X has not finished; it has in fact only begun. Two more books are planned to follow, completing a series of three.

My plan for part 2 of this story is to be completed and available in 2026. It will be called *The Historiscope*.

The third part of this story is to be called *The Apostle* and can be anticipated in 2027 if all goes to plan.

It is not the writing that takes much time, but the thinking and imagining. If the purpose was only to entertain that would be simple enough, but my goal is to present spiritual concepts in an entertaining way. I sincerely believe that in the same way some of the characters in this book had thoughts in their mind they believed were from God, I like to give God the same opportunity to give me thoughts too.

If you are a reader with faith, would you put your heart into words, and pray for me? If you are not a reader of faith, would you simply care, and let God know you care. That constitutes something similar to a prayer.

If you join the mailing list at davidalley.com.au you will be notified when future additions to the story are published.

A thousand blessings

David Alley

3 April, 2025

Gratiam

My appreciation goes to a few people for their help.

Thank you to Dr Noel Patson, Dr Chris Galloway, Esther Crossley, Grace Ricks, Sarah Crossley, Trinity Schwartz, Bithiah Alley, Leah Hood, Ashley Kerfoot and Elijah Alley. Thank you for taking time to help with reading the manuscript and providing feedback.

Special thanks to Hazel Alley for her extensive time in editing and checking grammar, and Bithiah Alley for providing assistance with edits.

Deep thanks to my parents who have always loved me, and to the Lord who dropped so many interesting ideas into my mind during a period of nine days of silence.

Promotio

In addition to this book, David has written two other books. The first is a series of stories outlining his time as a pastor in Mt Morgan, a unique parish. You can find *Sermons on the Mount* on Amazon, or at davidalley.com.au

David has also written *Flag on the Glacier*, a long letter written by a pastor to an atheist living a thousand years in the future. That book, also on Amazon and David's website, was the catalyst for this series of novels.

On YouTube you may find *Understanding the Bible with David Alley*. This is a series of 1202 videos created over four years with the goal of explaining the Bible. Those who have journeyed with David have come to know much more of the Bible than most people ever will. These videos are available at the Peace Apostolic Ministries youtube channel. This series is also available as an audio podcast from rss.com or spotify.

You can also find David on facebook, on twitter, on quora, and on his personal website davidalley.com.au. He also writes and preaches regularly on peace.org.au and on the Peace Apostolic Ministries YouTube channel.